By Angie Sage

Featuring
Septimus Heap

(in reading order)

Magyk
Flyte
Physik
Queste
Syren
Darke
Fyre

The Magykal Papers

Featuring
Araminta Spook

My Haunted House
The Sword in the Grotto
Frognapped
Vampire Brat
Ghostsitters
Gargoyle Hall

Look out for more titles coming soon!

PATHFINDER

ANGIE SAGE

BLOOMSBURY
LONDON OXFORD NEW YORK NEW DELHI SYDNEY

Bloomsbury London, Oxford, New York, New Delhi and Sydney

First published in Great Britain in October 2014 by Bloomsbury Publishing Plc
50 Bedford Square, London WC1B 3DP

First published in the USA in October 2014 by HarperCollins Children's Books,
a division of HarperCollins Publishers, 195 Broadway, New York, NY 10007

This paperback edition published in August 2015

www.bloomsbury.com

Bloomsbury is a registered trademark of Bloomsbury Publishing Plc

Copyright © Angie Sage 2014

The moral rights of the author have been asserted

A CIP catalogue record for this book is available from the British Library

ISBN 978 1 4088 5817 2

MIX
Paper from
responsible sources
FSC® C020471

Typeset by Hewer Text UK Ltd, Edinburgh
Printed and bound in Great Britain by CPI Group (UK) Ltd, Croydon CR0 4YY

1 3 5 7 9 10 8 6 4 2

For Tom Wishart

CONTENTS

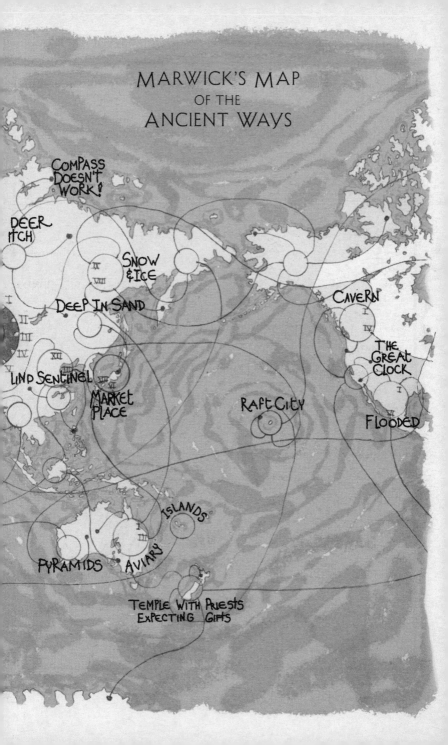

PART
I

ON THE BEACH

A distant bell tolled. On an ancient beach Dan Moon watched a line of flickering lights appear and disappear as they wound through sand dunes, heading towards him. It was three o'clock in the morning on MidSummer's Day. Holding his own lantern high, Dan stood in the middle of a circle of rugs on the sand, watching the lights move closer. Dan's bare feet were cold, and despite his heavy black cloak, he shivered in the pre-dawn chill.

Dan saw the first of the lights – a flickering candle encased in a glass lantern – emerge from the dunes. It was carried by a dark-cloaked figure, who was quickly followed by others. They walked slowly across the sand, heading towards what they called the MidSummer Circle. Silently, one by one they sat down on the rugs, making a circle around Dan.

The dark-cloaked group were not the only ones making their way towards the beach. In the shadows of the dunes the square figure of a woman moved hurriedly along a path she had marked out earlier that day. The woman, Mitza Dradden-mora Draa, was late. She had intended to be in her hiding place before everyone began to arrive, but she had been delayed by having to help Dan Moon pull out a pile of moth-eaten rugs from under her bed in the spare room. And, what was worse, she had to smile while she was doing it because Mitza had to be a good houseguest, and more importantly, be above suspicion. Consequently she was not in a good mood. She didn't like being late, she didn't like sand, she didn't like walking and she certainly didn't like what she called "dratted kids". Still, it would all be worth it – she hoped.

Covered in sand after losing her footing down a dune, Mitza found her hiding place behind a small hillock of sand. It was near enough to hear what was being said and yet far enough away to make a quick exit without being seen. She settled down among the spiky dune grass and tried not to think about sand snakes.

Dan Moon, whip-thin, tall and dark, fiddled with the lapis lazuli stone that hung from a string around his neck. He had performed the MidSummer Circle more times than he liked to remember, but that night Dan was nervous – because for the first time his only child, Alice TodHunter Moon, twelve years old (and so now considered to have come of age) was old enough to hear it. Alice, who insisted on being known as Tod, was sitting at Dan's feet, regarding him with an unflinching gaze. Her dark eyes were glowing with excitement as she twisted her long, thin plait – the traditional PathFinder elflock – that hung down from her mass of short dark hair. Just in time, she remembered not to chew the end of it.

Dan watched the last latecomer take his place. He did a headcount and saw that all those from the village, aged twelve to fifteen, were indeed present. He checked his timepiece. It was important to Dan that he timed his talk to the very second. His father had never bothered, but Dan loved the sense of wonder that timing it just right always produced. It still gave even him goosebumps. He looked around the circle at the solemn audience, sitting cross-legged, muffled in their black cloaks. The younger ones had their hoods up against the chilly offshore breeze, but the older ones – too cool to cover up – were toughing it out, and their faces and hair showed the typical PathFinder sheen that only became apparent in the dark.

Dan held his lantern high and saw the completed Circle of flickering points of flame. Silence had descended and with it an air of expectation. This was going to be a good night, Dan thought. The atmosphere was right. He was pleased for Tod's sake – everyone remembered their first Circle. Dan glanced at his timepiece once more, took a deep breath and, speaking slowly but loudly enough for all to hear – including Mitza Draddenmora Draa – Dan Moon began.

"Good morning, PathFinders. Welcome to our new people." Dan smiled down at Tod and two other twelve-year-olds, who were sitting in the space reserved for first-timers. Tod smiled shyly back. It was strange seeing her father in a new role – no longer a fisherman but someone who everyone was, literally, looking up to.

Dan continued. "Every year we meet in the early hours of MidSummer Morning to hear our history and to understand the secrets that made us PathFinders who we are, and why we are a little different from others. These secrets are kept among us, and when we leave the Circle we do not speak of them to anyone else. Does everyone here understand?" Dan did a 360-degree turn, looking at each person and getting a solemn "I understand" in return. Dan turned his gaze to the three sitting at his feet. "To begin, I will ask our first-timers to promise to keep our secrets from all who are not PathFinders, and more importantly, from all PathFinders who have yet to come of age and join our MidSummer Circle. You may have brothers and sisters or close friends who are only a little younger and you may feel there is no harm in telling them. But harm there is."

Tod blushed. She knew Dan was thinking of her best friends, twins Oskar and Ferdie Sarn. But there was no way she was ever going to break the Circle promise.

One by one, Dan asked each first-timer to say the promise. Tod was last and felt very nervous by the time it was her turn. "Alice TodHunter Moon," Dan said in a most un-Dad-like voice. "Do you promise to faithfully keep the secrets of our PathFinder Circle? For all time and in all ways?"

Tod spoke as loudly as she could manage. "I do promise to keep the secrets of the Circle."

Dan smiled. "Well said all." Then he addressed the rest in the Circle. "Let us welcome our new brother and sisters."

"Welcome, brother and sisters, to the MidSummer Circle," came the response.

Tod smiled. She belonged. It was a good feeling.

Dan relaxed. The serious part of the evening was done; now he could begin to do what he liked best – tell a story. He began to move around within the Circle, pacing slowly, speaking in his low, resonant voice while Tod listened, entranced.

"In the Days of Beyond, those distant days in the past, our ancestors went to the stars. Here on Earth they had great skills navigating what were called the Ancient Ways, and for this they were revered and called PathFinders. We no longer know what these Ancient Ways were, but we do know that because of their PathFinding skills, our forebears were chosen to leave this beautiful planet and find paths through the stars. They left willingly and went into a great closed metal container, a ship named

PathFinder, which they knew they would never leave. An explosion sent the *PathFinder* up into the sky, away from our planet, past the moon, and set her on a path to the stars."

Tod suppressed a gasp and exchanged glances of amazement with the other first-timers. She could hardly believe that Dan, such a great teller of stories, had managed to keep the most amazing story of all secret. She stared up at the dusting of stars above, trying to imagine what it would be like to walk into a huge metal tube, knowing that you would never see the sky or the sea again. Tod pushed her bare feet into the cold sand, as if to reassure herself that she was still firmly on Earth, and listened to the comforting sound of her father's voice continuing his story.

"These people were different from those they left behind. Because in order for the *PathFinder* ship to travel fast enough to reach the stars, at first the people had to live in fluid to protect them from the terrible forces of acceleration. This is where our beautiful sign language comes from, for it is not possible to speak in fluid. And neither is it possible to breathe. So in here –" Dan placed his fingers on either side of the bridge of his nose – "they had the things that fishes have. Gills. This was a deliberate change to the very essence of a human being, something that would be passed on to the next generation. This is why even now, many thousands of years away from our ancestors, some of us still have these gills."

Tod stared up at her father in astonishment – so *many* secrets. She tried to imagine what it would be like to immerse herself in fluid, what the first gulp would feel like. Even if she had gills, would she choke? Would she feel as though she were drowning? Tod told herself she was never going to find out. Because her

7

mother had not been a PathFinder, she was very unlikely to have gills. But even so, Tod had to fight hard to suppress a shudder. Like many fishermen's children, she had a horror of drowning.

Looking down directly at the first-timers, Dan said, "This is a dangerous secret that we keep from the younger ones for their own safety. As part of the Circle, you, too, will now keep the secret."

Tod and her two companions nodded solemnly.

"I know," Dan said, looking around the Circle, "that some of you will want to find out for yourselves whether you have these gills. And I know it is no good, my telling you not to do something, so I won't. But I will tell you that the only way to find out if you possess gills is –" Dan paused not only for dramatic effect, but also to make sure they remembered – *"to be prepared to drown!"*

A gratifying gasp came from the first-timers.

Well on form now, Dan continued. "And I will tell you why you must be prepared to drown. Because human gills do not activate until you breathe in a full, deep draught of water through your nose. If you do this and you are without gills, there is no way back. *You will drown*. And your chances of drowning are extremely high. We do not think that more than one in ten of us have gills now."

Dan looked around the group. He smiled. As usual, the first-timers were surreptitiously sniffing, wondering if they could tell. "And before you ask, no, I do not know if I possess human gills or not. And I do not want to have to find out."

Dan sneaked a quick look at his timepiece. He was going to have to speed up. "Our ancestors found the hidden Ways to the stars. For generations they travelled through distant galaxies,

8

looking for worlds like ours. They danced with moons and flew with comets. They visited countless planets. On one they found an ancient civilisation long dead; on another they found the stirrings of intelligent life but never, ever, did they find any creatures like us."

Dan surveyed his audience, who were gazing at him in rapt attention, the first-timers open-mouthed with amazement. "At last their expedition drew to a close and the *PathFinder* returned home. She landed on the very spot from which she had left, now marked by our PathFinder bell."

Dan paused, and right on cue the sound of the bell drifted over the dunes. Tod felt a swathe of goosebumps run over her.

Dan waited until the last echoes of the bell had faded. "When the crew emerged, they found nothing but windswept dunes and a hostile crowd from the Trading Post who had seen a ball of fire drop from the sky and had come to investigate. Thousands of years on Earth had passed, compared with a few hundred on board the ship – the *PathFinder* and her crew had been forgotten. The Trading Post people thought they were strange alien creatures and imprisoned them in a fortress in the Far." Dan waved his hand in the direction of the forest that bordered the village. "This is why we do not venture deep into the Far. It is not a good place for PathFinders.

"After many long years, the Trading Post jailers lost interest and they at last set our people free. The PathFinders returned here, built our village and lived peacefully. But the old mistrust between us remains to this day. They are a hostile people, quick to anger, and neither the Trading Post nor the OutPost is a safe place for a PathFinder to be.

"But enough of that!" Dan broke the sober atmosphere with

a sudden smile. "Now, it is story time. The PathFinders brought back many tales of the unbelievable places they had seen. At each Circle I tell a different one using our own sign language, which they passed down to us, their children's children. And tonight, Circle, I am going to tell you about the planet of the giant trees."

Dan placed the tip of his left index finger on the tip of his left thumb to make an O: the PathFinder sign for "OK" when used as a question. In reply, all in the Circle made the same sign with their right hands: *OK*, used to show agreement or that all is well. And so Dan began.

Tod sat entranced as her father wove his story with fluid hand movements, dancing around the circle on his long legs, taking them with him to the stars. She wished it would go on for ever, but when his hands began to slow and his elegant fingers fluttered less fast, Tod knew he was drawing to a close.

Now Dan began to speak as well as sign, slow and low. "And so, we PathFinders have travelled to the Great Beyond. We have seen many worlds, but we have seen none as beautiful as ours; we have seen many suns, but we have seen none as perfect as …" Dan turned around and pointed out to the sea. Exactly on schedule, a fingernail tip of orange broke the horizon, pushing its way up from the sea. "This! This is *our* sun. This is our Earth. This is where we belong."

A shiver ran around the MidSummer Circle. Dan Moon grinned. He had done it.

Enjoying their sense of being special, of belonging, the Circle watched in awe as the brilliant ball of light rose from the water; they saw the sky grow bright and the morning star fade away. It was, as Dan Moon had said, perfect.

Suddenly, Tod spotted a flash of gold in the sky. She looked up, shielding her eyes. There was another flash, green this time, and Tod's heart jumped in recognition. This was something she had seen long ago. Something she had dreamed about for many years, and something that no one, not even her father, believed she had seen.

"It's the Dragon Boat!" Tod shouted, leaping to her feet. "The Dragon Boat!" Everyone looked at her disapprovingly, particularly Dan. This was not how you behaved in the Circle. But now everyone was looking at the sky, and some were standing up to get a better view. The MidSummer Circle was broken.

The flash of gold and green moved ever nearer, and now they began to see what Tod already knew it to be – a beautiful green dragon that was also a golden boat. Or was it a beautiful golden boat that was also a green dragon?

The Dragon Boat approached steadily, her huge wings beating *up-and-down, up-and-down*, and soon she was near enough for everyone to see the dragon's neck stretched forward, her iridescent scales shining in the sunlight. They saw her tail arched high, the golden barb on the end glinting. And then her sleek golden hull was overhead; everyone was waving madly – and two figures at the helm, one in purple, one in red, returning their waves.

Dan Moon knew he had been upstaged, but he didn't mind. He was as excited as anyone to have seen such an amazing sight. He swept his daughter up into a hug and said, "So, Alice TodHunter Moon, you really *did* see that Dragon Boat."

"Put me down, Dad," Tod muttered. "Everyone's looking."

THE DRAGON BOAT

The pilot of the Dragon Boat – a young man with curly straw-coloured hair and green eyes so bright that you might expect them to shine in the dark – looked down at the first landfall since they had left their island.

"Hey, Jen," he said, pointing down to the beach. "There's that circle of lights again. That's another MidSummer tradition going on down there, I suppose."

Jenna Heap, a young woman wearing a fine cloak of red silk lined with white fur, her long dark hair kept in place by a circlet of gold, peered over the side of the Dragon Boat. "They've seen us," she said, returning the waves of the excited onlookers below. "It's already light. We must be later than usual."

The young man, Septimus Heap – Jenna Heap's adoptive brother – smiled. "I seem to remember someone was fussing about whether we had enough food." He pointed at two large picnic baskets strapped to the deck.

Jenna resisted the urge to stick her tongue out at Septimus. She was twenty-one now, she told herself sternly, she was the Castle Queen and it *would not do*. Particularly now, she thought, as she looked at Septimus's purple wool cloak lined with indigo fur and the thick gold-and-platinum belt he wore around his purple tunic, that he was the Castle's ExtraOrdinary Wizard. Which Jenna – and even Septimus himself – still found hard to believe.

Like those in the Circle on the beach below, Jenna was performing a MidSummer tradition. Every MidSummer Day for many thousands of years, Castle Queens had visited the Dragon Boat where she had lain in an ancient temple beneath the ground, hidden there by the Castle's first ever ExtraOrdinary Wizard, Hotep-Ra. And now that Jenna was herself Queen, every MidSummer Day she and Septimus took the Dragon Boat to see her old master, Hotep-Ra, in the House of Foryx. It was a time both Jenna and Septimus looked forward to, a precious space where they could be themselves once more – just brother and sister, plain Jenna and Septimus Heap.

This year was even more precious. Because Septimus was now ExtraOrdinary Wizard, he had been reluctant to go. But now, as the orange ball of the sun turned the sky a luminous pink and a flight of ducks flew quacking across their path, Septimus laughed out loud. He was *so* pleased that Jenna had insisted.

DISCOVERED

Later, as Tod and Dan were wandering home along the beach, watching the early morning sparkle of sunlight glancing off the MidSummer waves, Tod said, "Dad, why do you suppose Aunt Mitza was hiding in the dunes while we had our Circle?"

"Was she?" Dan Moon looked at Tod uneasily.

Tod nodded. "Yes. When everyone was waving at the Dragon Boat, I saw her get up and scurry away. And I know it was her, because she waddles like a duck. Like this." Tod did an accurate impression of Aunt Mitza's flat-footed walk, but Dan Moon was not amused.

"You must respect your elders, Tod."

"But I don't like her, Dad. And neither do you."

Dan Moon did not deny it. "Even so, Tod, you must give your mother's stepsister respect. We must both show her hospitality."

Tod fell quiet. Her mother had died when she was only five and Tod knew that anything relating to her mother was precious to Dan – as it was to her, too. She knew that was the only reason that Dan had made Aunt Mitza welcome when she had turned up on the doorstep the previous week, expressing a wish to meet "her darling little step-niece" after all these years. But Aunt Mitza's sharp-eyed looks when Dan was not around had not endeared her to Tod. Unlike Dan, she drew the line at Aunt Mitza. Tod could not believe her mother had ever liked her stepsister, and she was sure that her mother would not have tolerated Aunt Mitza eavesdropping on their secrets.

"But Aunt Mitza was listening in on our Circle, Dad," said Tod. "She heard our secret – the one we all promised never to tell. That's not respecting *us*, is it? Or our hospitality. Or Mum."

Dan Moon frowned. "What's heard is heard. It can't be undone. But you are right, Tod. She has not respected your mother. Tomorrow I will ask her to leave."

But it wasn't Mitza who left the next day. It was Dan.

PART II

PART
II

THE HOUSE OF FORYX

The Dragon Boat flew steadily eastwards. She knew the way perfectly, and all Jenna and Septimus needed to do was to watch the world going by and eat their way through the first picnic basket. It was late morning when they saw the grim fortress where Hotep-Ra lived. The octagonal granite towers of the House of Foryx, dark against the perpetual snow that surrounded them, reared up from a pillar of rock surrounded by an abyss. Both Jenna and Septimus shivered — it was an eerie place.

The Dragon Boat flew lower. She circled the House of Foryx once, then her long neck dipped down and she went in to land. Jenna shut her eyes — this part always scared her. The Dragon Boat was heading for a wide, white terrace of marble, and even though Jenna knew it would be all right, it felt as if they were about to crash into solid stone. But as the Dragon Boat's keel touched down, the marble changed into a milky liquid and they landed softly with a long, low *shishhhh*.

Septimus brushed down his purple robes and tightened his gold-and-platinum ExtraOrdinary Wizard belt. This was the first time he had met Hotep-Ra in his role as ExtraOrdinary Wizard, and he wanted to look his best.

Jenna put the landing ladder over the side and gave Septimus a hug. "You've got the **Questing Stone**?" she asked — as she always did.

"Jen, don't fuss. Of course I do."

"Show me," Jenna insisted, remembering the one terrifying day that Septimus had left the **Questing Stone** in the boat. She had gone racing after him with it and had only just reached him in time.

Septimus put his hand in his pocket and held out an iridescent black stone, round and smooth, with a gold "Q" set into it. This was Septimus's key to freedom; it allowed him to come out of the House of Foryx safely back into his own Time.

"Good," said Jenna. "Nervous?"

Septimus gave Jenna a strained smile. "A bit," he admitted. He swung himself on to the ladder and a few moments later was hurrying off across the marble terrace towards the forbidding grey fortress.

Jenna watched him stride up to a towering door made from great planks of ebony held together with iron bars and rivets. It looked, she thought, like the door to a prison — and it was, in a way. The House of Foryx, built by Hotep-Ra, was the place where All Times Do Meet. Here in the house, Time stood still, like a hub at the centre of a spinning wheel. And although those in the House of Foryx were free to leave whenever they chose, they could not choose the Time which they would step into. Only a person in possession of a completed **Questing Stone** could do this — and Septimus had the only one.

A flurry of snow swept across the terrace, and through it Jenna saw Septimus reach up and tug the bellpull. She saw the door open and the little bat-like doorman step aside to let him pass. Then the door closed and Septimus was gone.

Jenna hated this part of their visit; she was always afraid she would never see Septimus again. To take her mind off things, she set about rigging up a red-and-gold awning over the Dragon Boat. Then when Septimus came out, however hard the snow might fall, however chill the wind might blow, they would sit with Hotep-Ra under the awning and have the lunch that she had brought. This was how it always went, and this, she told herself, was how it would be today.

GOING OUT

Inside the House of Foryx, Septimus pushed open the lobby door – which always opened more easily than he expected it to – and hurtled into the candlelit entrance hall. He stood for a moment to collect his thoughts and breathed in the strange, stagnant air of a place where All Times Do Meet. The entrance hall was wreathed in candle smoke and crowded with people milling around, some plucking up the courage to go out, some disorientated by having just – or so it felt to them – come in, but most of them in a Timeless daze, hardly knowing who or where they were any more.

Septimus could see little through the smoky haze that always hung around this place, but he pushed his way through until he finally spotted the figure of Hotep-Ra. Standing tall in his faded purple robes with their intricate embroideries of Magykal symbols, his white hair held in a thick golden band, Hotep-Ra stood out from the crowd.

There are many things that a brand new ExtraOrdinary Wizard will want to ask the very first ExtraOrdinary Wizard, and Septimus was no exception. He spent what felt to him like many hours of House of Foryx Time with Hotep-Ra up in the old Wizard's rooms. When at last Septimus had asked all his questions, Hotep-Ra said eagerly, "I think it is time for lunch, do you not, Septimus?" Hotep-Ra had become rather fond of the picnics that Jenna made.

The two ExtraOrdinary Wizards threaded their way through the crowds of the hazy entrance hall and went into the lobby. The dragon chair was now occupied by a striking girl dressed in white furs. Septimus noticed she had brilliant blue fingernails and her white-blonde hair was dressed in tiny plaits gathered into a thick ponytail. The girl sprang to her feet and grabbed hold of Septimus's arm. "Tell me, please," she said in a heavily accented voice. "You are the man with the **Magyk** stone, aren't you? You always go out into the Time you came in?"

Septimus clutched the **Questing Stone** tightly in his hand, afraid that the girl might try to grab it. "Yes, I am. And I do."

The girl looked deep into Septimus's eyes. He was mesmerised. "Please, oh please, I beg of you," she said. "Take me Out."

Hotep-Ra did not like the prospect of his precious lunch with his Dragon Boat and his favourite Queen being disrupted. "Madam, you are in no need of being 'Taken Out', as you put it. You are free to leave at any time."

The girl glared at the old man. "I don't want *any* Time. I want *his* Time."

Septimus knew how the girl felt. He, too, had once been terrified of which Time he would step out into, but it was a terror that Hotep-Ra would never understand. "Of course you may Come Out with me," he said. "It would be a pleasure." He would have offered her his arm, but she already had it.

TAXI

Jenna was still trying to put up the awning when she saw Septimus emerge from the House of Foryx with – *who was that?* Jenna frowned. What was Septimus thinking, bringing someone – some new girlfriend, no doubt – to intrude on their precious time together? From the expression on Hotep-Ra's face she could see that the ancient Wizard was no happier about it than she was.

Their guest introduced herself as the Snow Princess Driffa, the Most High and Bountiful. "But I am known to my friends," she said, settling down in the Dragon Boat and kicking off her fur boots to reveal long, white feet with bright blue toenails, "as Driffa." She bestowed a glittering smile on her three companions. "And I hope that you will consider yourselves as my friends."

"Of course we will," said Septimus. Jenna and Hotep-Ra smiled icily.

Hotep-Ra thawed a little at the sight of the salmon mousse and elderflower champagne, but he said little – the Snow Princess spoke enough words for them all. She told them how she had gone to the House of Foryx to find an ancestor who had asked her to meet her there. After giving her a frightening message, her great-great- (and then some) grandmother had told Driffa to wait for "a beautiful blond young man in purple who had a **Magyk** stone". Driffa had waited for what felt like centuries until Septimus had at last appeared.

The Snow Princess put her thin, white hand on Septimus's and said, "I can never thank you enough for Going Out with me. Never." Driffa reclined languidly, so that snowflakes fell on to her upturned face. She breathed in deeply. "Ah," she murmured. "I had forgotten the smell of snow."

Septimus gazed at Driffa, entranced. Hotep-Ra and Jenna exchanged exasperated glances.

Hotep-Ra did not linger. Jenna was waving him goodbye, watching the dark door of the House of Foryx close upon the old Wizard once more, when she heard Septimus saying, "It would be our pleasure to take you home, Driffa. I have always wanted to see the Eastern SnowPlains."

Jenna bit back a retort of *Since when?* and gave Septimus one of her Queenly disapproving stares. It had no effect.

The Snow Princess Driffa, the Most High and Bountiful, was not a good passenger. She spent most of the journey lying prone on the deck of the Dragon Boat, groaning loudly. She protested whenever Jenna roused her to ask for directions, and when she looked out to see where they were, she was promptly sick over the side. "All down the lovely gold leaf," Jenna complained to Septimus. It took two swelteringly hot days and two bitterly cold nights to reach the Eastern SnowPlains. Night was falling when they at last reached the place that the Snow Princess recognised as home – a high snow-covered plain surrounded by mountains, where the air was thin and the wind blew with a low-pitched moan.

"There! I see it. Our Blue Pinnacle!" Driffa called out.

Septimus and Jenna peered out through the snow clouds and glimpsed what looked like a spire of pure lapis lazuli shooting up from the snow. Then the snow closed in and everything became a dull white once more.

Driffa turned to Septimus, her dark blue eyes shining with excitement. "Can you not feel its wonderful **Enchantment**?"

Septimus could feel an **Enchantment**, but he would not have called it wonderful. It felt **Darke** to him. Unwilling to upset the Snow Princess, he used the opaque Wizard-talk that he had recently acquired to get him out of situations he did not entirely understand. "I am sure there is many a wonderful **Enchantment** in this *enchanting* place."

"Oh," said Driffa, and she blushed.

"Oh, for goodness' sake," Jenna muttered under her breath. Ever since Septimus's longtime girlfriend Rose had dumped him for a certain scribe named Foxy, Septimus had turned into what Jenna considered to be an outrageous flirt.

The glimpse of the Blue Pinnacle – **Enchanted** or otherwise – was enough to guide the Snow Princess home. As the Dragon Boat dropped down through the clouds they caught a brief glimpse of beautiful snow-covered towers soaring up from the foothills and the welcoming glow of lanterns strung out along delicate walkways, but then a blizzard came howling in and they were lost from view.

There was nowhere for the Dragon Boat to land, but Septimus took her down until she was hovering a few feet above the snow. Jenna threw out the landing ladder and slipped into graceful-Queen mode, something she was extremely good at after seven years' practice. "Snow Princess Driffa, the Most High and Bountiful," she said. "It was our pleasure and privilege to return you to your beautiful country. We wish you much happiness among your kin. Farewell."

Determined to outdo Jenna's speech, the Snow Princess replied, "Oh, Castle Queen and ExtraOrdinary Wizard, you are truly the most generous of beings and I thank you from the soles of my feet to the top of my head. May your snowfall be soft and your skies be blue. May the Grula-Grula guide you true."

Septimus was puzzled at the mention of "Grula-Grula". He wanted to ask the Snow Princess what she meant, but one look at Jenna's expression told him that his Castle Queen wanted their passenger gone. Obediently, Septimus helped the Snow Princess on to the ladder. She held his hand for as long as possible and then she dropped down into the soft snow below and was gone, her white furs blending into the blizzard.

"I hope she will be all right," Septimus said.

"People like that usually are," Jenna observed.

Septimus took the Dragon Boat low across the centre of the SnowPlain to take another look at the intriguing Blue Pinnacle. As they drew near, the clouds briefly parted.

"Crumbs," said Jenna. "What's that?"

Beside the Blue Pinnacle was what looked like an ant nest. A huge mound of black spoil lay upon on the snow, and lines of figures were emerging from a great gash in the ground, slowly pushing barrows of dirt and rock.

Septimus frowned. "There is a **Darke Magyk** down there for sure," he said.

Suddenly a ball of flame shot into the air and headed straight for them. Septimus pushed the tiller across to take evasive action, but there was no need. The Dragon Boat had seen a

ThunderFlash before and she knew what was coming. She heeled over in a rapid turn and the ball of fire shot past, spinning as it went, the heat melting the ice on the deck.

Two more missiles came after them, but the Dragon Boat was out of reach. The snowstorm closed around them once more and Jenna made her way forward to the prow. She put her arms around the dragon's ice-cold neck and whispered, "Take us home."

WAITING

Two nights later the Dragon Boat flew over the PathFinders' sand-spit once again. This time there was no circle of lights. But down below on the beach in the darkness, someone was there.

It was Tod. She was sitting beside her father's empty boat, waiting.

At dawn the previous morning, Dan Moon had gone fishing. It had been a fine day and Tod had helped him stow the nets and push his boat, *Vega*, down the beach. She had watched him sail slowly out, and when his red sail disappeared around the headland Tod had wandered off to have breakfast with her friends, the Sarn family. Even though Aunt Mitza had gone out that morning, Tod had no wish to go home, in case she came back unexpectedly.

Many PathFinders had gone fishing that day. Tod returned to the beach in the evening with other villagers, watching the boats come in until the only one not come home was her father's. Darkness began to fall and the evening breeze blew in, but still there was no sign of Dan. Oskar and Ferdie Sarn joined her, bringing blankets and hot drinks. The long night passed slowly with nothing but an empty sea before them.

In the grey light of early dawn, Tod saw the unmistakable shape of Dan's boat drifting towards the shore. But one look told her that there was no one on board. *Vega*'s sail hung loose and she meandered along with the waves, rocking back and forth.

Jerra Sarn – Oskar and Ferdie's elder brother – took Tod out to fetch *Vega* and together, they pulled her up on to the sand. All that remained of Dan was his sodden fishing jacket lying in a pool of water at the bottom of his boat. There were no nets, no fish and absolutely no sign of Dan.

Tod put on Dan's fishing jacket and refused to leave the beach. The Sarns took turns keeping her company but Tod did not care who was with her – the only person she wanted to see was her father. She sat steadfastly staring at the sea, watching for Dan. Ferdie and Oskar did not understand why – for surely Dan had drowned? And Tod, keeping the Circle promise, did not tell them. But Jerra Sarn, who had been at the MidSummer Circle for the last time three days earlier, understood what Tod was hoping for.

And so, as the Dragon Boat flew overhead, Tod sat dreaming that any moment Dan Moon would break the surface of the water and come wading out to her to tell her that yes, he had PathFinder gills. Time and again Tod imagined how he would look – draped with seaweed, shivering, but alive. She dreamed of how they would help him up the beach and take him home, and how Dan would tell them stories of his strange walk home along the seabed, home to his little Alice, and that everything was all right now.

But when the sun rose over the sea for the second day, Dan had not come home, Tod was still waiting, and nothing was right.

PART III

A STORM BREWING

Dusk was falling. With her elflock flicking across her face in the wind, her short dark hair a tangled mess, Tod struggled to drag Dan's unwieldy fishing boat out of the sea.

A barefoot, red-headed boy wearing, like Tod, a hooded black-striped top and cut-off black trousers – or "trews", as the PathFinders called them – ran down the sloping beach towards her, the roar of the surf drowning out his voice.

"Tod! Hey, Tod! Wait. I'll help."

Suddenly Tod saw a pair of sun-browned hands next to hers on the rope, pulling hard. At once the boat felt lighter and began to break free of the tug of the backwash. "Oskar! Hey, *thanks*."

Together Tod and Oskar pulled *Vega* out of the waves and hauled her up the sand, until they reached a chain that snaked up the beach to a post driven deep into the dunes. Oskar's freckled, sunburned face glistened with salt water and his blue eyes with their distinctive yellow flecks crinkled into a smile. "She's heavy," he puffed. He waited while Tod roped the boat to the chain with two seaman-like knots. "Good catch?" he asked.

Tod ran her hand across her eyes, brushing away the sticky

salt. She smiled wearily. "Yeah," she said, and leaned into the boat to grab a large basket full to the brim with fish. "Not that Aunt Mitza will think so."

Oskar made a face. "No pleasing some people," he said. "Here, let me." He reached in and helped her haul the basket out. "You taking your nets in tonight?" he asked.

"No, they're OK."

Tod and Oskar trudged up the steep sandy beach, the basket of fish between them. At the top of the beach, where the sand dunes began, they put the basket down and turned to look back at the sea, wide and empty before them. The sun was setting, leaving behind a band of pale green cloud adrift in a pink sky. The afternoon wind had died away but the sea was what Tod called "edgy" – a dark, disturbed blue. "There's a storm coming," she said.

They followed the board path that led through the dunes to the settlement of houses scattered behind them in the lee of the wind. Made from tar-painted planks, the PathFinder houses were simple buildings, one room built upon another and set on to stilts, reaching up to the stars. Now, in the twilight, the houses looked like strange, dark creatures striding between the dunes, the candles in their windows flickering like watchful eyes.

Tod and Oskar came to Bell Square, a wide open space in the centre of which was a tall wooden frame that supported the PathFinder Bell. This bell was reputed to be from the ancient ship that had taken them to the stars. Many tracks led off from the square and one of these went to Tod's house, another to Oskar's. "I'd ask you to come and have supper with us," Oskar said, "but –"

"I'm not allowed," Tod finished for him. "Thanks anyway, Oskie. You know I'd love to." Tod thought of the ghastly Aunt Mitza waiting for her to come home. She thought of the scowl that would greet her and suddenly, without thinking, she found herself saying, "Why don't *you* come and have supper with *me*?"

Oskar looked shocked. "But what about Aunt Mitza?"

Tod shrugged. "What about her? I've caught *loads* of fish. I'm going to cook it – as usual. She's going to eat it – as usual. What's for her to complain about?"

Oskar thought that there would be *him* to complain about for a start, but he said nothing. If Tod wanted him to come to supper, then come to supper he would. Oskar guessed his mother would not be pleased – nowadays she liked all her children to be home before dark, but he knew he could win her over. "I'll go and tell Ma," he said. "I'll be at your place in ten minutes."

Tod smiled. "Great!"

Tod lugged the fish basket along the narrow track, damp and dark in the twilight. At the far end her house stood alone, tall and proud on its stilts, with bright green shutters and Tod's long, low attic room looking out to sea, crowned by a neat reed-thatched roof that Dan had renewed only a few weeks before he had disappeared.

Tod's arms were aching when at last she reached the foot of the stepladder that led up to her house. She put down the basket and looked up to the doorway above. The door was open and a light shone from inside. It looked so welcoming that for a moment Tod felt a flicker of hope that her father had come back – that when she walked through that door Dan would be there and once again sweep her up into his arms. It had been two months now since Dan Moon had gone fishing and never come back. Sometimes it felt like only yesterday, and sometimes it felt like for ever.

Aunt Mitza had compounded Tod's misery by staying on at the house. *Because it is my duty to be here, Alice, that is why*, she would say whenever Tod asked her why she didn't *go away and leave her alone*. And Tod knew that Aunt Mitza would indeed be there, sitting in her chair as ever, gazing out to the Far.

Tod shook away the sad thoughts about her father and picked up the basket of fish. She heaved it up the ladder and stopped in the doorway to get her breath back. Her father wasn't home, of course. *He* wouldn't have listened to her bringing up the fish without lifting a finger to help. She looked at the space beside the door where Dan's big seaboots had once stood – it was as empty as it had been when she left at dawn that morning. A wave of sadness overwhelmed Tod and she dropped the fish basket with a despairing *thud*.

From a winged chair in the shadows Aunt Mitza sprang to her feet. She stormed over to Tod, her black eyes staring out from her flat, red face, which was pulled taut by the dark hair scraped savagely up into a bun on the top of her head. She bristled with fury. "What do you think you're doing?" she demanded. "Banging the fish down like that – are you trying to give me a heart attack?"

"No," said Tod, thinking that wasn't such a bad idea. "I'm just bringing in the fish. Like I *always* do."

Aunt Mitza stared angrily at Tod. Tod returned the stare, determined not to blink first. Aunt Mitza looked away. "You'll be sorry," she said, turning on her heel and going back to the tall chair in the shadows.

Tod shrugged. She picked up the basket and went over to the cooking area. She selected three good-sized mackerel for the night's supper and laid them on the fish stone, then she took the rest out to the fish store – a box filled with ice (which every morning Tod heaved up from the icehouse and crushed) attached to the outside wall. Just as Tod had watched Dan doing, she gently laid the catch on the layers of ice, then sprinkled them with more ice. The fish would keep for about five days, although they always tasted best on the first day.

To the background *click-click-click* of Aunt Mitza's irritable knitting needles, Tod lit the fire in the stove, gutted the mackerel, and put them in the large black pan to gently fry. Then she went over to the table beside the window that looked out towards the marsh flats of the old lagoon at the back, which had once been one of her favourite places to sit and read. Tod threw her best red-checked cloth over the rough wood, laid three places for supper and waited for trouble. It wasn't long coming.

"*Three?*" asked Aunt Mitza, eagle-eyed as ever.

"I've asked Oskar Sarn for supper."

"Well, you can just *un*-ask him." Aunt Mitza threw down her knitting and set off towards the door. Tod knew what she was going to do – pull up the ladder so Oskar could not get in. She raced after her, but there was no need. At that very moment Oskar's cheery face peered in at the door.

It was not the most fun supper Oskar had ever had, but he would do anything for Tod, even if it meant spending a whole evening in the company of the dreaded Aunt Mitza. However, the evening was not as long as Oskar had expected. As soon as they had finished the fish – and before Oskar had time to point out that they hadn't even unwrapped the cake his mother had given him to bring for pudding – Aunt Mitza scraped back her chair and stood up. "It's late," she said. "Oskar Sarn, it's time you went home."

Tod frowned. "It's not at all late," she objected. "Oskar's only just got here."

Aunt Mitza folded her arms and stared at Tod. "Alice Tod-Hunter Moon. If I say it is late, it is *late*." She scowled at Oskar. "And if you know what's good for you, Oskar Sarn, you will go home *right now*."

Oskar felt terrible. He hated the thought of leaving Tod alone with someone who so obviously loathed her. And yet he knew if he stayed he would only make things worse for Tod. He got up from the table and, deliberately not looking at Aunt Mitza, gave Tod a strained smile. "I'll see you tomorrow," he said.

Aunt Mitza burst out laughing as though Oskar had made a joke. "Say goodbye, Oskar Sarn," she said. "Say *goodbye*."

Despondently, Oskar climbed down the ladder. The wind was blowing in from the sea strongly now, whisking sharp grains of sand off the dunes and sending them flicking across his skin. Oskar pulled his night cloak around him against the sand. His mother had insisted that Jerra came to meet him and walk home with him after supper, but his brother was not due for almost two hours, and there was no way Oskar was going to hang around waiting. His head down against the wind, Oskar set off quickly, following the track back along the sandspit.

As he trudged on, accompanied by the mournful rattle of the hollow dune grasses, all he could think about was the expression on Tod's face when she had waved him goodbye. She had looked so … Oskar tried to find the right word. The nearest he could come up with was "alone", but that didn't explain everything. No, he thought, there was something else – something new. Underneath it all, Tod had looked *scared*.

IN THE DUNES

Oskar, unlike Tod, still had both his parents – and until recently his home had been a happy place. But one dark night, a month after Dan Moon's fishing boat had floated back without him, Oskar and his little brother, Torr, with whom he shared his room, had been woken by their mother's screams. Oskar's twin sister, Ferdie, was *gone*. When he closed his eyes Oskar could still see Ferdie's bedroom window wide open and the soft summer rain blowing in on to her empty bed. All night Oskar and Jerra – along with his parents and their neighbours – had searched for her. They had found huge animal tracks in the sand outside Ferdie's window, which had led on to the main boardwalk, but after, nothing. The next day Oskar went out alone. Oskar was a skilled tracker, and despite the night's rain, he saw a few tracks going into the Far. An expedition set off but the trail disappeared. Ferdie was indeed gone.

But now, as Oskar pushed home against the rising wind, his mind was taken up not with Ferdie, but Tod. He remembered the scared look in her eyes, and Oskar had a feeling that, try as he might, he could not shake off: *something really bad was about to happen to Tod.*

Oskar needed time to think, time to work out what to do. He knew that as soon as he got home, any thoughts about Tod would be eaten up by his parents' sadness. He had plenty of time to walk home the long way by the salt marsh – a dried-up lake just beyond the village. He knew he could easily be home before Jerra left. Oskar loved the feeling of peace that the ancient PathFinder ghosts who wandered the marshes gave him. Maybe he would find some tonight; maybe he could even ask them what to do. Surely an ancient ghost would know?

It was the dark of the moon, a night when the PathFinders traditionally left lights in their windows until morning. As Oskar followed the boarded path, which weaved its way between the tree-trunk stilts of the houses, he felt as though he were walking through a mystical woodland, while above him the candle flames flickered like tiny stars falling to earth. It was beautiful, but it was also eerily empty. Since Ferdie had been taken, people did not go out much at night and all the ladders were drawn up so there were none of the easy comings and goings between the houses that had once happened.

With the quiet buzz of conversation in lilting PathFinder voices drifting down, Oskar headed along the track between the straggle of outlying houses. The wind was behind him and sent him quickly along. Soon he was leaving the lights and houses behind and following a narrow path as it dipped down into the cool darkness between the dunes. Even now, Oskar did not mind the dark; he knew the paths with his eyes closed and he enjoyed the feeling of invisibility that his night cloak gave him as his feet found their way across the weathered planks sunk into the sand. Silently Oskar padded along and soon the gentle *peep-peep* of waterbirds digging for worms on the marsh told him that he was very nearly there.

It was then, above the peepings, that Oskar became aware of a strange sound – a hoarse, breathy panting. He stopped dead. Knowing that, like many PathFinders, his skin and red hair had a sheen at night, Oskar pulled up the hood of his cloak; then he crouched down into the sandy darkness and listened.

Oskar could read the land like Tod could read the sea. He felt a few grains of sand skitter down; he heard the crackle of the dry dune grasses somewhere above him and he sensed the vibrations of large but light-footed creatures. Oskar reckoned that they were walking on all fours and, from the hesitant way they were moving, it seemed to him that they were unsure where to go.

The creatures drew to a halt and Oskar realised that they were almost directly above him. He froze. He suspected that the merest twitch of a muscle would get him noticed – and there was something about these creatures that made Oskar very certain that being noticed by them was the last thing he wanted to happen.

Click-clicker-click.

A low series of clicks were coming from the top of the dune. Oskar listened, recognising three distinct tones flicking in and out of what seemed to be some kind of discussion. He suppressed a shiver. The clicks were so foreign, so inhumanly mechanical, that they scared a very ancient part of his being. But what frightened Oskar most was something much more recent – the memory of a late-night conversation he had overheard between his parents not long after Ferdie had gone. "Jonas, I'm telling you, I heard *clicks*," he remembered his mother saying. "Like this –" Oskar's mother had made rapid

42

clicking noises with her tongue. "I thought it was one of Oskie's mechanical toys. You know how Ferdie liked – no, no, *likes* – to borrow Oskie's stuff. Oh, if only I'd gone in to see what it was. If *only* …"

Click. Click-clicker-click.

Oskar went cold. He knew that just a few feet above him were the creatures that had taken Ferdie.

Click-click-clicker-click.

And now they were back. Who had they come for this time?

Clicker-click.

He remembered Aunt Mitza's parting instruction: "Say goodbye, Oskar Sarn. Say *goodbye*."

Oskar knew the answer: they had come for Tod.

THE RACE

Click-click-clicker-click.

Oskar felt a rising terror. He decided that the only way to stop the panic was to see what was above him. The reality could be no worse than the images that were filling his head. Very slowly, Oskar looked up – and wished he hadn't.

Oskar's night vision showed him far more than he wished to see. Three beings, with wide, flat heads like those of a giant snake, stood at the top of the dune. Taller than a man, whip-thin yet muscular and as eerily white as deep-sea denizens that had never seen the light, they were half crouched on two powerful back legs; their smaller front legs – which had almost human hands – were off the ground, giving them an air of indecision. Their big heads were nodding in time with their *click-clicker-click*s and a sudden dart of a forked black tongue, glistening with slime, made Oskar's mouth go dry with fear.

Oskar recognised the creatures at once as Garmin. There was a drawing of them in one of his favourite books, *Magykal, Mystikal and Mythikal Creatures: Facts*. He was shocked. He had no idea Garmin actually existed.

Clicker-click. Clicker-click.

But the Garmin were as real as he was. Oskar could see the page in his book as though it were in front of him:

Garmin
Predator. Extruder. Non-venomous. Nocturnal. Cave-dwelling.
Covering: White skin. Minimal hair.

Oskar took a little comfort from "non-venomous", but that was outweighed by "predator". He was trying to remember what "extruder" meant when another shower of earth came flying down. Suddenly the Garmin took off, their powerful back legs sending them leaping swiftly across the top of the dunes – heading for Tod's house. A stab of fear ran through Oskar. The Garmin were going so fast that they would be there in no time at all. Oskar knew he had to get to Tod before the creatures did.

Oskar's only chance of reaching Tod first was to take the Burrows – direct routes through the dunes. Many were roofed over with planks and some actually burrowed through the sand. The Garmin would have to run up and down the hills, but by using the Burrows, Oskar could cut straight through. He raced off at top speed and was soon heading for the nearest Burrow. Oskar's parents had forbidden him to use the Burrows, as there had been a lethal sand-snake infestation some years earlier, but right then, Oskar didn't care about sand snakes. He reached the mouth of the Burrow, took his light stick from his pocket, snapped it open and dived inside. The dim green light of the stick showed just enough to stop him from cannoning into the sandy walls and, he hoped, to scare any remaining sand snakes away. Barefoot, Oskar ran fast, feeling the damp sand cold beneath his feet and hearing the muffled *thub-thubber-thub* of his footsteps. He was soon out of the Burrow and into the night air, heading for the next one, careering into a steep-sided canyon between two dunes, the sharp-edged grass cutting his legs as he ran. But Oskar felt nothing – nothing except for the terror of *being too late*.

Three long minutes later, Oskar emerged from a particularly low Burrow on to the old cinder track that led up from the rock pools at the end of the fishing beach. He paused very briefly to catch his breath and orient himself: *Tod's house should just be visible from here*, he thought. And sure enough, it was. To Oskar's surprise, the tall house standing alone was remarkably easy to spot – it was lit up like a MidWinter Feast tree, with candles blazing in every window.

Oskar was puzzled. Aunt Mitza was notoriously stingy – even at the dark of the moon she allowed only one window to be lit, but now every window had a whole line of candles blazing away on its sill, and the house shone like a beacon in the night. Suddenly, Oskar understood. The reason the house looked like a beacon was because that was exactly what it was: a beacon showing the Garmin where to come. *Aunt Mitza had planned it all*. Feeling sick with fear, Oskar raced up the track and hurtled down into a dark and particularly deep Burrow. Some thirty seconds later, he was pushing open a trapdoor and staggering out into the undercroft below Tod's house.

Oskar snapped his light stick closed and shoved it into his pocket. He stared at the brilliant window-shaped pools of light that the candles cast on to the sand surrounding the undercroft and listened hard for any clicks. All was silent. A sudden creak in the floorboards above sent his heart pounding until he realised it was just heavy footed Aunt Mitza moving across the room. Oskar knew he had to act quickly. Skirting the raised brick top of the icehouse, he padded soft and fast across the earthen floor of the undercroft, all the while listening, listening, *listening*. The sudden flap of a fishing net against the side of the house as the wind caught it made him stop dead – until he realised what it was and carried on.

Oskar reached the tree-trunk stilt at the front left-hand corner of the house, which was nearest to Tod's attic window. Carved into all PathFinder house stilts and continuing up the round corner posts on the sides of the houses were shallow footholds, cut so that nets could be easily hung up to dry. Oskar remembered Dan Moon scrambling up the very same stilt to hang out his nets after the day's fishing, cheerfully calling down to him and asking how he was. Oskar felt sad remembering Dan. Like Tod, he still found it hard to believe he was gone.

Silent as a cat, Oskar swung himself up on to a foothold and began to climb. Soon he was level with the first floor, where not so long ago, he had been having supper. Suddenly, in the window that faced the Far, Oskar saw the dark shape of Aunt Mitza outlined against the light, standing still and watchful, staring out into the night.

Like a lizard in the sun when a shadow passes over it, Oskar froze. He clung to the corner post, waiting for Aunt Mitza to go. But Aunt Mitza stood motionless – apart from her head, which she turned in quick, anxious movements. Soon Oskar's fingers and toes began to go numb and he knew he had to move or fall. Praying that Aunt Mitza didn't look around just then, he took a deep breath and carried on up, swinging from side to side, his bare feet finding the footholds, left … right … left … right, his strong hands pulling him ever upwards.

Tod's house was four storeys high if you counted the undercroft and the attic. By the time Oskar reached the bargeboard that ran below the reed-thatched roof, the muscles in his arms and legs were burning and his fingers were raw and bleeding from two broken nails. But Oskar felt nothing but triumph – *he had made it.*

Clinging to a net hook, his feet resting on the rim of the porthole that lit the attic stairs, Oskar considered how he was going to get across to Tod's window. It was only a short distance – no more than eight feet – but there was nothing to hold on to. Trying not to think of the drop below, Oskar put his right foot into the curve of the nearest net hook and levered himself up so he lay flat upon the thatch. Then, determined not to look down, he inched his way, crab-like, along the spiky reeds and was soon within arm's length of Tod's little dormer window. But, as he leaned across to get a handhold on the window sill, Oskar's heart leaped into his mouth. Far below, he glimpsed three white shapes flitting across a pool of window light on the ground.

Click-clicker-click.

The Garmin were here.

GARMIN

Alice TodHunter Moon was not a girl given to screaming. But it took all of Tod's nerve – plus her determination that Aunt Mitza was *never* going to hear her scream – not to yell out loud when she saw a bloody hand with broken nails clawing at her window. Tod picked up a net hook and advanced towards the window, ready to smash the hand away. She swung the hook back and was about to bring it crashing through the glass when Oskar's pale face – his mouth open in dismay as he saw the net hook swinging his way – came into view on the other side of the window.

With a deep *thud*, the net hook buried itself in the thick upright in the middle of the casement window and a shocked Oskar lost his grip and began to slide down the thatch. Tod threw open the window and in one easy, practised movement she grabbed hold of Oskar's shirt, pulled him in and deposited him on the floor – she had landed fish bigger than Oskar Sarn many times. He lay winded, staring up at Tod in much the same manner as her last Gooper fish had done.

Tod dropped to the floor. "Oskie!" she said. "Oskie, hey, what are you doing?"

"Tod," Oskar gasped. "You – we – we've got to get out of here. The things that came for Ferdie – they're Garmin, and they've come for you. *They're here.*"

Tod went cold. She jumped up, pulled Oskar to his feet and headed towards the attic ladder, dragging Oskar with her. Oskar protested. "No, no," he whispered. "The window. *Out of the window!*" Tod did not hear. She was already on the ladder, climbing down like a monkey and beckoning urgently to Oskar to *hurry up*. Oskar had no option but to follow. He swung himself after her and as Tod stepped on to the landing below, Oskar jumped lightly from the ladder and grabbed her.

"Tod. Stop. Listen. *They're inside the house.*"

Tod went pale. From the floor below came Aunt Mitza's familiar low growl followed by a terrifying new sound for Tod – a rapid series of *click-click-clicker-click-click-click-click*. Goosebumps went running over Tod and Oskar. The clicks were utterly inhuman – and frighteningly close.

But Tod still seemed not to understand. "Aunt Mitza!" she whispered. "They'll get her."

Oskar shook his head with a grim smile. "No, Tod. Aunt Mitza fixed this up. They'll get *you*."

Tod looked horrified.

A flight of open stairs led down to the kitchen. Suddenly, a bulky Aunt Mitza–shaped shadow, thrown into sharp definition by the blazing candles in the room below, moved across the bottom step.

Oskar was beginning to panic. "Tod," he whispered, "we've got to get *out*." Tod understood now. She grabbed hold of Oskar and propelled him through one of the two doors leading off the landing. As they hurried into the room, the stairs shook – Aunt Mitza was on her way. And on her heels, they both knew, were the Garmin.

The room smelled musty. It contained the big bed that Tod's parents had once shared and a small chair strewn with Aunt Mitza's clothes. Its flimsy door shook as Aunt Mitza crossed the landing. Tod was hurrying across to the furthest window when something happened that froze them to the spot: a heavy Aunt Mitza footstep loosened the latch and the bedroom door swung slowly open.

Tod and Oskar stared at each other in panic. Through the opening they saw Aunt Mitza's broad back. She was facing three-quarters away from them, holding a candle and looking down the stairs. Tod – who had spent many frightening evenings sizing up her step-aunt – stared at Aunt Mitza, trying to anticipate her next move. Never before had it been so important to get it right. From the solid immovability of Aunt Mitza's stance, Tod reckoned that she was too preoccupied with the Garmin to bother about an annoying door. But Tod also knew that any movement would catch Aunt Mitza's eye – they must tough it out, stay stone-still and hope. Tod glanced at Oskar and she could see he had come to the same conclusion.

From the shadows, Tod and Oskar heard the soft *thub-thub* of paw pads. Aunt Mitza raised her arm to hold the candle high to guide them, and it was now that Tod saw the Garmin for the first time. With some difficulty, she controlled a shiver that welled up from deep inside her. Aunt Mitza stepped back, crowded out by the huge creatures. She pointed at the ladder leading to Tod's attic room and one of the Garmin let go a thin stream of dribble from its mouth, as if excited by the prospect ahead. Surprisingly agile for its size, the Garmin headed up the ladder. The other two followed it, their huge, flat heads nodding with each step. Oskar clenched his fists. It made him feel sick to think that if he had been a few minutes later, right now Tod would be facing these creatures alone.

Aunt Mitza moved to the foot of the ladder and gazed upwards, waiting, Oskar knew, for Tod's scream. This was their chance.

He turned to Tod and mouthed, *Let's get out of here!*

GONE

Tod slipped the catch on the bedroom window and swung it open. The salt-scented night air swept into the musty room, and Oskar looked at Tod anxiously. Surely Aunt Mitza would smell the sea?

But out on the landing, Aunt Mitza had other things to worry about. She could hear the heavy thudding of running, jumping, padding paws as the Garmin paced the room, looking for their prey; she could hear the splintering of wood as furniture was hurled to the floor and increasingly loud *click-clicker-click*s. But she could hear no shrieks, no screams, no pleas for help. Nothing. Aunt Mitza knew enough about her step-niece to expect her to put up a fight. A worm of worry began to gnaw at her. Why was it taking so *long*?

By now Tod was out of the window, out into the rain that was coming in from the sea, out and swinging across to the fishing net that hung down the back of the house. Quickly, Oskar followed. As he scrabbled on to the net he heard the heavy *thub-thub* of the Garmin leaping down the attic steps. Then came a series of low, threatening clicks, quickly followed by Aunt Mitza's voice, sharp with panic: "She *is* up there. I *promise* you. She must be hiding in her secret cupboard. She's a devious little madam. I'll go up and get her."

As Aunt Mitza's hurried ascent of the ladder sent the window rattling, Oskar quickly clambered down after Tod, who was waiting for him below. He grabbed hold of Tod's hand and dragged her to the undercroft and trapdoor to the Burrow entrance. Tod shuddered. She hated the Burrows.

"Not down there," she whispered.

"Yes," hissed Oskar. "We have to."

Tod watched Oskar pull up the trapdoor and disappear into the dark, then she took a deep breath and followed him down the short ladder. The Burrow was as horrible as Tod had expected, but Oskar led the way in a very capable manner, and his light stick gave her some reassurance that she was not about to step on a sand snake. She followed Oskar as he headed steadily on through the cave-cold sand, and a few minutes later they emerged at the cinder track.

The rising wind and sharp spikes of rain took their breath away as they turned to look back at Tod's house. The lights still blazed out and nothing seemed to have changed. Tod stared at her home, trying to make sense of what had just happened, but it gave her no clues.

"C'mon," said Oskar. "We're not safe here. Follow me."

Tod nodded, but did not move. Oskar grabbed her hand and pulled. "Tod," he said urgently. "Please. Come on."

"Yeah. OK." But still Tod stood, mesmerised by her house.

And then a thin, terrified scream cut through the night. It flew out of the house, across the dark and windswept dunes, and it made the hairs on Oskar's neck stand on end.

The scream set Tod free. She and Oskar set off at a sprint; they hurtled down into the main Burrow, which was wide enough for two, and they did not stop until Oskar skidded to a halt at the tenth exit and jerked his thumb at a ladder that led upwards. He shot up the ladder, pushed open the trapdoor and waited as Tod tumbled out behind him.

Oskar let the trapdoor drop with a bang and sighed with relief. He was home. Safe. He took Tod's hand and led her out from the undercroft towards the outside steps. As they emerged from the shadows, the steps shook and two big feet came into view.

"Jerra!" Oskar called out.

Oskar's big brother spun around, a surprised look on his round, sunburned face. "Hey, Osk – what're you doing here? You're meant to be at Tod's. Mum will have a fit if she knows you came back on your own." Jerra stopped, aware now that Oskar was not alone. "Who's that?" he asked.

Tod stepped forward. "Me," she said. "Hello, Jerra."

"Hey, Tod," Jerra said. Puzzled, because he knew very well that Tod was not allowed out, he asked, "What you doing here?" And then, quickly, "Oh. I mean, it's really nice to see you. Really great, but you're not usually –"

"Shut up, Jerra," Oskar interrupted. "We've got to get inside. Fast. And bar the door."

Jerra looked shocked – Oskar was usually so calm. "OK, Oskie," he said.

Surprised at how shaky her legs suddenly felt, Tod climbed the steps and stepped uncertainly into the welcoming candlelit room. Oskar's mother was busy at the kitchen end of the room, but at the unfamiliar footstep on the threshold she turned around. Her face lit up when she saw Tod. She put down a bunch of sea kale she was chopping and, wiping her hands on her apron as she went, hurried over to Tod and enveloped her in a hug.

It was too much for Tod. To her dismay, tears welled up in her eyes. Since her father had disappeared, Tod had tried not to cry. She was afraid that if she started she might never stop.

The noisy entrance of Oskar and Jerra saved her. "Ma, we've got to bar the door," Jerra said, picking up the iron bar that hung ready on the wall.

"And the windows," said Oskar, hurrying across the room.

Rosie Sarn stared at her sons in dismay. "Oh my days," she said. "What has happened?"

LIGHT OF DAY

Tod woke slowly. It took her a while to understand why the grey light of dawn was coming into her room in the wrong place, why the howling wind was not making her window frame rattle and why the sea sounded so much quieter. A few long, drowsy minutes later, she remembered. She was in Ferdie's room – in Ferdie's bed. Warily, Tod opened her eyes and gazed around the plain, wood-shuttered room. She looked down at the floor just to check that Ferdie was not lying on the little spare truckle bed like she always used to in the happy days before Dan Moon had disappeared, when Tod had been allowed to sleep over at the Sarns'.

But there was no truckle bed and no Ferdie. Tod slumped back on the pillow and stared up at the wooden ceiling, from which hung the intricate kites that Ferdie used to sew and decorate. Something caught Tod's eye: a tiny, green felt dragon on the end of a little chain dangling on a hook just above her head. Tod reached out to stroke it. This was Ferdie's lucky mascot – she had carried it everywhere with her and kept it beside her at night. But Ferdie had had no time to grab her dragon the night she was taken by the Garmin. The thought of how horrific it must have been for Ferdie swept over Tod and mingled with her own terror of the night before. She knew she had been very lucky. Oskar had done for her what he had not been able to do for Ferdie.

As Tod listened to the sounds of the Sarn household beginning to stir, her fear ebbed away and she realised that for the first time since her father had gone, she felt safe. She drifted into a comfortable half-sleep, with the sound of the wind and the rain outside, luxuriating in the feeling of being secure inside.

At breakfast Rosie Sarn took charge. The long, scrubbed table was set for seven, and Rosie, small and round with her dark curly hair worn in a thick plait, sat at the end of the table, cutting slices of bread from a long loaf while Jonas Sarn fussed about the stove, frying the breakfast sardines. Ranged along benches on either side of the table were the Sarn family. Next to Rosie was little Torr, five years old, his dark hair sticking up on end as it always did, his bright blue eyes big with the knowledge that something exciting had happened last night that no one would tell him about. Next to him sat Oskar and next to Oskar was an empty plate that would stay that way all through breakfast – this was Ferdie's place, which Rosie Sarn laid for every meal.

Tod sat quietly opposite Torr. Beside her Jerra – tall, lanky and brown from the sea – fiddled awkwardly with his knife. No one spoke. It felt as though there was too much to say, that once they began to talk they would not be able to stop. Rosie passed the slices of bread along the table and Jonas arrived with a pan of sizzling sardines. They ate quietly, the clink of the knives and the bubbling of the coffee pot the only sounds to break the silence. Torr gazed from one face to another, trying to work out what had happened, impatient to know. In the middle of chewing his last sardine he said, "Tod, did Aunt Mitza go 'way?"

"Torr, please don't talk with your mouth full," said Rosie.

Torr swallowed his sardine. "But *did* she? Because Aunt Mitza doesn't like us, does she, Tod? That's why you can't come and stay with us any more. But now you are here." Torr smiled. "Which is very, *very* nice."

Tod smiled back at Torr. "Torr, you would not believe how nice it is to be here," she said, glancing uncertainly at Rosie. Tod was unsure how much to say in front of Torr. She didn't want to scare him. Rosie shook her head in warning.

But Torr was not to be put off. "So *did* Aunt Mitza go 'way?" he persisted, adding, "I hope she did, because she was *horrid*." He glanced at his mother, expecting her to tell him that he must not call anyone horrid, but his mother said nothing.

The memory of the thin, high scream that Tod had heard on the dunes played back in her head – and not for the first time that morning. "I think," she said slowly, "that maybe I ought to go and see ... see if Aunt Mitza really has, er, gone away."

Jonas, a man of few words, spoke for them all. "We will come with you," he said.

OUT OF THE BOX

Aunt Mitza was gone.

Tod, Oskar, Jonas and Jerra stood in the wreckage of the room where a little more than twelve hours before, Oskar had sat eating a very awkward supper. They had searched the house and found nothing but destruction. Tod thought it looked as though the storm had swept through the inside of the house, leaving the outside oddly untouched. Except, she thought, a storm left a freshness in the air when it abated, and the smell inside the house was anything but fresh.

Oskar wrinkled his nose in disgust. "It smells revolting."

"It smells of fear," Tod said sombrely. "Poor Aunt Mitza. She must have been terrified."

Oskar looked at Tod in amazement. "*Poor Aunt Mitza?* Tod, all this was Aunt Mitza's own doing. She brought those creatures here. And it was *you* who was meant to be terrified. And *you* who would have been gone this morn—" Oskar gulped. The thought of coming here and finding Tod gone was too much.

Jonas took charge. "Children, enough," he said in his soft PathFinder lilt. "We shall not think of what might have been, but of what is to be." He turned to Tod, addressing her by her formal name as the older ones always did. "Alice, you must not remain here. Our home is now your home. Is there anything you need to bring with you?"

Tod nodded. "A box. In my room."

"Oskar, go up with Alice and help her bring the box," said Jonas.

Tod was shocked when she saw her room. Its contents had been reduced to little more than matchwood. It reminded her of a wrecked ship she had once seen pounded into smithereens by the surf. She shuddered. Something had got very angry in this room. Oskar was equally dismayed. He guessed that Tod's box lay smashed on the floor along with everything else.

But Tod seemed unconcerned. She waded through the debris to the window and kicked away a pile of shredded bed-clothes mixed with the remains of a chair, exposing the bare floorboards beneath. Tod kneeled down and drew out what looked like a short pencil. She pressed the end of the "pencil" and it flipped out to become a screwdriver. Oskar smiled – it was the present he had given Tod for her twelfth birthday. Tod unscrewed a small section of floorboard, pulled the board up and reached in. She looked up at Oskar, smiling. "Still here," she said.

It was a small, exquisite box carved from lapis lazuli. It sat neatly on Tod's open hand, the lapis – dark blue with streaks of gold – glinting in a small beam of sunlight. Each corner of the box was protected by a tiny piece of curved silver and the edges reinforced with strips of battered darkened silver.

"It's so *beautiful*," said Oskar.

Tod smiled. "It is, isn't it? It's a family treasure. It belonged to … to Dad." Tod opened the box to show a bright blue felt lining with a moulded hollow in which lay a silver filigree

61

pointer shaped like a long, thin triangle with a delicate arrow-tipped point. It had a hollow lapis dome at the flat end of the triangle, which had a thick curl of silver on its opposite side with a hole in it. Beside it was a tiny padded leather triangle with a small onyx sphere on one of its points. Tod took out the pointer and showed it to Oskar. "It's called a **PathFinder**."

"Just like us," said Oskar.

"Yeah," said Tod. "Dad gave it to me just before the Circle, because that is when his father gave it to him. He said it had been handed down to the oldest child since the days before we went to the –" Tod stopped, realising she was about to tell Oskar a Circle secret. "Anyway," she said hurriedly, "it fits together like this ..." Tod picked up the onyx sphere and held its leather triangle between her finger and thumb. She placed the hollow dome of the **PathFinder** over the sphere. The filigree pointer pivoted gently, swinging back and forth, and Oskar had the impression that the dome was actually floating on the sphere.

"It's a compass," he said. "The most beautiful one I have ever seen."

"But it's not a proper compass, is it?" said Tod. "Because there are no compass points."

Oskar frowned. "I suppose. But it does look like it is showing you the way to somewhere, all the same."

Tod gave Oskar a lopsided smile. "Wish it would show me the way to Dad," she said sadly.

Oskar quickly changed the subject. "Hey, look. You've got a really cool snake ring, too."

Tod gently laid the **PathFinder** back in the box and picked up the ring, which was nestling in a corner. It was formed from two thick bands of gold and silver – the snakes – twisted together. The snakes' heads met in the front of the ring and curled around each other, looking up at the wearer. "It was my mother's," said Tod.

"Oh," said Oskar. He wished he hadn't pointed out the ring now. Everything reminded Tod of the people she had lost. Oskar hadn't thought of it before, but he suddenly realised that Tod was an orphan. "Orphan" was such a sad and lonely word, Oskar thought.

Tod was still holding the snake ring. "I'm going to wear it when it fits me," she said.

"I think it will fit *now*," Oskar said, hoping to cheer things up a little. "It will go on your thumb."

"Oh," said Tod. "I think it will." She slipped her mother's ring on to her right thumb and to her surprise, the silver and gold snakes sat snug and tight. It belonged, and Tod felt like she had somehow grown up. "Oskie," she said, "I've made up my mind."

"About what?" Oskar looked worried.

"Stuff."

"What kind of stuff?"

"Stuff … like not waiting around for things to happen. Like making things happen ourselves. Oskie, you and I are going to look for Ferdie. We are going to find her and bring her home."

A broad smile spread over Oskar's face. "You bet," he said.

PLANS

Jonas went to check his boat after the night's storm, while Tod, Oskar and Jerra set off back to the Sarn house. The storm had left behind a deep blue sky with white scudding clouds and the smell of damp sand. The sun was warm and the air felt fresh and clean. They stood on the beach, watching the wind cut across the dune grasses.

"Jerra," said Tod, "we are going to find Ferdie."

Jerra grinned. "Yes, we have a really good chance, I reckon." Then he stopped and looked puzzled. "But how did you know?"

Oskar knew when his brother was up to something. "Jerra, what's going on?"

"I think I've found out where Ferdie is."

"Why didn't you *tell* us?" Oskar asked, incredulous.

"Er ... well, it's a long story," Jerra mumbled. "I was doing my lobster pots and I fell overboard and – hey, you two, don't look at me like that!"

Oskar and Tod were staring at Jerra, shocked. It was considered shameful to fall out of one's boat.

"It wasn't so bad," Jerra protested. "I caught hold of the rope as I fell and this Trading Post girl, Annar, she was fishing nearby and she helped me get back in. So we got talking. And I told her about Ferdie –"

64

Oskar was cross. "You told a Trading Post *stranger* about our sister?"

"No one at sea is a stranger, Oskie. Anyway, why not? I want to find Ferdie as much as you do, you know."

"What did the girl – Annar – tell you?" asked Tod.

"She said that a ship called the *Tristan* is moored up the creek at the OutPost – you know, just along from the Trading Post. People say that it has weird, white creatures on board that only come out at night."

"Garmin!" Oskar and Tod said together.

Jerra carried on. "Annar says there have been rumours for some time that there are prisoners on the ship. A few weeks ago Annar's sister went missing and Annar sailed to the *Tristan* to see if she was there."

"Was she?" asked Tod.

Jerra shook his head. "No. But, this is the thing …" His voice dropped to a whisper. "One of the crew told Annar that the only girl on board was a red-headed PathFinder, a prisoner who had arrived about a month ago."

"Ferdie!" gasped Tod. "It *must* be."

"Yes," said Jerra. "That's what I think too."

Tod was suspicious. She remembered what Dan had told them at the Circle. "Jerra, can you really believe what someone from the OutPost says?" she asked.

"I believe Annar," Jerra said. "And Tod, we who fish for a living are different. At sea we are all brothers and sisters. It does not matter where we come from."

Tod remembered Dan saying something similar. And as they turned off along the track that led to the Sarn house, she said, "We have to go and find that ship. We *have* to see if Ferdie is on there."

Jerra looked a little sheepish. "Actually, it's all fixed up. I've already arranged to meet Annar at Goat Rock – it's an island near the OutPost. Annar is going to pilot me through the sandbanks."

"And Oskar and me," said Tod. "We're coming too."

Jerra smiled. "I was hoping you might say that. Actually, I was going to ask you both. The thing is, Annar can't go back on the ship; they'll recognise her. They have kids working there, and to older people all kids look the same. So all you need is to look like you belong and they won't give you a second glance."

"How do we look like we belong?" asked Oskar.

"Leave that to Annar," Jerra replied mysteriously.

The track rounded a dune and the Sarn house came into view. In the window Oskar saw Rosie Sarn looking out anxiously. "Ma's not going to like us going," he said.

"We'll tell her about Ferdie first," Jerra said. "Let me do it, OK?"

Rosie Sarn was overcome with joy at the thought that Ferdie might be found, but her happiness did not last long. When she heard that two more of her children were putting themselves in danger, Rosie put her foot down. "Jerra, Oskar, Tod – *no*. I am not losing you as well. Jonas will go."

It seemed to Oskar that his brother had grown up overnight. "No, Mum," Jerra said. "It's not for Dad to do. Oskie and Tod are coming. That is how it has to be."

Jonas reached out and took his wife's hand. "We must trust Jerra, dear." Rosie sighed. She knew she had lost.

At supper, Jerra outlined his plans. Jonas was worried. "That's all very well, Jerra," he said, "but you know how they are at the OutPost. They throw PathFinders into prison, no questions asked. Rosie's uncle was in one of their prisons for years. He was a wreck when he eventually got out."

"But why, Dad?" asked Oskar.

Jonas sighed. "It goes back a long way, Oskie. You'll hear about it next summer when you go to the Circle." Jonas fell silent. He suddenly remembered that Dan Moon was no longer there to lead the Circle. "You must take night gloves and cloaks, and always wear your hood up. You must not forget that we Sarns, Moons and Starrs have a sheen to our skin and hair that is easy to recognise."

"I'll be OK," said Tod. "I have my mother's complexion."

"True," said Rosie. "But you must still be careful, Tod."

"Anyway," said Jerra. "We'll be on our way home by nightfall. With Ferdie."

This was too much for Rosie Sarn. She buried her head in her hands. "Oh, Ferdie," she whispered. "My poor, poor Ferdie."

MEMORIES

Later that night as Tod tried to sleep, lying in Ferdie's bed, she remembered the first time she had seen the Dragon Boat. Her mother had still been alive then, although now Tod understood that she was already very ill. Tod couldn't sleep then, either. She loved to hear the happy sound of her parents' quiet conversation downstairs – even though it was punctuated by her mother's long bouts of coughing, which had worried her. Tod hadn't wanted to disturb them, so she had got out of bed, padded across to the attic window, stood up on her window seat and looked out. It was a beautiful starry sky, with a full moon riding high, and Tod had gazed at it for what felt like hours. She was beginning to get cold and was about to go back to bed when she saw what at first she had thought was a huge bird. And then she had realised that she was looking at a dragon. To her joy, the dragon swooped down and flew gracefully over the house. To her amazement Tod saw that the dragon was also a boat with a beautiful golden hull. At the tiller was a boy – a big boy even older than Jerra was then. He wore green robes with purple ribbons glinting on his sleeves, and she knew at once that he was **Magykal**. Tod had been entranced.

Tod's mother, Cassi TodHunter Draa, was from a **Magykal** family in the Hot Dry Deserts of the South. Her mother used to tell stories about how she had grown up in a big, round tent under the stars, and how the Draa family were the most powerful Wizards in the land. Tod had longed to be **Magykal**; she had decided that if only she could have purple ribbons like the boy with the dragon, then she would be. She had pestered her mother and father for purple ribbons, and when they gave her some for her seventh birthday, Tod was ecstatic. And when Ferdie's seventh birthday came around a few months later, Tod gave her one of her precious purple ribbons. Ferdie had been thrilled, and they had played **Magyk** games in the dunes all that summer.

Tod held up her arm and looked sadly at the thin, faded purple ribbon she still wore around her wrist – just as Ferdie did. Drowsy with dragons and purple ribbons, Tod fell into a deep sleep. Six hours later Oskar was shaking her awake.

"Time to go, Tod," he said. "Time to go and get Ferdie."

PART
IV

SKIMMER

It was three o'clock in the morning and four figures were making their way through the dunes in the darkness, heading for the sound of the gentle swells breaking on the beach. The tide was high but it was about to turn, and the ebb would take them quickly along the sandspit and out to sea. Jonas was going with them to help launch Jerra's boat, *Skimmer*, but Rosie had stayed home with little Torr. And when the house was silent and all were gone, Rosie felt a wave of despair wash over her – her family was disappearing so fast that it felt as though their house had sprung a leak.

Skimmer sped along, keeping close enough to the shore to see the lights from the PathFinder houses, heading for the Beacon that marked the end of the spit. The night air was cold and Tod and Oskar sat under the cuddy at the prow of the boat, wrapped in thick waterproof blankets. Oskar took the familiar tiny green felt dragon out of his pocket. "Look," he said. "I brought this. For Ferdie. For luck."

Skimmer cut swiftly through the dark water and they quickly reached the Beacon. Here, Jerra tacked the boat and headed into the deep channel between outlying sandbanks, which would take them to the open sea. In the east the sky was lightening to a milky green, and they knew that soon their boat would be all too visible. This would have spelled trouble for a traditional PathFinder boat in fishing waters so near the Trading Post and OutPost, but *Skimmer* was different. Some years ago Jerra had found her wrecked upon the beach and, with the help of his father, he had spent many happy summers repairing her. And now his boat was going to come into her own, for she was an OutPost boat with an OutPost name. Jerra had been teased about this because traditional PathFinder boats were given names of stars, but he had refused to change it. "That's what she's called and that's the way she stays. How will she know to answer to any other name?" he had said.

Jerra now set an OutPost ensign fluttering from the stern (which Rosie had stayed up all night sewing), spread a patterned rug from their kitchen on to the boat's rough wooden deck and asked Oskar to nail a strip of traditional OutPost gold braid along the edge of the cuddy. "There," he said with a grin. "Now she looks like all those other fancy-pants OutPost boats. Poor *Skimmer*."

The misty pale sun climbed higher in the sky, a brisk breeze sprang up and the ensign – dark blue with two big gold stars – fluttered importantly as *Skimmer* headed for Goat Rock, a tiny rocky island that, if seen with half-closed eyes and a lot of imagination, was the shape of a goat's head. *Skimmer* was well named. She skimmed across the water and soon they were near enough to Goat Rock to see an elegant little boat, its sails white against the grey granite, waiting for them.

"There she is," said Jerra, waving excitedly. "There's Annar!"

Through the telescope Tod saw a dark-haired girl in a thick blue fisherman's jersey. She handed the telescope to Oskar and whispered, "She looks OK, Oskie."

74

Annar and her boat, *Swan*, were waiting at a small stone quay on the sheltered side of Goat Rock, but as *Skimmer* approached she sailed out to meet them. "There's a thick mist up there this morning," she told them. "Follow close or you'll lose me."

As they drew near the mouth of the creek, a white mist came in and Annar raised a red pennant to make it easier for them to follow. Soon the wind died and both boats had to be rowed the rest of the way. They tied *Skimmer* and *Swan* together to the OutPost quay wall and moments later they were on the quayside. Annar and Jerra were hugging and smiling delightedly. Oskar raised his eyebrows at Tod as if to say, *Jerra's got a girlfriend.*

"This is my brother Oskar and our best friend, Tod," said Jerra, introducing them to Annar.

"Hello, Oskar. Hello, Tod," Annar said, a little shyly.

Tod noticed that Annar was standing beneath a large board on which was a written long list, each section beginning with: "DO NOT". One in particular caught her eye: *DO NOT land here if you are an undesirable alien. Undesirable aliens include: Path-Finders, Moth-Wardens and Carminators. Penalty: not less than ten years in prison.*

Across the word "PathFinder", someone had scrawled: *fish slime.*

Annar followed Tod's gaze. "I'm sorry," she said. "It's horrible. But we have to come here to get a pass for the creek."

But the Quay Office was not yet open. Annar glanced around anxiously. "Let's go somewhere quiet," she said. She led them to a line of deserted net lofts that backed on to the high wall that separated the OutPost from the woods and the creek beyond. They sat in the sunshine, watching the Quay Office and hoping that someone would soon arrive to open up.

75

"I've got your stuff here," Annar said. She handed Tod and Oskar two red-and-white-striped tops with *Tristan* embroidered across the back in big blue letters. "Put them on later," she said. "No one likes the *Tristan* people here."

Tod listened carefully while Annar described the layout of the *Tristan*. She did it so well that Tod could picture the ship as if she were there. Oskar, however, was having difficulty concentrating. He was ravenously hungry and longing for breakfast. Every now and then he glanced across at a hut with the words *SnakShak* scrawled across its black wooden planks. It sat in the middle of the quayside sporting a cheerful striped awning, and it was selling fresh bacon rolls. The smell of the frying bacon was driving Oskar crazy. As Annar once again ran through the layout of the hatches on the *Tristan*'s deck, Oskar's stomach let out a long growl – and before anyone could stop him, he was up and away, heading towards the SnakShak.

"Sheesh!" said Jerra, leaping to his feet. "What's he doing?"

Oskar had ducked in under the awning and was approaching the counter. Jerra looked at Annar in a panic. "He's got to get out of there."

"I'll get him," said Annar, setting off towards the SnakShak with Jerra and Tod in tow. "Nice and slow. No drawing attention to ourselves. We just act natural, OK?"

Jerra nodded and tried to walk nonchalantly. Tod followed, confused. Oskar seemed to be behaving in the most natural way of all, she thought. What was wrong with going to get a bacon roll? Tod soon found out.

Under the awning, a young seafaring couple looked up from their breakfast. They smiled at Oskar – as people who have spent time at sea do when they reach the safety of land. They both looked windswept and sunburned. The young man had friendly, bright green eyes, and a shock of tangled straw-coloured hair with plaits and beads woven into it. The young woman, with her white-blonde hair and blue eyes, was clearly from the Land of the Long Nights; on her lap was a small orange cat to whom she was feeding tiny fish. As Annar hurried in after Oskar, the couple smiled at her too, but Annar was too preoccupied to return their greeting. She put her arm around Oskar's shoulders and Oskar looked up irritably. He didn't think Annar knew him well enough to do that.

"Come now, Oskar," said Annar. "We must go."

"But I've just ordered four bacon rolls," Oskar said in his telltale lilting PathFinder accent.

"I'll get them," said Annar. "Go now, your brother wishes to speak to you."

Oskar frowned. "Can't it wait?"

"No," Annar said sternly.

Tod saw the cook behind the counter stare at Oskar's hand as he offered his payment of four big copper pennies. In the shadows of the awning the sheen on Oskar's skin and red hair flashed like the shine on a newly landed fish. Now Tod understood Jerra's concern.

The cook recoiled. "Put them there, *Fish Boy*," he muttered under his breath, indicating the zinc counter. But still Oskar stood waiting, taking no notice of Annar.

"I'm going to get him," muttered Tod.

As Tod joined Oskar and Annar at the counter she saw two OutPost officials wandering across to the Quay Office, their gold braid glittering in the sun and their elaborately curled white wigs bright against the black-painted sheds behind them. The SnakShak cook saw them too.

"Hey!" he yelled. "Fish slime here! Fish slime!"

Tod leaped forward and grabbed Oskar. "Run, you idiot!" she told him. With Annar on one side and Tod on the other, Oskar was propelled rapidly out of the SnakShak, protesting as he went. "Ferdie's dragon! You made me drop her dragon!"

Tod and Jerra pushed Oskar across the quay, following Annar as she dodged behind a line of net lofts. Behind them they heard the thudding of heavy footsteps. Annar dived under a tangled pile of old fishing nets, and Tod, Oskar and Jerra followed fast. In the rank, fish-smelling gloom they listened to the sound of the pursuing footsteps stop some distance away, wait a while and then walk off. None of the officials wanted to get their finery dirty.

Many long, smelly minutes later they warily crept out.

"You idiot!" Jerra hissed at his brother. "You stupid little know-it-all. You total —"

"That's enough, Jerra," Tod cut in. "Oskie knows it was stupid. There's no point fighting about it."

Oskar was distraught. "Ferdie's dragon. Her lucky dragon!"

"Oskie," said Tod, "you *have* to forget the dragon."

"Now please, follow me," Annar said.

Oskar hung back. "But the *dragon*," he wailed.

Jerra grabbed hold of Oskar's top and pulled him along. "Shut up, Oskar. You nearly got us all thrown in prison for *ten years*."

Oskar looked wide-eyed at Jerra. "Why?"

"Idiot boy. Didn't you read the sign? We're not allowed here, *get it*?"

Suddenly a shout from behind made them all jump. "Hey!"

They spun around and to their horror saw the young sea-faring man who had been at the SnakShak running towards them, closely followed by his girlfriend carrying her cat.

"Run!" said Jerra.

"No, wait," said Tod. "Look, I think she's got – yes, *she's got Ferdie's dragon!*"

Jerra hesitated. The young woman with the cat was holding out something very small and possibly green.

"Please, Jerra," Oskar pleaded. "Please wait."

"Let's wait," said Tod. "I think they're OK."

Jerra was not inclined to trust his brother's judgement, but he did trust Tod's.

The couple reached them. "You dropped this," the young woman said, handing Ferdie's felt dragon to Oskar with a smile.

"Oh, thank you," said Oskar. "Thank you very, very much!"

"It is my pleasure," she said in a sing-song Northern Trader accent.

The young man was looking around warily. He lowered his voice and said, "I saw you were having trouble. There are some strangers who are not welcome here, you know."

"We know," Jerra said shortly.

"Look," the young man said, a little awkwardly. "I think those two officials who saw you have gone to get reinforce-ments. They're not going to give up the search. You have to get out of here."

Oskar broke in suddenly. "But we can't! We have to rescue my sister!"

"Oskar, shut *up*, will you?" said Jerra.

The young man remembered a time when he and his little

brother had been searching for *their* sister. He remembered the desperation he had felt – the same desperation he could see now in the eyes of the kids in front of him. "So where's your sister?" he asked gently.

Jerra kicked Oskar to tell him to be quiet. No one answered.

"You can trust me," said the young man. "My name is Nicko. Nicko Heap. And this is my girlfriend, Snorri Snorrelssen. I know this place. I know how it works. And believe me, you are in danger."

"Which is why we're on our way out," Annar said, a little snappily. She pointed to the gate set in the high wall that surrounded the OutPost. As she did so four burly officials marched through, closed the gate behind them and stood on guard.

"Not that way, you're not," said Nicko.

"Come with us," said Snorri. "We have a boat. We will get you out of here."

Jerra glanced at Annar, who nodded. "Thanks," Jerra said. "Thanks, Snorri. Nicko."

As they approached the quay they saw another knot of officials – in their usual array of white wigs and too much gold braid upon their jackets – staring down at the boats tied up below. They had discovered *Skimmer*. As they drew nearer, Jerra could see his beloved boat being trampled in by two heavy-footed men laughing at her hand-sewn flag and her rough disguise while they tied her – and *Swan* – to an OutPost launch.

"Hey!" Annar yelled. "Leave my boat alone!" And before anyone could stop her, Annar had darted away to argue with the officials.

Jerra had to be stopped from going after Annar. "Don't," said Nicko, grabbing his arm.

"You will put her in danger if you go after her," Snorri told him sternly.

Nicko and Snorri hurried them on, heading for a large, weather-beaten red boat called *Adventurer*, moored with the bigger fishing boats. In seconds they were on board and Snorri was casting off the mooring lines. As they sailed off from the quay, Jerra had to watch his beloved *Skimmer* – along with *Swan* – being towed away by the launch. But what was even worse was seeing Annar marched off to the Quay Office, her slight figure dwarfed by the prancing OutPost officials with their ridiculously tall white wigs.

From across the water came the conversation of the two sailors towing *Skimmer* and *Swan*.

"No escape for them now," they said, laughing. "Stupid Fish Slime."

THE LEMONADE STALL

The Adventurer *was moored* at a jetty in the creek safely past the OutPost, and Nicko was cooking breakfast. Up on deck Snorri was showing their Visitor Pass to a pair of officials who had arrived as soon as they tied up. Down in the cabin, Oskar's stomach was rumbling loudly.

Over breakfast – a deliciously heavy soup of beans and fish with crusty pieces of cheesy bread floating in it – they exchanged stories. Snorri told them how she had met Nicko in his country across the water, and how after a few years she had gone back home to the Land of the Long Nights. Nicko told them about his long voyage to find Snorri and that she was now coming back to his home – which he called the Castle – where they planned to get married. Tod thought this was very romantic indeed. Oskar thought it was a long way to travel just to find a girl, but he knew better than to say so.

Then it was the turn of the PathFinders to tell their story. Tod did the talking while Nicko and Snorri listened increasingly sombrely. She explained about Ferdie, the Garmin and Aunt Mitza. And the more she explained, the worse Tod thought things sounded. By the time she had finished, Tod was feeling seriously scared. A glance at Oskar told her he felt the same.

Jerra, too, looked serious, but he was thinking about Annar.

What would she think of him, watching her being taken away and doing nothing about it? And without Annar, they did not know where to find the *Tristan*.

There was a lemonade stall set up at the end of the jetty run by a big woman with a friendly smile. After breakfast, Tod and Oskar decided to ask the lemonade seller about the *Tristan*. Tod made Oskar stay in the sun while she ventured into the shadows of the awning. She handed over a couple of copper pennies and the stallholder took two thick green bottles out of a tub of ice and gave them to her.

"Excuse me," Tod said. "We are looking for a ship. She's called the *Tristan*."

The woman frowned. "The *Tristan*?"

"Yes. We have an, er, appointment there. I wonder if you know where –"

The lemonade seller leaned so close that Tod could smell her sweet, lemony breath. "Look, ducks, here's some advice. If you have an appointment on that ship, *don't keep it*. Go home. Got that?" Suddenly she screamed out, "Get off, you vermin! *Get off!*"

Oskar froze. He'd been discovered – but how? He was standing in full sunlight. He turned to run but Tod grabbed him. "No," she said. "It's that. Look."

A small monkey wearing a red jacket was leaping across the pile of lemons, skillfully avoiding the lemonade seller's swipes. It picked up a lemon and then jumped into the sugar barrel, scooped up a fistful of sugar and crammed it into its mouth.

"Filthy, filthy animal!" yelled the woman. She lunged at the monkey and set the pile of lemons tumbling to the ground. The monkey screamed with laughter and ran off.

"Tod!" said Oskar. "Look. Look what the monkey's got!"

"What?" said Tod, who was busy picking up the lemons and handing them back to the lemonade seller.

"Thank you, ducks," said the woman. "You see, nothing but trouble comes from that ship."

"*Tod!*" Oskar said urgently.

Tod ignored him. "So," she asked the lemonade seller, "is that where the monkey's from – the *Tristan*?"

"Yes, ducks. And it's not the only filthy creature on board, either." She leaned forward confidingly. "There are abominations on the ship. *Abominations.*" The woman rolled the word around her mouth like a sour lemon.

"Sorry," Tod said, looking at the fallen lemons, "but we have to go now."

Oskar was impatiently hopping around in the sun. "Did you see what was on that monkey's arm?" he said.

"No, what?"

"It was *Ferdie's purple ribbon.*"

"Oh, Oskie!" Tod spotted a flash of red scuttling through the stalls. "There it is! After it!"

Oskar dithered. "But what about Nicko and Snorri? They won't know where we've gone."

"There's no time," said Tod. "We have to follow the monkey."

Snorri saw them go. "They are chasing a monkey," she said to Nicko as she climbed down into the cabin. "They are a little peculiar, do you not think?"

THE MONKEY

Following the monkey was not as difficult as Tod had feared. As it scampered along the dusty path beside the creek, people leaped out of the creature's way. Tod noticed that many of them crossed their index fingers against each other and held them in front of their faces, making the seafarer's sign to ward off the Evil Eye.

Suddenly the monkey sat down and bit into the lemon. It leaped up squealing and hurled the offending fruit out into the creek.

Oskar chuckled. "Serves it right," he said.

The monkey dropped down off the path and set off along the sand uncovered by the low tide. The flash of its red jacket against the dark yellow was easy to see, and Tod and Oskar jogged along the path keeping pace with it. They had left the market behind and the creek was now bordered by a dense wood, which curved into a steep left-hand turn ahead. As they rounded the bend, Tod and Oskar no longer had any need to watch the monkey. In front of them lay a beautifully elegant ship, her paintwork shining blue and gold. Her white sails were neatly furled, her woodwork shone, her ropes were perfectly coiled and the line of windows in her broad stern – their blinds down – gleamed in the sunlight. And just below the stern rail, proud curlicues of gold proclaimed the ship's identity: *Tristan*.

Tod was shocked. "But … she's *beautiful*." She had been convinced that somehow the ship would show the evil that lurked within.

Oskar, too, was dismayed at his inability to read the ship. He had been convinced that as soon as he saw the *Tristan* he would feel that Ferdie was close by. But Oskar felt nothing at all. His twin could just as easily be thousands of miles away on the other side of the world.

Down in the deep cut of the creek, the monkey was scampering towards the ship. Her blue hull reared up like a cliff face and they watched the monkey run into the shadows of the ship's overhang.

"Look!" said Tod. "There's a rope ladder for the monkey!"

"We could use that to get on board," Oskar whispered.

There were some ivy-clad ruins deep in the shadows of the trees. In an old, eerily dark archway with the figure *IV* carved into it they put on their *Tristan* tops.

"This is some kind of tunnel," whispered Tod.

Oskar peered into the depths of the archway. "Yeah, you're right."

"Can you see a spooky white mist way down there?"

"Weird," said Oskar with a shiver.

"Yeah," said Tod. "Let's go."

THE PRISONER

Balanced at the top of the rope ladder, Oskar peered into the ship. It was just as Annar had said. The only person on deck was a sailor guarding the gangplank on the far side, and he was facing away. Oskar looked down at Tod and gave the Path-Finder "OK" sign. With a movement as sinuous as if he were tracking dune rats, he pulled himself up over the gunnels and slithered silently down on the deck, which was warm and smooth to his bare feet. He crouched behind a raised hatch and waited for Tod.

Tod was up the ladder as fast as the monkey. In thirty seconds she had slipped over the gunnels and landed lightly beside Oskar. They began to crawl slowly forward, keeping hidden behind neatly stowed coils of rope, upturned boats and a stack of packing crates. Soon they reached a long, raised skylight, which concealed them from view and allowed them to head fast for the open cargo-hold hatchway that Annar had described.

The cargo-hatch ladder took them two decks down into hot, stuffy gloom. As they descended they smelled something nastily familiar – the damp-dog stench of Garmin. As Tod and Oskar crept warily off the ladder, they saw three large cages in the shadows. Each contained a Garmin. The creatures got to their feet, their eyes glinting yellow out of their broad, white faces, their monkey-like front paws gripping the bars. They opened their mouths to show a row of flat, white teeth and two long, tubular fangs from which thick spittle was dropping in a shining thread. One of them flicked out a lengthy, flat, forked black tongue.

Clicker-click-click. Click-click.

"C'mon," whispered Oskar.

Tod and Oskar dropped down the hatchway into the lowest cargo hold. There were no portholes here, and all Tod could see was the sheen of Oskar's hair. She took a light stick from her pocket and bent it. Its soft green light showed many more cages lining the sides of the hold.

"They're empty," whispered Oskar, who could see much better in the dark than Tod. "And they don't smell of Garmin."

A horrible thought struck Tod. "You don't think they keep *people* in these?" she whispered.

"I dunno," Oskar said miserably. He couldn't bear to think of Ferdie imprisoned like a dog. "Ferdie," he said in a hoarse whisper. *"Ferdie."*

A faint rustle of straw from somewhere in the darkness set Oskar's heart pounding. "Ferdie?"

There was no response. "Did you hear that?" Oskar whispered to Tod.

Tod nodded. They crept slowly along the dark, silent row. At every cage they stopped, and the eerie green light from Tod's light stick lit up no more than rough wood and straw. They headed forward towards the prow of the ship and at the very last cage, by the forward bulkhead, a voice said, *"Hish!"*

"Who's there?" whispered Oskar.

"Hish. Hish. Water. *Water.*" The voice was harsh and parched and Oskar knew there was no way it belonged to Ferdie. Tod's light showed a man sitting cross-legged on the straw, a thin hand gripping the bars. He stared at them, sizing them up. "Water," he whispered.

From his backpack, Oskar took his precious bottle of lemonade and handed it to the man. The man fumbled awkwardly with the top and Oskar realised with a shock that he had only one arm. Oskar reached in and flipped the top open. The man drank greedily, gulping down the liquid while Oskar and Tod exchanged glances, both imagining Ferdie in the same condition. The man finished drinking and handed the empty bottle back to Oskar.

"I thank you. I thank you."

"Can we help you – can we get you out?" asked Tod.

"Out?" The man's wide eyes stared at them, shining in the dim green light. As the water and salts from the lemonade spread to his parched brain he began to think once again. And he realised that the two children in front of him were not the regular crew. And they were as desperate as he was.

"Aye, ye can. Bolt at the side. Simple mechanism. Release it and the front slides up."

The front of the cage slid open easily and the man crawled out. He stood up slowly and painfully – he had not stretched out straight for many days. He looked at Tod and Oskar. "My heartfelt thanks to ye," he said. "Samuel Starr, at your service." He bowed his head.

"Are you the only one here?" asked Tod.

"In these pernicious cages, I am the only one left," he said, running his hand along the bulkhead, searching for something. He grinned. "No use to them with but one arm."

"Oh, Oskie," Tod whispered miserably. "I was so sure we'd find her."

Oskar was too desolate to speak.

Clink. Something metallic fell to the floor. Samuel swore.

"I beg your forgiveness for my foul words," he said. "Please, I was trying to discover a key they keep hanging here on a hook. But it has fallen. Can you see it with your light?"

With the glow of her light stick, Tod found a large iron key lying on the floor. She handed it to the man, but he waved it away. "I pray you do it, for my hand is shaking still. Place it in the lock there." He pointed a trembling finger to what Tod and Oskar could now see was a small door in the bulkhead – the entrance to the chain locker, the place deep in the prow of a ship where the anchor and its chain were normally kept. In the right-hand side of the door was the dark shape of a keyhole.

"My family were PathFinders, way back. And one of us is in there – a child. A PathFinder child. She was here when I came. I cannot leave knowing that she is still here."

Oskar went deathly pale. Tod handed him the key.

"Here, Oskie," she said. "You do it."

THE CHAIN LOCKER

Oskar's hands were shaking as he turned the key in the lock. The door swung open and a dim light lit up their faces. Oskar felt sick. He was afraid of what he would find. If it wasn't Ferdie, he couldn't bear it. And if it was Ferdie, what state would his sister be in after one long month as a prisoner in a place like this?

The heavy door – thick, riveted metal just like the bulk-head – swung silently open. Tod handed her light stick to Oskar and nudged him through the door.

Oskar stared, trying to make sense of what he saw: a lantern hanging from the ceiling showed a tiny figure – surely too small and thin for his robust sister – sitting with its back to the door, surrounded by a sea of shimmering gold. The figure's right arm was methodically moving in and out, in and out. Oskar was puzzled for a moment and then he realised that, bizarrely, the figure was *sewing*. It reminded him of a scene from the book of fairy tales that his mother used to read to them on dark winter nights, but it made no sense at all. The figure had not looked around at the opening of the door and Oskar had the feeling that this was deliberate, for something in the tense alertness of the figure told him that whoever it was knew that someone was there and was deliberately ignoring them. And that raised

Oskar's hopes – that was just the kind of way Ferdie would behave.

Oskar's throat was dry as dust. He swallowed hard and managed to croak, "Ferdie?"

The figure sprang to its feet and swung around; cascades of golden cloth fell to the floor like softly billowing waves.

"Oskie?" came a whisper.

"Ferdie! Oh, *Ferdie*." Oskar leaped towards her and Ferdie looked horrified.

"No! Oskie, the cloth, mind the gold, it's –"

But Oskar didn't care; all he wanted was to grab Ferdie and take her home. He trampled across the soft gold cloth and hugged Ferdie hard. Oskar was shocked: Ferdie felt like a bag of sticks.

Ferdie's deep, dark-shadowed eyes stared at her twin and she broke into a sob. "You've ruined it. What's going to happen to me now?"

Oskar didn't know what to say. Behind him came Tod's voice.

"You're coming home, Ferdie," she said gently. "You don't have to worry about that stuff any more."

"But it's my Lady's ball gown," said Ferdie. "I have to finish the buttons by tonight."

"Ferdie, please – you don't have to finish *anything*," said Oskar. "Because by tonight you'll be home with Mum and Dad."

"Mum … Dad …" Ferdie tried out the words as though she could not quite remember what they meant.

Tod was becoming apprehensive. "Ferdie, we must go before someone finds us." To the accompaniment of a gasp from

Ferdie, Tod now also trampled across the fine gold fabric. "Ferdie's in shock," Tod whispered to Oskar. "We'll have to just grab her and go."

Oskar nodded. He took one arm and Tod took the other, and together they tried to walk Ferdie forward.

"No! Oh, *stop!*" gasped Ferdie, as if in pain.

Oskar began to feel scared. He had dreamed of the moment he would find Ferdie so often that it had almost become reality. And in each dream, every time, she had hurtled into his arms and they had run away home together. Never, ever, had he imagined *this*. What was wrong with Ferdie? Why wouldn't she come with them?

Ferdie snatched at the shiny gold fabric and for a moment Oskar thought that his sister had gone mad and wanted to take it with her. And then, as she lifted up the fabric to reveal her feet, he understood the awful truth – Ferdie's ankle was shackled to the floor.

A hoarse voice behind them swore once more. "To do that to such a little one!" said Samuel Starr. "It is a bad thing. A bad, bad thing."

Oskar kneeled down at Ferdie's feet. A thick, tight band of steel was fixed around her left ankle and linked to a chain that was welded to a metal plate set into the floor.

"*Hish!*" came a hiss from the doorway. "*Hish, hish.* I hear someone a-coming." Samuel stepped into the chain locker and pulled the door closed behind him. He hurried over to Ferdie, took the shackle in his hand and shook it angrily. "We must shift it. We *must!*"

Oskar felt in his pocket. *Please*, he thought. *Please let it be here.* Outside they heard the light *thub* of bare feet on boards as someone jumped off the ladder, followed by the rattle of something being dragged across the bars of the cages. In the light of the lantern, Tod saw Samuel Starr go pale. "It is feeding time," he whispered. "The turnkey will see I am not there. I – I must go. I will give myself up. It will buy you time to release your sister."

"No," whispered Ferdie. "Don't go. Please, Samuel."

Ferdie had spent many a lonely night and day listening to Samuel through the thin bulkhead walls. The rasp of his voice had travelled through the tiny grille in the door and while Ferdie sewed, she had listened to his stories, his soft sea shanties and his rambling yarns. The knowledge that not far away there was someone good had kept the worst of her fears at bay and given her hope. And now she could not bear the thought of Samuel giving himself up – to what fate she could not imagine.

So Samuel Starr stayed. And when they heard the turnkey's gasp of surprise to see his empty cage and heard the running of his feet and the rattle and rush of him ascending the ladder, they knew there was little time left.

"Escape! Escape!" They heard shouts from above and the *thub-thub-thub* of more feet.

In the last pocket he had left to try, Oskar's frantic fingers closed around his lock-picking key. He grasped the shackle around Ferdie's ankle. "It won't come off, Oskie," Ferdie said quietly. "You should go now before they catch you, too. Go back to Mum and Dad. Tell them I am OK and that somehow, one day I will come home. I will. I *promise*."

"Just keep still, will you, Ferd?" Oskar muttered.

Above their heads they could hear the cry spreading through the ship. "Escape. Escape!" Oskar ran his fingers over the seemingly smooth fetter until he found the telltale line of the join. He ran his fingernail along the join until he came to a small dip, and this was where he pushed his lock-picker in. With two deft twists and a press downwards, Oskar felt something within the fetter give and it sprang open. Ferdie gasped in amazement. She shook her foot and she was free.

Everyone stared in astonishment at the sprung shackle lying on top of the billows of gold. Then the sound of bare feet in the cargo hold beyond brought them back to reality. They were not out of danger yet.

"Did you not look in the chain locker, you fool?" demanded an angry voice.

"N-no sir. I thought it best to tell you first, like."

"And let him hide until you'd gone and then let him creep out nice and easy, eh? Like you had planned it all cosy together? My Lady will be very interested to hear of your new friend."

There was terror in the voice that replied, "No! No friend of mine, sir. I *swear*."

"Well, let's have a look, shall we? Let's see if your fine feathered friend really has flown."

The steps advanced towards the chain locker. Tod and Oskar looked at each other in panic – they were trapped. Samuel threw his weight against the door. "They won't get in," he growled. "Over my dead body."

It was Ferdie who took control. "No!" she whispered. "Let them open the door. Let them come in. You all hide under the ball gown. You, too, Samuel. Now hurry, *and get underneath*!"

Oskar was back to being little brother. "OK, Ferdie. Come on, Tod, Samuel. *Quick*."

They held up the swathes of cloth for Samuel, who crawled

underneath with some difficulty, and then Tod and Oskar dived in. Meanwhile Ferdie had seated herself on her stool and resumed sewing. When the door burst open to reveal a burly sailor in whites followed by a tall man in dark blue, Ferdie looked up calmly.

"Yes?" she said imperiously.

Underneath the folds of cloth, Oskar smiled. So this was how Ferdie had behaved – as though her prison was her palace. His heart beating so loud that he was afraid someone would hear it, Oskar listened.

"Your door is unlocked," he heard a voice saying suspiciously.

Oskar felt scared. How was Ferdie going to explain that?

Ferdie answered calmly. "Yes," she said. "A horrible man with one arm came in. He wanted to set me free."

Oskar shut his eyes tight in terror. What was Ferdie doing, giving Samuel away?

"Did he indeed?" said the voice.

"Yes, he did." Ferdie sounded disapproving. "I told him to go away. I have my Lady's ball gown to finish."

"Oh." The voice sounded somewhat thrown.

Oskar smiled. He'd forgotten how clever his twin was. But now Ferdie scared him even more.

"Shall I tell you something?" he heard her say confidentially.

"Yes?" came an eager reply.

"That man was really *bad*. He came rushing in and very nearly *trod on my Lady's gown*. He didn't care one bit. He would have ruined it. I told him to shut the door and leave me alone."

"Well, well," Oskar heard the man say.

Oskar could feel his twin give a careless shrug. "Good riddance, if you ask me. Nasty man."

"You are right in your judgement, miss. He is indeed a nasty man. We will leave you to finish my Lady's gown. I apologise for interrupting you."

"Apology accepted," Ferdie said loftily.

The door closed, and beneath the stifling folds of the gown three people lay very still, listening to retreating footsteps and full of admiration for Ferdie Sarn.

A STARR

As the sound of retreating footsteps died away, Tod and Oskar crawled out from under their golden cloud. Samuel followed slowly. With a stifled groan he stood up and bowed stiffly to Ferdie. "Magnificent," he murmured.

Ferdie grinned and returned the bow. Oskar smiled too, pleased to see that the old Ferdie was still there.

But Tod was edgy. "We've got to get out of here before someone else comes," she said.

"Aye, so you do," said Samuel. "There are loading hatches on the next deck up with ropes there you can use to climb down."

On the upper cargo deck the *click-clicker-click*s started up as they hurried past the cages. Everyone stared deliberately ahead, determined not to look into the yellow eyes that were watching their every step. Quickly, Tod, Oskar and Ferdie followed Samuel, who led them to a cargo door in the hull of the ship. Two large bolts secured the door at the top and a short, thick rope was tied to a handle set in its centre. Under Samuel's instruction, Tod, Oskar and Ferdie held the rope taut while Samuel shot the bolts open. The weight of the door surprised them. It dropped outwards and a bright strip of light appeared. Slowly they let the door fall and as it moved down, the strip of light became a beam of brilliance that spilled into the dingy cargo hold, sending the *click-click-click*ing wild with anticipation. Ferdie squinted in the brightness. After two months of living in lantern light, sunlight hurt.

The cargo door stuck out from the side of the ship like a drawbridge, but it was a drawbridge going nowhere. However, this did not worry Samuel. He took a rope and with a deft sailor's knot he one-handedly secured it to a ring set into a beam in the ceiling and threw the other out over the side of the door.

"Go!" Samuel told them. "And when you get down, you run for it."

Tod went first so she could hold the rope for Ferdie. In a few seconds she reached the grassy footpath, cool in the shadows of the ship. Weak from her imprisonment, Ferdie slowly climbed down, then Oskar followed quickly. They all looked up, waiting for Samuel.

Samuel leaned out from the cargo hatch and made a flapping, shooing movement with his hand. Tod realised what Samuel meant. "He's telling us to go without him," she said.

"No," Ferdie whispered. "No!"

"Ferdie, he's going to be really slow down the rope with only one hand," Tod said. "He wants us to get away. *Now*."

Ferdie gazed miserably up at Samuel, who was standing in the cargo hatch. Samuel waved briefly and Ferdie blew him a kiss. Suddenly, Samuel was pulled back into the darkness of the ship. A shout sent them running: "My Lady, my Lady! Your sewing girl! She's out!"

Tod risked a quick glance backwards and saw the Lady for the first time. A large, round woman, with a swathe of silver-and-gold cloth wound around her head and a thick rope of blue stones around her neck, was staring down at them, her blue silk robes billowing in the breeze, her red mouth open in a shout. "Get her!" she screamed. "Get her!"

Behind them they heard heavy feet pounding down the gangplank. The chase was on.

THE CHASE

Ferdie's feet hardly touched the ground as Tod and Oskar carried her between them, racing along the path that would take them back to the jetty. Behind them they heard their pursuers drawing ever closer, and as they rounded the bend, disaster struck. Their only hope of escape – Nicko and Snorri's boat – was not there.

"They've gone!" Oskar gasped in dismay. "What are we going to do *now*?"

One glance at the water told Tod what had happened. The *Adventurer* was anchored in the mouth of the creek – Nicko and Snorri had had to move out into deeper water in order not to be stranded by the falling tide. Oskar had slowed down in despair and Tod found that she was dragging not only Ferdie along but Oskar, too. Tod yelled at him fiercely, "Get a move on, Oskie! They're out in the creek. We can get to the jetty. There's a rowing boat!"

Now Oskar understood. He picked up speed, but the long dusty path stretched out before them. The jetty seemed a million miles away and Ferdie was tiring fast.

The pounding of the pursuers' feet was drawing ever closer. Tod glanced back and wished she hadn't. Rounding the bend were four sailors in striped *Tristan* tops, their knives glittering in the sun.

"Those kids don't stand a chance," the lemonade-stall woman said to a customer.

"Oh!" said her customer. "They've got her. *They've got her!*"

"Got who, ducks?" asked the lemonade seller as her customer sprinted off. "Hey, you forgot your lemonade!"

Tod saw a familiar figure running towards them and then Jerra was there, sweeping Ferdie up into his arms as if she weighed nothing at all. "Follow me!" he yelled, and set off at a run back to the jetty. Tod and Oskar followed him down the steps and Jerra hurried them into a battered red rowing boat with *Bucket* scrawled across her stern. Gently, he lifted Ferdie in, then he and Tod pushed the *Bucket* into the water and jumped aboard. As they rowed away, their pursuers pounded on to the jetty.

Tod and Jerra pulled hard, but behind them the pursuit party had piled into a vicious-looking pointed blue boat with *TT Tristan* engraved upon the stern. They were setting off fast, and both Tod and Jerra knew that four rowers would soon easily outpace one. Meanwhile the *Bucket* was living up to her name, rocking and twisting in the turbulent waters of the outgoing tide, taking them whirling towards the *Adventurer*. And their pursuers were rapidly closing the gap.

Nicko had pulled up the anchor and Snorri was edging the *Adventurer* towards the *Bucket*. As soon as they were within range, Nicko threw a rope. Oskar caught it. He hung on tight and Nicko pulled the *Bucket* alongside the *Adventurer*. Snorri threw down a ladder and Jerra carried Ferdie up it as fast as he could.

Craaack! The pursuit boat hit the *Bucket* and the little rowing boat went cannoning into the side of the *Adventurer*.

Undeterred, Jerra was down the ladder again. He hauled Oskar up by his jacket, then helped Tod to scramble up.

The *Bucket* did not look pretty, but she was built to last, unlike the thin pursuit boat, which, in the collision, had split from end to end. Immediately *TT Tristan* began to sink and the four pursuers found themselves ignominiously clinging to the ropes that were looped around the sides of the *Bucket*, begging for help.

Nicko loved the *Bucket* but he knew what he had to do. He cut the rope and set her free. The *Bucket* was swept into the outgoing tidal stream and as the *Adventurer* set her sails and headed out to the channel through the sandbanks at the mouth of the creek, the *Bucket* followed slowly and sadly until one of its four unwilling crew managed to climb aboard and began the long row to the shore.

Sound travels easily across water, and as the *Adventurer* left the mouth of the creek and began to carefully pick its way through the sandbanks, Ferdie heard the Lady's scream drifting down the creek.

"I want her back! Get her!"

PART
V

THE *ADVENTURER*

As the Adventurer *nosed into* the deepwater channel that would take them out to sea, Jerra saw something he had not expected to see again – *Swan*. Annar was waiting for them. Jerra grinned. Suddenly, everything was pretty near perfect.

Annar waved and brought *Swan* skimming towards them. Soon she was sailing alongside. "OK?" she shouted.

"Yes, yes!" Jerra called down. "We've got Ferdie!"

"Wow!" Annar had not really expected them to find Ferdie. She had not even expected to see Jerra again, so convinced had she been that the Lady would capture them all. But while they were gone, Annar had been determined to do something. "I've got *Skimmer* back!" she called up. "I'll take you to her!"

Jerra laughed out loud. Everything was totally perfect now.

The *Adventurer* and her crew arranged to meet up with Jerra and *Skimmer* at Goat Rock later, and then free at last, they set sail. Ferdie sat at the prow with Tod and Oskar, savouring the sun, the salt spray and the heady sense of freedom. No one said a word. They sat with their arms around one another, luxuriating in the feeling of utter happiness and relief.

They settled down to wait at Goat Rock quay. Nicko and Snorri, with the accustomed patience of those who had been at sea for a long time, occupied themselves with fishing and letting down a lobster pot on to the seabed, but Oskar was more impatient. He borrowed the telescope and climbed Goat Rock to watch for *Skimmer*, but it was not until dusk was falling that he saw a little green boat with a white sail bringing – to his surprise – Annar as well as Jerra skimming across the waves.

"No one's following?" Ferdie asked anxiously.

Oskar shook his head. "Nope. No one."

It was nearly dark and the sea was choppy with the onset of the evening breezes when *Skimmer* jauntily rounded Goat Rock. The smell of cooking – Nicko was making a fish stew – drifted appetisingly up from below, but Jerra refused all invitations to stay.

"We've got to get back," he said. "I promised Mum we'd be home by nightfall."

Oskar looked dubiously at *Skimmer*, which seemed very small after the *Adventurer*. "We won't all fit in there," he said.

"Of course we will," Jerra said impatiently.

Ferdie was as hesitant as Oskar. She longed to see her parents, but the thought of five of them in *Skimmer* out on the open sea in the dark scared her. "Jerra," she said. "It's too dangerous. After all this I … I just want to get home *safely*."

"Ferdie is right," said Annar. "*Skimmer* will be slow and low in the water with five of us. If the wind freshens any more it could be difficult."

Tod agreed. "The winds around the headland are always strong at this time of year," she said. "I don't think it would be safe."

"It would be downright *dangerous*, if you ask me," said Nicko. "Snorri and I will bring Tod, Oskar and Ferdie home tomorrow morning."

"That is very kind of you, Nicko, but I promised we'd be back *tonight*," said Jerra.

"And you will be, Jerra," said Annar. "But Nicko is right, it is too risky for more than two people in *Skimmer* tonight. We will go now; *Skimmer* will be light and fast and you will soon be home to tell your parents that Ferdie is free."

And so Jerra and Annar sailed away. Tod, Oskar and Ferdie watched them until no one could see the white sail any more, then they went below to large bowls of steaming fish stew.

GOAT ROCK

In the early hours of the morning, Ferdie woke. She stared up into the darkness, wondering why the *Tristan* was rocking and pitching so much. A flash of panic ran through her. What if the ship was sinking? How would she escape, shackled as she was to the floor? Ferdie's hand found her right ankle, where the hated shackle lay, and to her amazement, *it wasn't there*. She sat up with a start – and then she remembered where she was and a flood of joy rushed through her. Too excited to sleep, Ferdie crawled out from under her blanket and, stepping gently over Tod, climbed up to the hatch, which Nicko had left open to let the air in.

Tod was suddenly awake, aware that the space next to her was empty. She glanced up and saw Ferdie's bare foot disappearing through the hatch. Very quietly, Tod tiptoed past the sleeping Oskar and followed Ferdie outside. She found her friend sitting on the cabin roof, gazing up at the beautiful dusting of stars – stars that she had not seen for more than two months. Ferdie smiled at her. "Hey, Tod," she whispered. "Can't you sleep either?"

Tod shook her head and sat down next to Ferdie. The warmth of the late summer's night, the gentle creaking of the boat and the *swish-swash* of the swell lulled them into a contented silence. Behind them rose the comforting mound of Goat Rock, hiding them from the OutPost and its sinister creek. In front lay the wide expanse of the sea, and in the distance on the unseen horizon was home. Dreamily, Tod watched the water moving past the anchor chain, entranced by the tiny points of phosphorescence.

Ferdie could not take her eyes off the sky. "Aren't the stars beautiful?" she whispered.

Tod looked up. "They are," she agreed.

"They were like this the night ... the night I was taken," Ferdie whispered, her nervous fingers playing with the little green dragon that Oskar had jubilantly returned to her.

"Oh, Ferdie, don't think about it," said Tod.

Ferdie shook her head. "I ... I don't *want* to think about it, but I can't stop. I keep seeing those horrible white heads. Hearing those clicks ... I thought it was Oskie fooling around with one of his mechanical things. So I opened the window to see. And then ..." Ferdie shuddered. "And then I saw them. Huge, white snake heads bobbing ... I remember one of them jumping up towards me and then something white and ... and slimy, falling over me, sticking to me like glue and ... I couldn't move. I couldn't shout. I couldn't even *breathe*. Everything was so tight. And so, so cold. Like being trapped in ice. Argh!" Ferdie screamed, leaping to her feet. *"What's that?"*

Tod jumped up, heart beating fast. "What?" she gasped. "Where?"

In the cabin below, Nicko sat up fast and hit his head on the ceiling above his bunk. Snorri managed to fall *up* the ladder. Two anxious faces appeared at the hatch.

"What is it?" Nicko asked.

"There – there's something up here," stammered Ferdie, pointing to the prow. "An *animal*."

"Ullr." Snorri sounded relieved. "Come, Ullr, come and say hello." The black shape of a panther stood gracefully and padded silently across the deck to Snorri. She patted the panther. "Ullr keeps watch for us at night," she said.

Both Tod and Ferdie looked puzzled – where had the panther come from?

"Your cat is called Ullr too," Tod said.

Snorri smiled. "This *is* my cat," she said. "Ullr is a **Transformer**. At night he becomes a panther. In the day he is my little orange cat."

Ferdie's shout had unsettled Nicko. After Snorri, Tod and Ferdie had gone below, Nicko climbed to the top of Goat Rock and for the rest of the night he kept watch, leaving Ullr to guard the boat. He stared out to sea but all was quiet, just the gentle *splish-splash* of waves slopping up against rock. On the horizon, where Nicko supposed the PathFinder Village to be, he could see a red glow like the first rays of the rising sun – but surely it was too early for sunrise? Nicko frowned. He had an uneasy feeling that something was wrong.

LETTERS

The morning dawned clear and bright. Quietly and efficiently, Nicko and Snorri weighed the anchor, raised the sails and were soon away with the rising sun behind them.

With Snorri at the helm, Nicko brought his **FlickFyre** stove up to the cockpit. Although Nicko came from an ancient Wizarding family, he found **Magyk** somewhat boring. He could manage a few simple spells if he needed to, but he was a practical person and preferred to work things out for himself. The **FlickFyre** stove was one of the few **Magykal** gifts Nicko had accepted for his voyage, and he had only done so on the grounds of safety. The stove used a flame contained within a **Magykal** field, which did not allow any sparks to escape and burned steadily whatever the strength of the wind. Ten minutes later Tod, Oskar and Ferdie were up on deck drinking Nicko's hot chocolate.

While Oskar and Ferdie talked excitedly about how happy their parents would be to see them home and how amazing it was that Ferdie had actually escaped, Tod sat quietly in the prow of the boat, stroking Ullr, who had now **Transformed** back into the small orange cat that Tod had first met. Tod watched the flat horizon growing more distinct as the *Adventurer* swished through the waves, taking her ever closer to home. Except, thought Tod, it didn't feel like home any more. What was there left for her back at the village? Nothing more than an empty, wrecked house. And although Tod loved the Sarns and knew that they would insist she live with them, she felt she would always be a stranger. Their history was not hers. And Rosie and Jonas, however lovely they were, could never be her mother and father.

It was then that Tod realised that she had given up any hope that Dan would come back. She stared down into the fast-running water breaking from the prow and watched her silent tears drop into the salt water below.

Two hours later, as the *Adventurer* sailed past the Beacon, her crew saw columns of smoke rising above the dunes. As they drew closer they smelled the acrid scent of burning. Silently, they passed the telescope from one to another and saw to their horror the charred remains of PathFinder houses, black against the clear blue of the sky.

Snorri came in as close to the shore as she could, turned the *Adventurer* into the wind so that the boat slowed to a halt and Tod threw out the anchor. The *Adventurer* swung around on the chain so the prow was facing the shore.

Minutes later, they saw a flash of white sail and the green prow of *Skimmer* as she cut through the water, heading towards them. As Jerra drew near, his drawn expression and the soot on his clothes and face told them all they needed to know. Wearily, he took *Skimmer* alongside, let the sail down and threw a rope to Tod. Willing hands helped him aboard and he collapsed on to the deck. Snorri offered him some clear liquid that smelled of dead leaves. Jerra drank a little, spluttered at the taste and sat up.

"Fire," he said. "Almost everything burned to the ground."

"But … but how?" whispered Ferdie.

"Garmin – a whole pack," said Jerra. "They came last night and set fire to the village."

Nicko shook his head. "*Garmin?* How can Garmin use fire?"

"There were men with them," Jerra said. "They had some kind of liquid they threw on to the stilts, then they set fire to it with what old Morris-next-door called Fire Sticks and the flames just shot up into the air – twenty, thirty feet high. No one in the attics had a chance."

"Was anyone in *our* attic?" Ferdie asked quietly.

"It's all right, Ferdie, no one was in the attic. Mum, Dad and Torr all got away, old Morris said. By the time Annar and I pulled *Skimmer* up the beach, most of the houses were on fire. We helped put out as many as we could but it was too late. By then they were just charred stumps."

Tod shook her head. "Why? *Why* did they do this?"

"Revenge," said Oskar.

As soon as he said it, Ferdie knew Oskar was right. By escaping from the Lady it was she, Ferdie, who had caused this terrible destruction.

The *Adventurer* rocked quietly on the gentle swell and the morning sun sent sparkles dancing on the top of the waves. It was – despite the destruction on shore – a beautiful day. A gust blew from the west and slowly the *Adventurer* swung around on her anchor chain so that she was facing into the wind – and towards the Castle. Nicko felt a stirring of restlessness. He wanted to set sail right now and take Snorri home.

His hands sooty and shaking, Jerra fished two crumpled folds of paper out of his pocket. "I found these," he said. "Mum and Dad stuffed them into the old lead pipe at the bottom of the steps." Jerra flattened one out on his knee and handed it to Oskar and Ferdie. It was their mother's writing. Even without reading the words, the hasty pencil scrawl and the sooty smudges told a story.

Darling Jerra, Oskie, Ferdie,

   In great haste. May you all be safe and with Ferdie. Garmin have come with men and fire. Do not worry, we are all right. A wise woman has come to show us a place where we can be safe for now. We will come back soon.

   Love, Mum xxx

Ferdie shook her head in despair. She could not believe she had come so close to being reunited with her parents, only for them to be snatched away at the last moment.

"I want to be with them," Ferdie said with a sob. "I just want us to be *together* again. As a family."

Tod listened sadly. When Ferdie spoke of family, it made her feel even more alone.

Jerra held out the other sooty piece of paper. "It's for you," he told Tod.

Tod unfolded it and read the words with a growing feeling of wonder.

Darling Tod,

   Your mother used to speak of a tower with a golden roof somewhere across the water. She wanted you to go there. This

116

was very important to her, but I don't know why. Dan was
going to tell you on your fourteenth birthday. So I tell you now,
just in case …

Love, Rosie x

Tod was sitting so still, so silent, that Oskar was worried. "Tod, what is it?" he asked.

Tod read out the letter and Nicko and Snorri exchanged glances.

"Wow," Oskar said. "A tower with a golden roof. I wonder where that is."

Tod shook her head unhappily. "I don't know," she said. "And there's no one I can ask now."

"It's the Wizard Tower," said Nicko.

Tod stared at him, amazed. "How do you know?"

"It must be," Nicko said. "It all fits. It's across the water and it's got a golden pyramid on the top. Like a roof."

"Have you been there?" Tod asked.

Nicko grinned. "Yes. It's where my dad works. And some of my brothers."

"Nicko has a lot of those," Snorri said with a wry smile.

"Yeah." Nicko said. "I lose count sometimes."

Snorri looked at Tod quizzically. She saw a thin, dark-haired girl twisting her elflock in her fingers, staring stonily at the smoking ruins of her village. Snorri knew that sometimes you had to leave the place where you grew up. She put her hand on Tod's and said, "The Wizard Tower is in the Castle, Tod. The Castle is a fine place, full of good people. This is where Nicko and I are going."

Tod twisted her gold-and-silver snake ring. She thought of her mother's wish for her. She thought of the house now

117

wrecked by Garmin and the emptiness that awaited her on the shore. And Tod realised that, for the first time since her father had disappeared, she felt something good – a flicker of hope. She turned away from the devastation of her village and said to Snorri, "Take me with you. Please?"

GOODBYE

Arms around each other, Oskar and Ferdie stood among the charred remains of their house. Nothing was left but four blackened stilts, the tangled metal reinforcements of the ladder and the old message pipe half-buried in the ground. They watched Jerra poking about, picking out a few objects that had escaped the fire. He laid them on the flat stone and surveyed them gloomily. "Three forks, Dad's old penknife and a couple of fish-gutters. Not much to show for the Sarn household, is it?" Jerra kicked the ground angrily and an acrid cloud of ash rose into the air, sending them all coughing. Then he saw Ferdie's face, desolate and drawn – this was not the home-coming he had wanted for his little sister. He forced himself out of his anger.

"But we'll show them, won't we, Ferdie? We'll build the house just how it was before. And Mum, Dad and Torr will be back soon and we'll all be fine. Hey, Annar!"

Annar arrived, breathless. Jerra put his arm around her. "Annar and I want to build a house here too. Down by the marsh so that Annar can see the Trading Post lights at night."

"Build a house? *Together?*" Oskar and Ferdie looked amazed.

"Yes. We are very happy together," Annar said.

"Yes," said Jerra. "We are."

Ferdie and Oskar looked at each other – suddenly the Sarn family felt different. Oskar wasn't sure if he liked the difference, but Ferdie hugged Jerra, then more shyly, Annar. "That's lovely," she said. "I can't wait for Mum and Dad and Torr to come back. They'll be so excited."

"Thank you, Ferdie," Annar said with a bashful smile. "But I came to tell you, there is a meeting. There is a house with green shutters at the far end of a track. They missed that one. People are going there now."

"That's Tod's house!" exclaimed Oskar. "Oh, Jerra, do you think she'd stay if she knew her house was OK?"

Jerra shook his head. "I don't think so, Oskie. There are bad memories here for Tod. She wants a new start."

"But Tod loves her house. And now that Aunt Mitza is gone it belongs to her. Oh, please, Jerra, *please* can we go and tell her? *Please?* Before it's too late!"

Jerra hated seeing his little brother so upset. "We can go if you really want, Oskie," he said. "But I don't think it will make any difference."

"Please, Jerra," Ferdie said quietly. "I miss Tod already."

Leaving Annar to go on to the meeting, Jerra headed off to the beach with his brother and sister. But as they reached the top of the dunes and looked out to sea they saw the *Adventurer*'s sails filling with the freshening wind.

"The tide has turned," said Jerra. "They're going."

Landsman that he was, Oskar did not understand. He raced down the dune, shouting to Jerra, "Hurry, Jerra! We've got to catch them! Hurry, hurry!"

Jerra and Ferdie caught up with him. "The *Adventurer*'s caught the wind and the tide together," Jerra said. "She sails fast. There's no way *Skimmer* could catch her. It's impossible, Oskie. I'm so sorry …"

Oskar was suddenly overwhelmed at the thought he might never see Tod again. He raced back up to the top of the dune, and frantically waving both arms he yelled, "Tod! Wait! Don't go. Please don't go! Tod, Tod!"

From the *Adventurer* Tod saw Oskar waving at the top of the dune. She waved back.

"Bye, Oskie," she whispered. "Goodbye."

PART VI

TO THE CASTLE

Tod woke early the next morning and, hearing Nicko still snoring in his cabin, tiptoed up the ladder and padded on to the deck. She stopped and took a deep breath – it was beautiful.

It was just before dawn and through the dim twilight, Tod saw a thin layer of mist hanging over a green river, enfolding the *Adventurer* in a soft blanket of silence. She stood for some minutes, listening to the *peep-peep* of river birds and the soft *slip-slop* of wavelets caused by the dive of a duck. After the restlessness of the sea, Tod was entranced by the stillness of a river. As her eyes became accustomed to the dimness, Tod saw that Snorri and Ullr were already on deck, sitting quietly at the prow. She went forward and sat down beside Snorri and her panther, sleek and black in the darkness – apart from a bright orange tip to its tail.

Snorri looked up and smiled a welcome. "It is a beautiful morning, Tod," she whispered.

Tod smiled. It *was* beautiful, even though all she could see was the mist surrounding them and the tops of trees poking out of it. But as she settled down next to Snorri, Tod saw a small gap between the mist and the water, which sat green and still. Everything felt so mysterious – just how it should be when you were on your way to a **Magykal** tower with a golden pyramid for a roof. A sudden *plip* of a fish breaking the surface made Tod laugh. "It's so different," she said. "I've never seen a river like this."

Between Snorri and Tod lay Ullr: peaceful but watchful, as if waiting for something to happen. Tentatively, Tod rested her hand on Ullr's back, feeling the strong muscles below the warm, smooth fur. She found it hard to believe that such a powerful beast was also Snorri's daytime scraggy orange cat.

The mist was slowly clearing now and Tod could see the sky – a pale greenish yellow – and as she gazed towards a low, flat land Nicko had called the Marram Marshes, the first glow of the sun broke above the horizon and Tod felt a shudder pass through the panther. She snatched her hand away in surprise.

"Do not be concerned," Snorri murmured, stroking Ullr's head. "Ullr is about to Transform."

Tod watched the orange tip to the panther's tail begin to spread, changing Ullr's fur from black to a brindled orange. With the tide of colour, Ullr began to change shape, shrinking before Tod's eyes so that in no more than a few moments the creature sitting beside her was once again a small orange cat with a black-tipped tail.

Snorri patted Ullr. "Good morning, little cat," she said.

Tod shook her head in amazement. This was the first Magykal creature she had ever been close to. Dimly remembered tales told to her by her mother began to come back to Tod – stories of Magykal Transformations that Dan had laughed about, but Tod had always believed, however strange they had seemed.

An hour later, after a breakfast of eggs and bacon, the wind freshened and the *Adventurer* set off up the river once more.

Tod sat in the prow, leaning against the bowsprit, watching the green water rushing past. The mist had disappeared in the early morning sunshine and Tod gazed dreamily as the scenery sped by. On the right was farmland with meandering tracks, wide green fields and orchards dotted with round, woolly grazing sheep. It was quiet, but occasionally Tod glimpsed a farmer going about his work or saw smoke emerging from a chimney of an isolated farmhouse.

On the left of the river a much less welcoming scene presented itself. Ranks of trees crowded the bank, dark and tall and so thickly set together that Tod could see no further than a few yards in. Every now and then the distant howl of a creature drifted across the water and set the hair on the back of her neck prickling. But sitting on the *Adventurer*, Tod felt happily secure. There would be no more lonely, fearful evenings with Aunt Mitza, and although she still had a sad pit of emptiness when she thought of her father, she no longer felt that she was falling headlong into it.

The hours wore on, and as the sun rose higher in the sky a feeling of nervousness began to creep up on Tod. They were sailing ever deeper into a new country and she could not help but wonder what awaited her in the Castle. What were the people like? Where would she live? And *how* would she live? Nicko had told her not to worry, that he and Snorri would make sure she was OK, but it began to dawn on Tod that she had only met Nicko and Snorri two days ago. She hardly knew them.

By the time the *Adventurer* rounded the last bend and a tall, forbidding escarpment of rock reared up on their left, Tod had some very large and energetic butterflies in her stomach. But when the *Adventurer* cleared the rock and Tod saw a huge Castle, bright in the sunlight, spread out before her, the butterflies vanished. Sitting on the bowsprit, her feet dangling over the water, Tod watched, spellbound, as the detail of the Castle began to unfold before her – the ancient walls surrounding it, with houses clustered along them, colourful and bright in the afternoon sun. As they drew closer Tod saw a long, low crenellated building of mellow old stone, which Nicko said was the Palace. Its lawns stretched down to the water, where a landing stage sported red-and-white-striped poles with gilded tops. And there, walking across the grass, Tod saw a young woman in red wandering down towards the river. On her head was a circlet of gold that flashed bright in the sun.

"Hey – Jen!" Nicko yelled.

The young woman stopped dead. She stared as if in disbelief, then she let out a piercing shriek and broke into a run, hurtling down to the landing stage, waving and yelling, "Nicko! Nicko!"

"My sister, Jenna," Nicko said to Tod with a smile. "Very undignified behaviour for a Queen, if you ask me."

Tod nearly fell off the bowsprit. "A *Queen*? So you're a prince?"

Nicko laughed. "Oh, I must tell Jen that. No, I'm not a prince. It's not like that."

"Hey, Nik!" yelled the Queen, running along the landing stage, her red-and-gold cloak flying out behind her. "Tie up here, Nik!"

Nicko looked at Snorri. "OK?" he asked.

Snorri grinned. "OK!"

"Hey-ho," Nicko said, pushing the tiller across. "Around we go."

128

Tod scrambled on to the deck to help Snorri with the sails and the *Adventurer* swung in gently towards the landing stage, the sails flapping as they lost the wind. Snorri threw the ropes to the Queen, who caught them easily and tied them around the gilded poles, pulling the *Adventurer* alongside the landing stage as she did so.

Snorri put down the landing ladder and to Tod's amazement, the Queen hitched up her long red silk tunic – revealing a pair of very sensible brown leather boots – clambered aboard and threw her arms around Nicko. "Nik, oh, Nicko, you're back safe after all this time. We thought you were gone for ever. Oh, I can't wait to tell Mum! Oh, *Nicko!*"

Suddenly, something caught Tod's eye – something very big, green and shiny was moving behind a tall hedge on the far edge of the Palace lawns. Tod heard frantic shouting and a young man wearing a leather jerkin came running through a gap in the hedge, dragging a fat hosepipe towards the river. Behind the hedge, flames were rising.

"Oh," Snorri said. "It is that wretched dragon. I hope he is not coming near the boat."

"Spit Fyre!" the Queen gasped. "He's set light to the Dragon Kennel. *Again.* 'Scuse me –" she flashed an apologetic smile at Tod – "got to go!" The Queen leaped from the boat and raced towards the flames, but the young man – who Tod rightly took to be the dragon's keeper – stepped into her path to stop her.

"Barney, let me pass!" Tod heard the Queen shout.

The young keeper stepped aside and Tod saw the most magnificent dragon, the sun shining on his smooth green scales, his head held high, his huge, leathery wings slowly moving up and down, rising up into the clear blue sky.

"Come down, Spit Fyre, you bad dragon!" the Queen yelled, jumping up and down. "Come down *right now*!"

Tod saw the dragon tilt his head to one side, as if considering the matter. Then he opened his mouth and a great stream of flame came roaring out, dancing up into the sky. To Tod's excitement, the dragon swooped down low across the Palace lawns and headed straight towards the *Adventurer*.

"No!" yelled Snorri. All on board threw themselves on to the deck but at the last minute, the dragon curved upwards, his pale green tummy no more than a few inches above the top of the mast. And then he was gone, flying out across the river, leaving behind a strong smell of underwing dragon sweat.

"Come back!" the Queen yelled. "Spit Fyre, come back, you stupid dragon!"

But Barney Pot, the dragon keeper, knew his charge was not coming back. "Queen Jenna," he said, "it is seven years now since Spit Fyre grew his adult spurs. He has gone to find a mate."

Jenna sighed. "I know, Barney. You did warn me. But we'll miss Spit Fyre so much."

"Aye, that we will," said Barney. He threw the end of the fire hose into the river and then raced away to start turning the pump, leaving the Queen gazing sadly up at the sky.

On board the *Adventurer*, they picked themselves up off the deck and Nicko chuckled. "Welcome to the Castle, Tod," he said.

THE PALACE

Tod spent the rest of the day at the Palace, meeting more new people in one afternoon than she had ever met in her life. By the evening, when Nicko's family were gathered together in a large room overlooking the lawns that swept down to the river, Tod's head was spinning. It seemed to her that Nicko had a very large family indeed, and he had introduced her to every one of them. "Except my little brother, who can't get away from work," he explained. "You'll meet him tomorrow when we go to the Wizard Tower." Nicko smiled. "I've booked you in for a tour."

They had a noisy, happy supper at a long, narrow table. At either end were Nicko's mother and father, both with curly straw-coloured hair, just like Nicko's – except a little faded with age. Sarah and Silas Heap were surprisingly scruffy for parents of a Queen, Tod thought. But everything in the Castle seemed a little odd to Tod – surely as the Queen's parents were still living, *they* should be the King and Queen of the Castle?

At supper, Tod sat next to Sarah Heap. Sarah was ecstatic at having her second-youngest son home after four long, uncertain years and she was very talkative. "You see, Alice," said Sarah – who thought Tod was a very strange name for a girl – "my seven are lovely boys, but boys will be boys. I hardly ever have them all here, safe with me. And for the first ten years I thought my youngest was *dead* – yes, it was shocking, Alice, shocking, poor little Septimus – and then just as I found him, my eldest, Simon, went a little bit wild. You know, like they do at that age sometimes. And by then my other four were living in the Forest with some *very* disreputable witches. It was not ideal, I can tell you. And then Nicko got trapped in another Time and I thought I'd never see him again. But he came back eventually, thank goodness."

Tod stared at Sarah in amazement, her spoon suspended in mid-air. She was rendered speechless, which was fortunate, because Sarah Heap still had a lot to say.

"For a while, Alice, all my boys were doing really well. The twins, Edd and Erik, they were Apprentices at the Wizard Tower. Simon had married a lovely girl, Lucy; Nicko worked at the boatyard; my fourth son, Jo-Jo ..." Tod saw a flicker of dis-approval cross Sarah's face. "Well, Jo-Jo got himself a job at a very interesting shop here, and my second oldest, Sam, decided to go out to the Marram Marshes and help young Marwick out there. And of course my youngest, Septimus, he's always done *very* well; we're very proud of him indeed. But nothing lasts, does it? Nicko decided to go over the seas and find his old girlfriend, Snorri – who is a lovely girl, Alice – but he was gone for *four whole years*. Can you imagine? We thought he was never coming home. And then to top it all off, Sam and Marwick disappeared. Gone. *Gone*. And now poor little William. I still can't believe it ... I was such a proud Grandma ... Oh dear." Sarah got out a large white handkerchief and blew her nose loudly. "*So* sad ..." To Tod's relief, the flow was stopped by the Queen passing Sarah a bowl of something stodgy floating in custard.

"Mum! Look, here's your favourite pudding."

While Sarah protested that she couldn't eat a thing and passed the bowl down to Silas, the Queen turned politely to Tod. "So, Tod, what would you like to do now you have come to the Castle?"

Tod's head was spinning and for a moment she had no idea why she was at the Castle at all. And then she remembered Rosie Sarn's note. "Well ... my mother wanted me to come to the Wizard Tower."

"Well, that doesn't surprise me. Your mother must realise you have some **Magyk** about you," the Queen said.

"Really?" Tod said, pleased.

"Yes. You really do have that **Magyk** something. And I should know – I grew up with a whole *ton* of **Magykal** brothers, and I can tell." The Queen shook her head and looked puzzled. "It's a strange thing. It's not just the green eyes, it's something else too. I don't have it, of course."

"But I don't have green eyes!" Tod said, dismayed.

Queen Jenna peered at Tod in the candlelight. "So you don't. But that doesn't matter."

Tod was confused. "But I thought you said you had to have green eyes."

"Not right at the beginning," the Queen explained. "If you have that **Magykal** thing – whatever it is – then your eyes will begin to turn green when you are exposed to **Magyk**. And I don't suppose you had any where you come from, did you?"

Tod smiled. "No," she said. "We only had the sea. And fish. *Lots* of fish."

"There you are, then," said the Queen. "Fish aren't at all

133

Magykal, from what I've heard." She smiled. "I'm sure your mother is right. Mothers generally are."

Tod was not used to talking about her mother. "Are they?" she asked.

The Queen gave Sarah an amused glance. "Well, usually," she said. "So, Tod, you must let your mother know you have arrived safely."

"My mother's dead," Tod blurted out.

The Queen looked shocked. "Oh!" she said.

"I'm sorry," Tod said. "I didn't mean to …" Her voice trailed away. She realised she had never spoken those words before.

"I do understand," said the Queen, leaning across the table confidentially. "My mother is dead too. She was killed when I was only a day old."

"Oh!" said Tod. "Oh, that's awful."

"It is," said the Queen. "Well, it is for her. But I was lucky. I found another mother." She nodded towards Sarah Heap, who was now sipping some herbal tea. "And another father – even though I found out later I still had my first one. And of course I've got a whole *load* of brothers." She looked at Nicko, who was flapping his hands like seal flippers and making barking noises. "And very noisy, silly brothers they are, too."

Nicko's seal impression was being directed at a young man who was sitting next to the Queen. He had earlier been introduced to Tod as the Chief Hermetic Scribe. Tod had no idea what a Chief Hermetic Scribe might be, but she thought the young man looked really nice. He had dark floppy hair, which every now and then he pushed back from his eyes. He was wearing a long, deep-blue jacket with gold cuffs, which Tod thought suited him very well. He had spoken to Tod a few times – asking her where she had come from and how she knew Nicko, but Tod had felt shy and had only managed one-word answers. But the Queen had no such trouble. She took the young man's hand and said, "Beetle."

Tod was surprised; she couldn't see a beetle anywhere.

The young man obviously didn't care about a stray beetle. He gave the Queen the kind of smile that Tod had seen Jerra give Annar. It made Tod feel strangely lonely.

"Beetle," said the Queen again. Tod stared at the young man, trying to spot the beetle but with no luck. "Why don't we show Tod the Wizard Tower after supper? It's a beautiful evening." She turned to Tod. "The Wizard Tower looks wonderful at night. You'll be amazed."

"Thank you," said Tod. "I would love to see it." She twisted the gold-and-silver snake ring on her thumb. *I'm going to the Wizard Tower,* she silently told her mother. *Just like you wanted me to.*

THE WIZARD TOWER

No one ever forgets their first sight of the Wizard Tower at night, and Tod was no exception. As she walked out of the Palace Gate and looked along Wizard Way, the wide, torchlit avenue that led to it, Tod gasped in wonder. The Wizard Tower rose high into the clear night sky, eclipsing the stars. It was tall and elegant, shimmering with a silver sheen over which played a myriad of coloured lights – fleetingly blue, purple, green and pink. The golden pyramid had become a pyramid of many colours reflecting the lights that glanced off it, so that it seemed to be almost transparent at times.

Tod walked up Wizard Way, flanked by Nicko, Snorri, the Queen and the Chief Hermetic Scribe, whom, she now real-ised, was actually called Beetle – although she found it hard to believe that this was his real name. Why would anyone name a baby after an insect? But Tod reminded herself she was in another country. For all she knew, lots of people in the Castle were named after insects. Maybe there were Millipedes, Bugs and Bees wandering around all over the place.

The nearer Tod got to the Wizard Tower, the more unreal everything felt. Only a few days ago, with her mother and father both gone from her life for ever, she had been marooned in her house with a woman who hated her. Now she had a new life, new friends and a very precious message from her mother – and every step she took was bringing her closer to the place her mother had wanted her to go.

The party progressed slowly up the middle of Wizard Way – a beautiful broad avenue lined with silver torch posts, tall as trees. The torches were lit and the flames burned high and steady in the still night air, sending shifting shadows across the smooth limestone paving. On either side of Wizard Way was an interesting mixture of small shops – mainly to do with **Magyk** – all shuttered for the night.

Tod was silent, content to be surrounded by the easy talk of her four companions. Even though they were so much older than her, their happy, joking friendliness made her feel part of the group. Their easy chatter reminded her of the Sarn family, and suddenly Tod missed Oskar and Ferdie terribly. How much she would love them to be with her right now, for them to be walking with her towards this **Magykal** place.

They were approaching a magnificent silver gateway – the Great Arch, which led into the Wizard Tower courtyard – when they stopped outside one of the shops. Written on its signboard were the words: *Number Thirteen: **Magykal** Manuscriptorium and Spell-Checkers Incorporated*. The window was brightly lit with lanterns and stacked with neat piles of papers and books. It seemed that this was where Beetle lived, for he was putting a large key into the lock of the shop door.

"I'm off," Beetle told everyone. "It's an early start tomorrow. I've got to sort out a Grula-Grula."

Nicko laughed. "You're kidding me!" he said.

Beetle looked rueful. "I wish," he replied. "But unfortunately there's one taken up residence over there." He pointed across the Way to a shop on the other side: *Bott's Wizard Cloaks: New and Pre-Loved*. "I promised Miranda Bott I'd fix it for her."

"Isn't that a job for the Wizard Tower?" asked Nicko. "They've got safe places to put creatures like that."

"Miranda won't let them in," Beetle explained. "She's a bit against Wizards in general, you know, ever since her uncle Bertie got eaten by that **Darke** Dragon."

Tod listened, amazed. So much seemed to happen in the Castle.

"That wasn't their fault," Nicko said.

"Try telling Miranda that," said Beetle, who clearly had. "So I have to get the wretched Grula out myself and take it to the Stranger Chamber in the Wizard Tower."

"Rather you than me," said Nicko.

"Yeah," Beetle said ruefully. He turned to Tod and shook her hand. "It's been very nice meeting you," he said, smiling. "Welcome to the Castle. May your stay be a happy one." Tod watched Beetle hug Snorri and Nicko goodbye, give the Queen a kiss and then he was gone, the door to the strange little shop closing behind him with an exuberant *ping*.

The four now headed into the Great Arch. As they walked between the two burning torches on either side and stepped into the shadows, Tod was amazed to see that the inside of the arch was lined with the same brilliant blue stone shot through with gold that her precious box was made of. The huge amount of the **Magykal** stone, glittering in the light of the torches, amazed Tod.

"Lapis lazuli," the Queen told her. "It's lovely, isn't it?"

Tod nodded, lost for words. Her hand closed around her precious lapis lazuli box safe in the deep, buttoned pocket of

Dan's fishing jacket. She thought of the strange **PathFinder** with its lapis dome that nestled inside it and she knew she had a connection with the place she had come to. If only her parents were here to ask, Tod thought, they could have told her as much. But whatever they knew was lost now. She must find it out for herself.

The Queen was chattering on like a tour guide. "There's a lot of lapis here," she was saying. "It's one of the things that makes the Castle special. Ooh, look, doesn't the tower look fabulous tonight!"

Tod stepped into the courtyard and stopped dead. The sight of the Wizard Tower suddenly so close made her feel dizzy. Twenty-one storeys high, it reared up into the night sky, alive with silently flashing, popping, prancing, dancing lights of every colour. The tower's hundreds of tiny windows glowed purple and Tod had a vivid impression of many lives being lived behind them. Feeling as though she were wading through water, Tod walked across the courtyard in a daze, following the Queen's red cloak as she moved towards a flight of brilliant white marble steps, which led up to the tall silver doors of the Wizard Tower.

Slowly, silently, the doors swung open, and there, standing at the top of the steps, Tod saw a long-robed figure dark against the lambent lights behind. As though from a great distance, Tod heard the Queen call out, "Hey, Septimus!"

A river of brilliant sparkles streamed out from the doors and danced towards her. She heard ringing in her ears. *Is this*, Tod thought, *the sound of* **Magyk?** A roar from afar filled her head and everything went dark.

"Oh, crumbs," said the Queen. "She's fainted."

AWAKE

Tod opened her eyes and realised that she had no idea where she was. She lay still, looking at the strange shifting patterns all around her, trying to make sense of things. She could smell something sweet and heady. She could hear tinkling sounds of tiny bells, or was it faraway singing? Or both? Slowly, the world began to swim into focus. Tod realised that she was in bed – a bed high off the ground with a tall headboard that rose up behind her. The bed was in some kind of dark-coloured tent, the walls of which seemed to move as though in a breeze. Blearily, Tod considered things. So … she was in bed. In a tent. Which meant she must be outside. But *why*?

Pushing away fears that she had somehow been caught by Garmin, Tod sat up. *A tent is not a good prison*, she told herself, and besides, the bed was far too comfortable. She threw back the featherlight quilt and swung her legs over the side, her feet not reaching the floor. She noticed that she was wearing a long, green nightgown, which felt very soft and extremely strange. Tod had never worn a dress in her life; she was a typical Path-Finder girl raised in hooded canvas smocks, tightly woven Fisher jumpers and sailcloth trews.

Tod slipped down from the bed, and the floor felt surprisingly soft and warm. Although her other clothes had disappeared, her father's old fishing jacket was neatly folded at the end of the bed. Anxiously, Tod checked the pockets, then smiled with relief – her PathFinder box was still safe. In another pocket, her fingers closed around something almost as precious – a pebble splashed with green paint from the last time Dan had painted the shutters, which she had taken from underneath her house to remind her of home. Tod put the salt-stained jacket on over her nightgown, then she parted the curtains and peered out.

The scent of incense and the taste of spices on her breath greeted her and gave her the strange feeling of remembering something long forgotten. To her amazement Tod saw that she was indoors; and what was even stranger, she was in a huge room *full* of tents. Tod stepped out of the tent, letting the soft cloth fall closed behind her, and looked up at the high, vaulted ceiling, which glimmered with a dull blue light like a cloudy night sky. She gazed around and saw that her tent was part of a circle of twelve tents, themselves circular, with the points of their roofs strung from the ceiling on long, shining ropes. Tod shook her head in amazement. Was she still dreaming? And if she wasn't – *where was she?*

Tod padded into the centre of the circle, the floor feeling oddly soft and squashy beneath her bare feet. As she stood quiet and still, she became aware of the sound of breathing all around her and she realised that each tent contained its own sleeping occupant. All traces of sleep had now left Tod and a feeling that she was in a good place began to grow within her.

In the dimness, the shape of a door shone out. Tall and arched, it was outlined in a shimmering, greenish blue. Tod decided to see what was on the other side of it. Treading quietly to avoid disturbing any of the occupants of the other tents (although there was no need, because the soft floor dampened all sound), Tod reached the door and gave a tentative push. It swung silently open and she stepped outside.

Tod found herself in a wide corridor, dimly lit with a low blue light. Four other arched doors led off it and the signs on them read: *Senior Girls' Apprentice Dormitory*, *Junior Boys' Apprentice Dormitory*, *Senior Boys' Apprentice Dormitory* and *Apprentice Common Room*. Tod turned back to look at the door she had come through and read the words *Junior Girls' Apprentice Dormitory*. So, thought Tod, she was in some kind of school.

A movement caught Tod's eye and she stepped back against the wall, not wanting to be seen. She watched from the shadows and saw that a purple window at the end of the corridor had suddenly lit up, revealing what looked like a huge silver corkscrew going from the ceiling to the floor, steadily turning. Intrigued, Tod crept forward through the blue-black shadows and then stopped – *there was something on the corkscrew and it was coming through the ceiling*. Pressed against the wall, Tod watched. She realised that she was looking at someone's feet: they were rotating around, moving slowly further and further down until Tod could see the whole figure, long-robed in blue and silhouetted against the purple window, travelling ever downwards so that soon it was moving through the floor. As the head finally disappeared Tod crept forward and stared at what she now realised were revolving silver spiral stairs.

The light from the purple window faded and Tod guessed that the window only lit up when there was someone on the stairs. As she watched the now silver stairs still slowly turning, Tod began to piece together a jigsaw of memories. She remembered a wide avenue with burning torches high on their silver torch posts. She remembered going through an amazing blue archway and seeing a flight of brilliant white steps leading up to two tall silver doors. She remembered how the doors had swung open and a stream of purple and blue stars had come tumbling down towards her. She remembered the buzz of **Magyk** all around her ... and then she remembered nothing more. Nothing until she had woken up inside her tent.

I think, Tod said to herself, *I'm in the Wizard Tower.*

DANDRA DRAA

Buzzing with excitement, Tod watched the stairs revolving downwards and wondered if she was brave enough to step on to them herself. She saw each flat, grooved slab of silver briefly meet the edge of the floor and then move on down, a few seconds later to be replaced with the next tread and then the next. Tod decided to go for it. She was about to step on when she became aware of someone above on the stairs. Quickly, she moved back into the shadows.

Tod saw a solid, well-worn pair of shiny brown boots appear through the hole in the ceiling. Grazing the top of the boots was a purple robe edged in a shimmering purple silk ribbon. Remembering that only the ExtraOrdinary Wizard wore purple, Tod gazed in awe as the young man with purple ribbons hanging from his sleeves slowly rotated down. He was immersed in a book, oblivious to his watcher in the shadows. Her gaze took in a belt of gold and platinum, embellished with Magykal signs and symbols, a teardrop-shaped lapis-and-gold amulet around his neck, and as his face came into view she had to suppress a gasp of astonishment. *He was Nicko.* Except ... Nicko had shaved. And he had taken the plaits out of his hair. And was a bit taller. No, he wasn't Nicko, and yet he so very nearly was. And then, as Tod stared at the young man's curly straw-coloured hair haloed in purple light she remembered something Nicko had said about the Wizard Tower: *Yeah, some of my brothers work there.* Tod grinned. *So the ExtraOrdinary Wizard was one of Nicko's brothers. Trust Nicko not to mention it,* she thought.

The ExtraOrdinary Wizard disappeared from view and the stairs were now clear. Taking a deep breath, Tod stepped on to them – and felt as though someone had pulled a rug out from under her. She clung on to the central post, determined to get off at the next possible opportunity. What Tod did not know was that the Apprentice dormitories were only one floor above the main entrance hall – known as the Great Hall. She would very soon *have* to get off.

The dim night lighting of the upper domestic floors of the Wizard Tower grew ever brighter as the Great Hall came into view. Down Tod went, past the golden vaulted roof with its night-time stars (a recent installation of the new ExtraOrdinary Wizard), past the flickering pictures on the wall depicting brave deeds and important moments from the Wizard Tower's history and into the peace and calm of the night-time Great Hall.

The tread and the floor met and, unsteadily, Tod stepped off on to what felt strangely like sand. Puzzled, she looked down and saw her name slowly appear in the grainy surface: WELCOME, ALICE TODHUNTER MOON, APPRENTICE.

Tod gasped. She was an *Apprentice*? How had that happened? She could remember nothing about it. As she stared at the wobbly green letters, the words faded and were replaced with: SORRY. SHOULDN'T HAVE SAID THAT. MY MISTAKE. Tod was still staring at the floor, wondering what it might decide to say next, when she became aware of someone at her side. A tall woman with an aquiline nose and thick, short dark hair – through which ran a striking streak of white – had appeared from nowhere. She wore a long, somewhat formal pale blue robe with shiny red ribbons on the hem and elaborate green snakes embroidered up the sleeves. She smiled at Tod delightedly.

"Alice!" she said, grabbing both of Tod's hands in her own. "Are you feeling better now?"

Tod nodded.

"Still wandering around at night," the woman-with-snakes said with a huge smile. She let go of Tod's hands, stepped back and smiled. "Ah, I can see you do not remember me. But then, you were only four."

But Tod did remember. She remembered the shining green eyes and the half-amused smile.

"I am Dandra," the woman said. "Dandra Draa."

"My mother's friend," said Tod.

"Indeed I was." Dandra corrected herself: "No, Alice, I *am* your mother's friend. And I will always be. I promised her that I would be a second mother to you and that when you were fourteen – which is a good age to begin to be acquainted with Magyk – you could come to the Wizard Tower and see how you liked the old trade." Dandra took in Tod's bemused look. "The old trade – what some call Wizarding. Or Magyk. Sorcery. Bewitchment. Conjuring. Call it what you will. If you have a talent for it, this is the place to be." She shook her head. "How the time has flown. I can hardly believe you are fourteen already."

"I'm not," Tod said. "I'm twelve."

"But you have the ring – the snakes upon your thumb," said

146

Dandra, puzzled. "That's how I recognised you when they brought you upstairs." She smiled. "But even if I hadn't seen your mother's ring, I would have known you for your mother's daughter. You are *so* like Cassi. But why, Alice, are you here so soon?"

"Something happened," said Tod. She didn't want to say any more right then.

Dandra saw Tod's closed expression – her lips pressed together, her eyes suspiciously bright. "I understand," she murmured. "Things happen." Dandra looked at her best friend's daughter and her heart flipped in a little twist of pity. The child looked so thin and dishevelled, her black hair sticking up on end, standing there twisting her strange elflock, the same as her father wore, and with such black circles under her dark eyes.

"Come, Alice," Dandra said. "I will take you back to the dorm. I don't suppose you'll be able to find your way back to the right bed now that they've stuffed the place with those silly tents."

Tod was reluctant to go. Greedily, her eyes took in the amazing space around her – the unbelievably tall silver doors rearing up to the full height of the vaulted hall, its seven golden beams arching up from the floor like graceful trees dividing the luminous dark blue ceiling and its dusting of stars into segments like slices of cake. She gazed at the pictures around the walls that faded in and out of view, and her attention was taken by one particularly bright one that showed a small green dragon and rider fighting a monstrous, six-winged, six-eyed dragon.

"Couldn't I just stay here for a bit?" asked Tod.

Dandra was taking her position as Tod's second mother very seriously. "It's very late," she said, "and you need your sleep. You can see it all in the morning."

Tod looked crestfallen. She hated the feeling of being the little kid sent back to bed. Dandra reversed the direction of the stairs and Tod was about to step back on to them when a cold draught of air swept into the hall. The great silver doors were opening. The ExtraOrdinary Wizard strode in, across the message that the floor had written – WELCOME, SEPTIMUS HEAP, EXTRAORDINARY WIZARD – and made straight for Tod and Dandra. Before Tod could catch her breath he was standing right beside her and Dandra Draa was saying, "ExtraOrdinary, this is our new guest, Alice TodHunter Moon –" Dandra looked at Tod questioningly – "who still likes to be known as Tod?" she asked.

Tod smiled. "Yes, please," she said.

The ExtraOrdinary Wizard smiled in return. "Hello, Tod," he said. "I hope you're feeling better now?"

"Yes, thank you," Tod said politely.

"I am taking Alice – I mean, Tod – back to bed," Dandra said. "I shall be down soon. We have ten minutes still, I think?"

"Eight," the ExtraOrdinary Wizard said, glancing at his timepiece. "Well, goodnight, Tod." He smiled at Tod, and her expression caught him by surprise. It reminded him of how he had once been – lost and confused. It seemed cruel to send her back upstairs to a lonely dormitory. He also knew that it was rare for someone to be so sensitive to **Magyk** that they fainted. He looked at the skinny, wild-looking girl and for a brief moment thought he saw a glint of green in her dark eyes. "But perhaps, Tod, you would like to come and see what we are doing tonight?"

One look at Tod's face told him what her answer was going to be.

"Yes, please."

MARCIA OVERSTRAND

Tod followed the ExtraOrdinary Wizard down the wide, white marble steps determined to keep her mind clear of the **Magykal** buzzing and singing that threatened to invade it. At the foot of the steps an elderly Wizard with white hair tied back into a ponytail drifted over to join them. He, too, wore purple, and for a moment Tod was confused. She had been told that there was only one ExtraOrdinary Wizard in the Castle – so why were there suddenly two? Through his faded purple robes, Tod saw a stream of brilliant blue lights that were dropping from the top of the Tower, and when the old Wizard moved she saw he was floating some inches above the ground. With a flash of excitement, Tod realised that she was looking at a ghost. She had never seen a ghost before. People said there were some ancient PathFinder ghosts from the Days of Beyond down by the marsh in her village, but they rarely showed themselves and were reputed to look very strange. But this ghost looked like a kindly elderly man. Noticing her gaze, the ghost smiled at her, his friendly green eyes crinkling as he did so.

"A new Apprentice, Septimus?" he said, addressing the ExtraOrdinary Wizard in a voice that sounded, Tod thought, as though he were talking in a large, empty room.

The ExtraOrdinary Wizard caught Tod's embarrassed look and grinned. "Maybe, Alther. Maybe. But for the moment she is our guest. She is, Dr Draa tells me, the daughter of an old **Magykal** family. Alther, allow me to introduce Alice TodHunter Moon. Alice, this is Alther, a wise friend and the old tutor of someone we are about to meet. Well, we hope we are about to meet."

Alther bowed. Tod was not sure what to do. She guessed you couldn't shake hands with a ghost, so she bowed too.

"How are we doing for time, Septimus?" Alther asked in his oddly distant voice.

Septimus looked at his timepiece again. "We are approaching the Midnight Minutes," he said.

They gathered at one side of the smooth white marble steps that reached high above their heads, in front of what Tod could see was the outline of an archway sitting beneath the steps like a cupboard under the stairs. The archway had *VII* inscribed on its keystone, which Tod knew was number seven in the ancient PathFinder numbering system. She peered into the arch and saw an eerie white mist swirling deep within it. It reminded her of the one in the woods where she and Oskar had put on their *Tristan* tops.

"It's weird," she whispered to Dandra Draa. "It's like there is something really deep and strange in there."

Dandra looked at Tod. "In where?" she said.

"Inside the arch," said Tod.

All eyes turned to Tod and she felt embarrassed. Clearly it was not a time to be chatting. Something serious was about to happen. "Sorry ..." she whispered.

To Tod's discomfort the ExtraOrdinary Wizard was looking

at her in a very unsettling manner. *"You can see the arch?"* he asked.

Tod nodded.

"What can you see inside?"

"Er. Well, it's like a tunnel with a kind of swirly white cloud deep inside …" Tod's voice trailed off. She wished he would stop staring at her like that.

"And does the arch have a symbol anywhere?" the Extra-Ordinary Wizard asked, testing her.

"Er, yes. Number seven. But it's written the ancient way: 'V,' One, One."

"How do you know these numbers, Tod?"

"We're taught them when we are little. They are Path-Finder numbers. Oh! There's someone in there!" Tod gasped. In the depths of the white mist, she saw the dark shape of a figure.

The arch began to glow with a dull purple light, which became ever brighter. Tod saw the figure coming towards them and then suddenly a tall dark-haired woman in a richly embroidered cloak was striding out into the night air, her green eyes glittering with the reflections of the **Magyk** around her.

"Marcia!" The ExtraOrdinary Wizard sounded relieved. "You made it!"

"Of course I did," she said. "Alther! Dandra! What a wonderful welcoming committee." She swung around and threw her arm out somewhat theatrically towards the archway, which was still shining a brilliant purple. "So, *now* can you see it?" she asked.

"Well, I can *now*," the ExtraOrdinary Wizard said – a little grumpily, Tod thought. Slowly the purple light began to fade and Tod watched the archway return to just a dark space within the white marble. "It's gone again," he complained.

Marcia Overstrand regarded him with impatience. "Of course it hasn't *gone*, Septimus," she said. "It is still there, but *you* can't see it."

"Neither can I," said Dandra.

"Well, Dandra, I'm sure you have more important things on your mind," Marcia said diplomatically. She turned towards the ghost. "Alther?"

The ghost sighed. "I can Feel the disturbance, Marcia. But I, too, can see nothing. Sorry."

"You will eventually," Marcia told them. "It's a skill you have to learn." She took a stick of purple chalk from her pocket. "I will draw the outline. That way, if anyone wants to come and see me –" she looked pointedly at the ExtraOrdinary Wizard – "there is no excuse not to."

While Marcia drew around the archway, the ExtraOrdinary Wizard turned to Tod. "Do you still see it?" he asked.

Tod nodded.

"Of course I still see it, Septimus," Marcia said as she stood on tiptoe to reach the highest point of the arch. "How would I draw around it otherwise?"

"Actually, Marcia, I was talking to our young guest here," Septimus said.

"Oh?" Marcia spun around and peered into the dimness past the steps. She saw for the first time a slight, barefooted girl wearing a scruffy old jacket covered with pockets, pulled over an Apprentice nightgown. "Goodness," she said. "Who is this?"

"Marcia, this is Alice TodHunter Moon, the only one of us

153

who can see your elusive archway. Tod, this is Marcia Overstrand."

Tod felt quite overawed by the ExtraOrdinary Wizard including her in the "us" of his group of high-powered Wizards.

Marcia frowned. "You can *still* see the archway?" she asked Tod.

"Yes," said Tod, trying to sound sure. She had the feeling that Marcia did not believe her.

"Well, well," Marcia said. As she spoke, the tinny chimes of a distant clock drifted in on the still night air: *ting … ting … ting …* Silence fell as they all stood counting the chimes. Tod glanced at the ExtraOrdinary Wizard. He looked nervous, she thought. On the twelfth chime Marcia turned to him and said, "Septimus, I know we had arranged for you to **Go Through** on your own tonight on the Midnight Minutes, but this is very interesting *indeed*. Perhaps we could leave that for now and have a little chat with Tod instead? Upstairs, Septimus? In your rooms?"

Tod saw momentary relief flicker across the ExtraOrdinary Wizard's features before he managed to suppress it. She didn't blame him for not wanting to **Go Through** the archway. There was something unnerving about its misty depths.

"With pleasure, Marcia," he said.

A few minutes later, Tod found herself escorted up the spiral stairs in some style, accompanied not only by the current ExtraOrdinary Wizard, but by the previous two ExtraOrdinaries as well. It felt unreal – and just a little bit scary.

THE TOP OF THE TOWER

On the seventh floor of the Wizard Tower, Dr Dandra Draa did the last rounds of the night in her Sick Bay and tutted to herself about her protégée being whisked away by the Extra-Ordinaries. Dandra was of the opinion that twelve-year-olds should not be up after midnight. She decided to go to the ExtraOrdinary Wizard's rooms as soon as she had finished and insist Tod come back to bed.

"What would Cassi say?" Dandra muttered to herself. "Letting the girl stay up so late?" She sighed. The honest answer was that Cassi, a free spirit, would have been perfectly happy about it. And she would have been thrilled that not only had her daughter shown signs of inheriting the Magykal skills of the Draa side of the family, but that it had been recognised so soon by two powerful Wizards.

Poignant memories of the very last time she had seen her friend came rushing back to Dandra. Dandra – a Wizard and a skilled Physician, who came from the Hot, Dry Deserts of the South – had some years ago received a request from Marcia to help with a difficult DisEnchantment. Dandra had been only too pleased to leave her home, where things had become very dangerous for her. On her way to the Castle, she had stopped off at the TodHunter Moon household and Dandra still remembered the shock of seeing her old friend. Pale and thin, with a hacking cough and streaming red eyes, it was obvious that Cassi TodHunter Draa was seriously ill. Dandra knew there was nothing she could do to help her. Cassi had the dreaded Sand Sickness, caused by inhaling a small but deadly sand fly – common in Dandra's homeland, but previously unknown in the PathFinder village. Dandra had stayed a few days with Dan and Cassi and had got to know their little girl, Alice, who was, she remembered, a very determined tomboy. It was one of the saddest moments of Dandra's life when she said farewell to the little family, for she knew she would never see them together again. Her heart ached for Dan and Alice – or Tod, as the young Alice insisted on being called – as she waved goodbye from the Trading Post shuttle boat and began the very last stage of her journey to the fabled Wizard Tower. Dandra had promised Cassi to be a second mother to her little girl if ever she decided to follow the Magykal Draa side of the family and come to the Wizard Tower, but Dandra had never expected to see Tod again. She doubted Dan would ever let his one reminder of his beloved Cassi out of his sight. Dandra sighed. But now poor Dan was gone too. Who would have thought it? Forlornly, Dr Dandra Draa continued her midnight rounds of the Sick Bay.

Meanwhile, in the rooms of the ExtraOrdinary Wizard, Tod's head was buzzing with Magyk and excitement. She was ensconced on a small stool next to the fire, which burned with Magykal multicoloured flames. The room was filled with dancing shadows and fleeting purple lights that Tod could see only at the very edge of her vision. The room had an odd, echoing quality to it. It felt quite bare, apart from the heavy purple curtains on the windows and a small, furry rug beside the fire. It was sparsely furnished, as though someone had only recently moved in.

There was, however, an unusual purple sofa in front of the fire, on which Marcia had settled herself. She leaned back, kicked off the most astonishing pair of shoes that Tod had ever seen – purple snakeskin with tiny green jade buttons – and gave a contented sigh. "It's nice to be back," Marcia said, wiggling her toes. "It's so *warm* here."

The ghost of Alther Mella floated down next to Marcia, and to Tod's surprise, the young ExtraOrdinary Wizard sat on the floor beside her. "Now," he said to Tod. "If I am calling you Tod, then you must call me Septimus. OK?"

Tod smiled shyly. "OK," she said.

"Likewise, Marcia is just Marcia and Alther is just Alther. We don't use our titles when we are among people who understand **Magyk**."

"Unless they are being *very* annoying," Marcia put in.

"Marcia was ExtraOrdinary Wizard here up until six months ago," Septimus explained. "But she has now found more interesting things to do. Like go wandering through all kinds of strange arches that none of us can see. Except for you, Tod, it seems."

"Oh!" said Tod, somewhat lost for words. She could not quite believe what was happening. She sat very still, breathed in the **Magykal** air and listened to Marcia and Septimus bicker in the way that only old friends can do.

"Septimus, you exaggerate," Marcia was protesting. "It is just this one archway at the Wizard Tower that you can't see. All the others are perfectly clear; I don't know what you are fussing about. I suspect there has been some kind of Invisibility screen put on this arch, and you know how Invisibility soaks into marble. You just can't get it out however hard you try. But it is only a matter of practice before you see it."

"Maybe." Septimus sounded unconvinced.

Marcia was now in full flow. "And to set the record straight, Septimus, I did not 'find more interesting things to do', as you put it. It was time for me to go. The worst thing an ExtraOrdinary Wizard can do is to outstay her welcome. Look at that Brynna Jackson woman, she hung on until she was ninety-three. The Wizard Tower was a complete mess for years after that."

"You had a little way to go until you were ninety-three," Septimus pointed out.

"A little," Marcia agreed. "But I was in the job for twenty-one years; it's best to go when your powers are at their height." She sat back and sniffed the air appreciatively. "You know, Septimus, you must be doing something right – I have never felt so much Magyk in the air. It's quite exhilarating."

A companionable silence fell as they watched the multi-coloured flames of the fire leap and dance in the darkness and Tod supressed a yawn. It had been a very long day and it was beginning to catch up with her.

Alther spoke, and Tod felt goosebumps run down her neck. It struck her that there was no warning when a ghost was about to speak, because there was no intake of breath – it was very peculiar. "We should not keep this child up for any longer than necessary," Alther said, his voice drifting into the room.

"No, of course not," said Marcia. "Now, Tod, tell me. Are you by any chance a PathFinder?"

Tod stared at Marcia in astonishment. How did she know? It wasn't as if Tod's skin showed up shiny at night like most PathFinders. "I'm half PathFinder," she said. "My dad is — I mean, was — a PathFinder."

Marcia nodded. "And your mother is from a **Magykal** tribe?"

Tod felt almost spooked. How did Marcia know so much about her? "My mother was a Draa. But she is not alive now. Dr Draa is a distant cousin. And she was my mother's friend, too."

Septimus understood that it was not easy to talk of one's dead mother and father. "Enough questions about parents, Marcia," he said. "I am sure Tod doesn't want to talk about that tonight."

"Of course," Marcia agreed. "But you *are* from a PathFinder village, Tod?"

Relieved not to have to talk about her parents, Tod began to speak about her PathFinder village and the terrible things that had happened. A solemn silence fell in the room as the three ExtraOrdinaries listened to her story.

As Tod drew to a close, Septimus said, "Tod, this is terrible. You must consider the Wizard Tower your home for as long as you wish."

Marcia leaned forward impatiently. "But the reason I asked if you were a PathFinder is because a few years ago a friend of ours named Marwick found something rather exciting — a system of Ancient Ways that stretch across the world. And you get into them always through an archway. Most of these arch-ways are in what is called a Hub — like a crossroads, really, where some Ways meet. Anyone can see the archways in a Hub. Even Septimus." Marcia flashed Septimus a smile. "But there are other arches that are not in Hubs and they tend to be

Hidden. These arches are always, Marwick said, at the end of what he called a blind Way – a Way that does not go to a Hub, but to one place only. And, you see, Marwick once said a very strange thing to me. He said he wished he were a PathFinder. I asked him what he meant and he said that PathFinders can see all the **Hidden** arches."

"Have you seen any other arches, Tod?" Septimus asked.

"No," said Tod. And then she suddenly remembered the creepy arch where she and Oskar had put on their *Tristan* tops – which felt like a lifetime ago. "Well, maybe I *did* see one," she said. "In a wood near the OutPost."

"The OutPost, eh? Now let's see if we can work out which one that would be." From a pocket inside her voluminous cloak, Marcia extracted a long, silver tube. She pulled a cork from the end of it and eased out a scroll of grubby, crinkled paper. She carefully unrolled it to reveal what looked to Tod like a drawing of a fishing net made by someone with her eyes closed.

"This," said Marcia, "was drawn by Marwick. It is, he told me, a map of the Ancient Ways and it covers the whole world."

"The whole *world*?" Tod breathed.

"Amazing, isn't it? I didn't believe him at first," Marcia said. "And neither did you, did you, Septimus?"

Septimus shook his head. He felt bad about that still. But at least, he thought, his older brother Sam had believed Marwick. Septimus gazed at his old friend Marwick's spider-like scrawl with a pang of sadness. The paper circle began to roll itself back up and Marcia quickly passed her hand over it. A flicker of purple light followed her hand and the paper obediently unrolled and lay as flat as a piece of glass.

Marcia put on a pair of small, round spectacles and joined Septimus on the rug. Unsettlingly, Alther floated off the sofa and hovered above the map, looking down at it. Tod found it hard to concentrate on the map with the ghost hanging in the air, his robes showing no sign of being affected by gravity at all.

The map was nothing like the sea charts that Tod was used to. At the very centre was a circle carefully coloured in blue. It was numbered like a clockface with twelve Roman numerals and contained a spiral and a heart-shaped symbol. Marcia placed a long, elegant finger on it. "Marwick told us that this is the Heart of the Ways. It's the very centre of the network and is reputed to be made of solid lapis lazuli and built by a snake or something. *Very* strange. He never found it, though. Well … not as far as we know."

"Maybe he and Sam are there now," Septimus murmured.

Tod had a question. "But if Marwick never got there, how did he know what it was like?"

"Well, Marwick lived on an island on the Marram Marshes," said Septimus. "You would have come past the marshes on your way up the river. It's a wild and weird place where the Dragon Boat used to lie hidden in an old temple beneath the ground."

"But why was the Dragon Boat under the ground?" asked Tod.

"That," said Marcia firmly, "is another story for another time."

Septimus continued. "So, in this old temple Marwick found a sphere of lapis lazuli covered in a network of lines. He borrowed my best Enlarging Glass to have a closer look at it and he never gave it back." Septimus grinned ruefully. "He was a little scatty, was Marwick. Anyway, he realised that the lines all joined up and he reckoned it was a map. So he drew it out flat and thought no more of it – until one day at the back of a shelf, he found a little book called *The Ancient Ways of the World*. And in the book was a map just like the one he had drawn. It turned out to be a kind of guidebook, and that's how Marwick got interested. It seemed from the map that there was an archway somewhere on his island, so he started looking. He eventually found it when he was sweeping out the old temple. He said he just saw a kind of dent in the wall, walked straight at it and ended up in a jungle somewhere.

"He was stunned. He was thousands of miles from home, yet he had travelled there almost in an instant. He discovered that he was in an overgrown circle of twelve arches, each one numbered, one to twelve –" Septimus smiled at Tod – "with your PathFinder numbers. He explored a little and found that each arch led to another Hub – or sometimes to a single Hidden arch. Marwick was hooked. He and my brother Sam began to explore and they ended up all over the world. Marwick said it was easy to find your way back home as you just took note of the number of the arch you had come out of. He and Sam took the map with them and noted down all the numbers and where everything went and which Ways still worked – not all of them do, he said. And of course, really the map should be in three dimensions. Even so, it's pretty amazing."

Tod peered at the map, fascinated. She could see the faint numbers in different colours and the wiggly descriptions of some of the Hubs – *Beware Snake Pit*, *Deep in Sand*, *Temple with Priest Expecting Gift* – gave Tod the strange feeling of a whole world laid out before her.

Marcia took over. "Every now and then, Marwick and Sam would come and see me and update my map. It was so fascinating, Tod. And, after years of being at the Castle I began to get itchy feet. I longed to travel and see the world too."

Tod was beginning to understand how Marcia felt.

"So, Tod, last year while I was still ExtraOrdinary Wizard, while I was travelling with a dear friend, I found a beautiful old tower called the Keep. And deep in the basement of the Keep, to my amazement, I found what I knew was a Hub. It was choked with earth and had been used as a rubbish pit but I could not stop thinking about it. Here was my chance to have my own entrance to the Ancient Ways. My chance to travel the world. So I sold what was left of my collection of Fragile Fairy pots – they had suddenly become very popular – and bought the Keep."

A ghostly voice from above the map made Tod jump. "But not until she had made sure I had been to a party there. In my wild youth." The ghost chuckled.

This was all too strange for Tod to take in. She leaned back against the wall beside the fireplace, and it was only the pressure of the warm stone behind her that told her she was not dreaming.

Marcia laughed. "Alther is not as crazy as he sounds, Tod," she said. "One of the rules of ghosthood is …"

"A ghost may only tread once more where, Living, he has trod before," Alther finished for her. "Which means I can't go somewhere new any more. Ever. So remember that, young Tod. Go to as many places in your life as you possibly can. Goodness, Septimus, if I had known about these Ancient Ways then you wouldn't have kept me out of them for one moment. Think of all the places I could go to now."

163

Septimus shook his head. "It's not *all* good, Alther. I am concerned that using these Ways opens us up to all kinds of Incursions. Who knows who or what might come through to the Wizard Tower."

"I should have thought it was *more* secure now I'm living at the Keep," Marcia countered. "Anything that comes here has to come through my Hub first."

The heavy purple door to the rooms swung silently open and Dandra Draa walked in.

"Oh, Dandra!" Marcia said, rather guiltily.

"Marcia, it is very nearly one o'clock," Dandra said sternly. "I do think Alice should come to bed now."

Tod thought so too. Her head was fuzzy with **Magyk** and the new ideas she had been trying to take in. She felt so tired she could have fallen asleep right there.

Marcia, Septimus and Alther wished her goodnight and as Dandra shepherded her out, Septimus and Marcia headed out towards a little brightly lit kitchen. "I have some really wild new coffee," Septimus was saying. "Would you like to try some?"

"I'd love to," Marcia replied.

Tod watched Septimus and Marcia together. Septimus was half a head taller than Marcia and he wore his ExtraOrdinary Wizard robes well, Tod thought. His long, purple tunic hung from his broad shoulders and the ExtraOrdinary Wizard platinum-and-gold belt sat easily around his waist. As Septimus stood back to let Marcia go first, Tod saw Marcia put her hand on his shoulder and say, "I hope that coffee pot is behaving properly now."

Septimus groaned. "That coffee pot is in disgrace. I've

locked it in the cupboard. It's a one-woman pot, Marcia. It's yours to take home."

Marcia laughed. "Poor old pot. Septimus, how *could* you lock it away?"

"Easy," said Septimus. "Just one turn of the key." Tod heard the smile in his voice as he disappeared into the kitchen.

Tod could tell there was a private space between Septimus and Marcia that no one intruded upon. It made her feel suddenly lonely; there was no one she was close to now. She was very far from home indeed.

And then Dandra put her arm around her shoulders and drew Tod out of the room. "Time," she said firmly, "for bed."

On the first floor in the Junior Girls' Apprentice Dorm, Tod was asleep, but in her dreams she was awake and running, slow and scared, beneath the water. She was looking for Dan, just as she did every night, but now she was pursued by the dreaded sounds: *clicker-click-click ... click-click ... clicker-click*. And in her dreams she understood what the clicks were saying.

"We know where you are, Alice TodHunter Moon. We know where you are and *we are coming to get you*."

TOWER TOUR

Tod woke late to a feeling that she was the last one in the dormitory. She lay still for a while, listening to the purposeful hum of **Magyk** as the day-to-day work of the Wizard Tower proceeded, then she pushed back her covers and jumped out of bed on to the soft, warm floor. At the end of the bed were her clean sailing trews, striped top and canvas shoes. Tod smiled, pleased to see the adventurous part of herself back once more.

Ten minutes later she bumped into Dandra Draa in the Apprentice corridor.

"Aha," said Dandra, "I thought you'd be up. I'm your Wizard Tower guide for today. How does breakfast and then a tour sound to you?"

It sounded pretty good to Tod.

By the end of the day, Tod's head was in a whirl. Dandra had shown her every part of the Wizard Tower it was possible for a non-Wizard to see, and much that wasn't. Now Tod felt tired and frazzled. The constant presence of **Magyk** – as much as she loved it – was exhausting. So when, on her way back with Dandra from viewing the **Sealed Cell** lobby, Tod saw a familiar face in the Great Hall, she felt almost tearful with relief. "Nicko!" she called out.

Nicko was sitting on the waiting bench. Hearing his name, he jumped to his feet. "Hey, Tod!" he called out. "How's it going – weird?"

"A bit," Tod admitted.

"I'm not surprised," Nicko said. "Ever since Sep – I mean, the new ExtraOrdinary Wizard – took over, this place has been buzzing like a swarm of bees." He grinned at Dandra. "*You* may not notice it, but personally, it gives me a headache."

Dandra smiled. "You've been away on your boat for too long, Nicko."

"Maybe," Nicko said. "And talking of boats, Tod – Snorri and I wondered if you would like to have supper with us on the *Adventurer* and get out of all this fizzy-fuzzy **Magyk** stuff."

"I would love to have supper on the *Adventurer*," said Tod. "And to see Snorri. And Ullr." She turned to Dandra. "May I?"

"Of course," Dandra said. She reached up to a small box high on the wall, pulled a long, thin purple card from it and handed it to Tod. "The night password. You will need this to get back in."

Tod buttoned the card into one of the many pockets in Dan's fishing jacket. It was good to feel part of the Wizard Tower – to have the password just like she truly belonged.

On the *Adventurer*, everything seemed happily simple and familiar. Tod sat in the cabin dipping crusty bread into the big pot of stew that Nicko had cooked, while the Night Ullr lay in the doorway keeping guard.

"So, Tod," Snorri said in her sing-song accent. "How was today?"

Tod took a gulp of lemonade. "Amazing," she said.

"And your mother's friend?"

"I love Dandra. Look, she did this. It's real **Magyk**!" Tod took her paint-splashed pebble out of her pocket and held it in her palm. Nicko glanced at Snorri with a smile. He guessed what was going to happen.

Very gently, Tod stroked the pebble. It slowly opened two little black eyes and stretched out four stumpy legs. "It's a pet rock," she said.

"So it is," said Nicko. "And they are greedy little things, pet rocks, so don't feed it too much because it will get very heavy and lazy."

"Oh! Have you got one too?" asked Tod.

"No, but Jen – I mean, the Queen – has lots. They live in the Rockery at the Palace. You must take yours down to meet them. With those green splashes all over it there is no chance of losing it."

"Does it have a name?" asked Snorri.

"Not yet," said Tod. "I'm going to get to know it first." She stroked the pebble once more and it closed its eyes, drew in its stumpy legs and became just a green-spattered pebble.

"So, Tod," said Nicko, "it's been a good day?"

"Yes, it has," said Tod. "Dandra told me so much about my mother and about … about Dad, too. She'd like me to stay if I want to. I can live with her and decide what I want to do. It's what she promised my mother." Tod sighed. "But … oh, it's silly, I know. But I've been thinking …"

"About home?" asked Snorri.

Tod nodded. "I … suppose I didn't really understand that I was leaving, maybe for ever. But now that I'm here, I keep thinking about Oskie and Ferdie. And Rosie and Jonas and little Torr and Jerra and … and how good they were to me.

But I just ran away and left them. I can't believe I did that." Tod put her head in her hands.

Snorri put her arms around Tod. "You did not run away. You left because it was your parents' wish."

Tod shook her head. "I ran away. And left my friends in a total *mess*."

Nicko leaned forward. "Tod, you chose between two courses. And that is the trouble with choosing – there is always the one you didn't take. It may have been better, it may have been worse, but that's not the point. You could not choose both. And sometimes, when the tide is running fast, you have only one chance to decide. You do your best at the time, with what you know then. It's tough, but that's how it goes. Personally, I think you caught the tide just right."

Tod shook her head. She wished she could feel so sure.

"You see, Tod, life is like a sea passage," said Snorri. "You sail your boat the best you can, but sometimes there is a storm. All you can do is to keep a steady hand on the tiller and hope for better weather."

Nicko grinned. "You're doing pretty well so far. Not hit any rocks yet."

But somewhere in the middle of a dark forest, rocks were appearing. Mitza Draddenmora Draa was nervously standing in the middle of a prowling circle of Garmin, clutching one of Tod's old tops. She threw it into the pack with a yell. "Find!"

PASSWORD

It was late in the evening when Tod walked back through the boatyard with Nicko and Snorri. They headed along the tunnel that burrowed through the thick Castle walls and out into a lantern-lit path that wound behind a straggle of typically tall, narrow Castle houses. The path came to an end at an impressive wall, beyond which Tod could see the Wizard Tower rising up, awash with lights. There was a gate set into the wall and Nicko gave it a push. It swung open into the Wizard Tower courtyard and Tod felt her worries fading as the exhilaration of the **Magyk** swirling beyond took over.

She turned to Nicko and Snorri and hugged them both. "Thank you," she said. "Thank you for *everything*."

"We shall come with you to the doors, Tod," said Snorri.

But Tod wanted to be alone with the night-time **Magyk** chasing through the courtyard. Proudly, she held up her purple password card. "I'm fine, thanks. I've got my night password."

Nicko understood – sometimes he just wanted to be alone with his boat and the sea. "Tod's OK," he said to Snorri. And then to Tod, "We'll be at the boatyard tomorrow. Come and see us, yes?"

Tod smiled. "Yes, please."

Nicko gave her a thumbs-up and closed the gate.

Tod wandered slowly across the courtyard, savouring the sensation of moving through **Magyk**, feeling as if she were walking underwater. A delicate purple light suffused the air; long, slow, lazy arcs of indigo, green and orange were dropping down from the Wizard Tower like pinpoints of light from an enormous firework. Tod walked dreamily through the lights, some of which landed at her feet, bouncing up into the air again and then zooming away, flashing upwards like shooting stars in reverse. The air felt sharp and alive, popping and fizzing as she drifted through it, heading towards the shimmering marble steps that rose up to the silver doors.

At the foot of the steps, Tod stopped and looked up at the Wizard Tower, entranced by the myriad of purple windows flickering so subtly that she could only see the movement when she looked away from them. One in particular – the **UnStable** window that Dandra had showed her that morning – caught Tod's attention. As she gazed at it, trying to figure out whether it was there or not, she became aware of another kind of movement. She swung around and to her horror, Tod saw the unmistakable pale, flat-headed shape of a Garmin lurking in the shadows at the base of the Wizard Tower.

A flight of steps had never felt so long and so exposed. Tod raced up them, and at the top, with a stab of fear, she realised that she had forgotten the password and *she no longer had the purple card in her hand*. Near to panic, Tod guessed she must have dropped it as she fled up the steps. Slowly, she turned around and there was the slip of card lying dark against the white of the lowest step. But not far beyond it stood the tall, unwieldy shape of a Garmin.

Confused by the onslaught of the courtyard **Magyk**, the Garmin was standing still, its big, heavy head swaying from side to side. Tod could tell it had not seen her. She had a few moments to retrieve the password – and she knew that if she hesitated, those moments would be gone. Going against all her instincts Tod crept down the steps, towards the slip of purple and towards the Garmin. Reaching the last step but one, she snatched up the card and turned to run back up. Her sudden movement was her downfall.

Click-click-click.

A metallic flash of yellow eyes caught her gaze. Tod tried to look away but all her strength had left her. Nothing seemed to work any more.

Click-clicker-click. Click-clicker-clicker-click.

No more than half a minute later, the tall silver doors to the Wizard Tower opened and Dandra Draa came hurrying out. She stopped and listened, then she hurried down the steps. The **Magyk** was disturbed – *something was wrong.*

PART
VII

AN INCURSION OF ILL INTENT

Marcia Overstrand was sitting in her favourite place in the world – a window seat high up in the circular, central room of her Keep.

Marcia rarely went to bed before the early hours of the morning, and many a night would she wander through the Keep with only a lighted candle for company, getting to know every night-time creak, every shadow, every strip of moonlight that glanced in through its arrow-slit windows. After the thrum of the Wizard Tower, so full of people demanding her time, Marcia savoured the luxury of being alone, of having space and time to think and maybe – when she finally unwound from the frenetic years of being responsible for everything – rediscovering her own personal **Magyk**.

To reach her window, Marcia had climbed some narrow steps set into the window alcove, which nestled inside the ten-feet-thick walls, and was now sitting on the rug and cushions, gazing down at the scene below. The nearly new moon cast little light, but lanterns illuminated the lumps and bumps of the ancient, earth-covered outer walls that surrounded the Keep. Beyond these was a fine stone quay – newly constructed with a line of lanterns placed along it, ready to guide a ship called the *Cerys* safely home up the wide and wild estuary.

Revelling in the silence, the peace of the old stones and the knowledge that no one was going to bang on her door and demand that she *do something right now*, Marcia gazed dreamily out at the night. The water was high and Marcia – who had once paid very little attention to tides and all things concerning boats, but who now knew the tide times backwards – wondered if tonight she would see the *Cerys* coming home once more.

The evening mist began to roll in. Soon it covered the white stone of the quay and was creeping up the grass. It lay low like a blanket so that above it, Marcia could still see the star-filled sky. With the arrival of the mist, Marcia supposed she had her Keep to herself for another night. She settled herself among the cushions and picked up a much-thumbed book, Marwick's house-warming gift to her, a precious copy of *The Ancient Ways of the World*. Marcia drew her thick woollen cloak around her against the night chill that was creeping in. She turned to chapter thirteen, ominously titled "Incursions of Ill Intent", and began to read.

Marcia was not entirely alone in her Keep. On the lower levels lived three Drummins. Drummins were small humanoid creatures who originally came from the Great Chamber of Fyre below the Castle. Marcia had been deeply suspicious of Drummins when she had first encountered them, for they were the result of the ancient Alchemists tinkering with human life, of which she did not approve. But over the seven years since their rediscovery, Marcia had grown to like and respect them. And so, when she had moved into the Keep and three elderly Drummins had offered to come with her, Marcia had not needed much persuading. They were quiet, practical creatures and she knew she could rely on them.

Fabius, Lucius and Claudius Drummin preferred not to venture above ground. Their domain was beneath the earth and they were perfectly happy guarding the Hub and tending the fire in the kitchen. So when Marcia heard a soft, apologetic cough beside her, she looked up to see a pair of ginger eyebrows beneath which the large dark eyes of Fabius Drummin gazed at her. The Drummin's broad, suckered fingers gripped the deep stone window sill and his face was anxious beneath his long, plaited beard.

Marcia put her book down at once. "What is it, Fabius?" she asked.

Fabius was a Drummin of few words; like most Drummins, he preferred to use signing. "Trouble," he said.

Marcia was down the window steps in an instant. The Drummin scurried across the main chamber and Marcia hurried after him, heading through the archway and on to the stone spiral stairs that would take them down to the lower levels. Fabius turned around and placed his finger to his lips to caution Marcia to be quiet; Marcia was glad that she was wearing her soft, purple fur boots, which allowed her to pad as silently as any Drummin – although clearly not quite as silently as Fabius would have liked. They descended through three levels. The first level was the entrance chamber, and once they were past that and heading down to the second level, the temperature began to rise. This was what the Drummins called the Fire Pit, though it was actually the kitchen where they tended the fire, cooked very simple food and slept.

Marcia and Fabius continued down the narrow, gently curving stairs, with a musty smell of damp earth becoming ever stronger as they headed for the Hub.

The Hub itself was relatively small. Down in the foundations of the Keep, the walls were extremely thick, but radiating into them like spokes from a wheel were twelve vaulted tunnels, each with a stone arch at its opening. The arches were labelled with PathFinder numbers one to twelve. The tunnels did not appear to be long – about twenty feet at the most – because each one ended in strange swirling white mist, which Marwick had called the Vanishing Point.

Marcia hurried into the Hub to find the other two Drummins waiting, their notoriously sharp flick-knives held ready to open in the blink of an eye.

What is the thing? Marcia signed. She was not as good at Drummin signing as she wanted to be and her attempts provided the Drummins with much amusement, though they appreciated the fact she was trying to learn.

Garmin out of Way Two, Claudius signed, pointing at the arch behind him with the figure *II* on the keystone.

Into Seven, added Lucius, rather unnecessarily pointing at the almost opposite arch sporting the number *VII*.

Unfortunately, finished Fabius.

Marcia was horrified. Too flustered to sign, she whispered, "*Garmin?* Are you sure?"

The three Drummins nodded in unison.

Shh, Fabius signed. *They are coming*.

Which road? Marcia signed.

Seven.

A feeling of relief washed over Marcia. If the Garmin were coming back from the Wizard Tower so soon, surely they would not have had time to do anything terrible. Marcia's relief did not last long – a moment later a streak of white burst out of Way VII. She was aghast. The creatures were terrifying – and far bigger than she had expected. They hurtled across the Hub, oblivious to its occupants, and then they were gone, white skin and sinew disappearing into the shadows of Way II.

Marcia was shocked. She raced across to Way II and, summoning all her energy, she pulled a shimmering purple Magykal Seal across its arch to protect it against any more Incursions of Ill Intent. Marcia was just beginning on the next arch – for she had no idea what else might be coming through – when a shout from the Drummins made her swing around. Coming out of Way VII was another Garmin, but this one was in great distress. Limping, its mouth hanging slackly open with thick drools of saliva dripping down, its flat, forked black tongue lolling out, the creature blundered blindly towards Way II, hit the Seal and bounced off, stunned. Marcia and the Drummins froze, revulsion prickling their skin. They watched the creature stagger in circles with its great flat head drooping down and then wander unsteadily out of the Hub and up the stairs.

Three Drummin flick-knives snapped open. "We will get it," Fabius said.

Stunned, Marcia watched the Drummins race up the stairs in pursuit. She took a deep breath, trying to calm herself and stop her hands from shaking. She must Seal the other Ways – and fast. Marcia was renewing her attention to Way III when she heard a hollow, echoing sound coming from Way VII – footsteps. *Human* footsteps. Hurried. Panicked.

A moment later, Dandra Draa came racing out, carrying a large, shiny silver cocoon in her arms. "Alice!" cried Dandra.

"What?" said Marcia.

"*Alice*. Oh, I mean, Tod. She's in here – in a Garmin cocoon. Oh, Marcia. I promised Cassi I'd look after her and look what's happened! Oh, please help. *Please!*"

"Upstairs," Marcia said briskly. "We need warmth, fire. We must hurry." It was only as she headed across to the stairs that Marcia remembered the lone, injured Garmin at large somewhere above. She stopped, unsure what to do, and at that moment something huge and white appeared, airborne, heading down the stairs towards her. Marcia leaped out of the way just in time. The creature hit the flagstones with a *crunch* and lay immobile. A heavy footfall came thundering down the steps after it and, to Marcia's astonishment, a piratical-looking man came into view, brandishing a heavy stick. "Milo!" she cried.

"Marcia!" gasped Milo.

Marcia looked down at the Garmin, leaking thick, black fluid across the white flagstones of the Hub. "Is it dead?" she asked.

Milo poked the creature with his foot. "Yes."

"Good," said Marcia. "Come on, Dandra. Quickly now."

Dandra gave Milo a strained smile as, bemused, he stepped back to let them pass. It took Milo a few seconds to recover his wits, and then he yelled up, "Marcia! What's going *on*?"

"No time! Explain later!" Marcia called back.

From the foot of the stairs, Milo watched his wife of one year to the day disappear around the first spiral. He shook his head in bemusement. He had hoped that life here would be more simple, but he now realised how silly that had been. Marcia didn't do simple.

COCOON

The silver cocoon lay on the rug in front of the impressive fireplace in the Great Chamber. Thanks to Milo the flames were roaring up into the tall stone chimneypiece, sending out the heat that Marcia wanted.

"I can't believe there is a human being in there," Milo said, sombrely gazing at the cocoon. "It looks so tiny."

"It has been **Compressed**," said Marcia. "A **Darke** art, showing no respect for human life whatsoever. You'd be surprised how small the human body can become."

"And still live?" asked Dandra anxiously.

"For a while." Marcia was running her hands over the cocoon, trying to find a way in through the tough membrane, which felt as unyielding and strong as steel. "Milo, would you lend me your silver knife, please?"

Milo took out a small knife folded into its ebony handle and handed it to Marcia. She opened it and breathed on the blade, muttering, **"Unbind the thing that binds, unwind the thing that winds."** Then she pushed the tip of the blade – like all Milo's knives, razor-sharp – in between what she judged to be a join in the membrane. To her relief, she was right. Marcia plunged her hand in and felt the body of a small human beneath. "Milo, Dandra. Take hold of this horrid stuff. Pull it away before it sticks back together again."

Milo and Dandra both took hold of the unpleasantly sticky substance and pulled. It resisted but neither was going to be defeated. They tugged at the membrane so it stretched out like a long, transparent piece of silk. Marcia began frantically sawing at it with the blade. Suddenly, it was cut and like a spring released from tension, the cocoon fell apart.

Inside was the folded-up form of a girl, legs and arms crossed like, thought Marcia, a dressed goose ready for dinner.

"Good Lord," said Milo.

"Oh, *Alice*!" gasped Dandra.

Milo had never seen Marcia "at work", as he called it. He watched in awe as Marcia lifted Tod's head, which was limp and heavy, and gently moved her damp, matted hair away from her bluish-white face. He saw Marcia take a deep breath in, and in, and in, until it seemed impossible that she could breathe in any more without bursting. He saw her lean over the girl's face and begin to breathe out in a slow, steady stream, her warm, Magykal breath a soft, pale pink against the night air.

As Marcia was breathing out, Milo realised that he was doing the same. But Milo ran out of breath long before Marcia did. On and on, the long, thin stream of pinkish air curled out from her mouth and settled over Tod's pale, damp features. And just as Milo was convinced that Marcia could breathe out not a moment longer, he saw Tod's eyelids flicker and then suddenly, her dark grey eyes were wide open, staring straight at him.

"You're safe. Sleep now," Marcia murmured.

"Oh. Oh, thank goodness," Dandra whispered.

Tod took in a long, deep, shuddering breath; the air tasted sweet and smoky and felt wonderfully warm. The coldness of the reptilian slime had chilled her to the bone and now the heat set her shivering. She wanted to ask where she was, what had happened, but her teeth were chattering uncontrollably. Someone put a blanket around her shoulders and Tod pulled it tighter. She felt as though she would never be warm again.

"Alice … oh, *Alice*." Someone else put her arms around her and Tod found herself being gently laid down on soft cushions and blankets. Slowly, she began to feel more human. She looked up and saw three worried, pale faces smiling down at her and she savoured the presence of humans — their body warmth, the expressiveness of their faces. Someone placed another blanket over her and Tod closed her eyes, knowing that she was safe.

Dandra got shakily to her feet. "She's sleeping now," she whispered, gazing down at Tod, who looked very small and thin beneath the blankets. Dandra hugged Marcia. "Thank you, oh, thank you," she said. "But I must go. I have a patient in Sick Bay, dying, I think. And I've left the Apprentice on his own. Oh, I don't want to go, but I must."

"Dandra, it's all right," Marcia said. "We will look after your Alice. We'll stand guard all night, don't you worry." She stood back and looked at her friend. "You could do with some rest yourself. Goodness, what have you done to your hand?" Blood was dripping off Dandra Draa's knuckles.

Dandra looked at her hand in surprise. "I must have hurt it when I punched that Garmin on the nose."

"You hit a Garmin?" Marcia was amazed.

"Well, I had to get Alice away from it somehow. Couldn't think what else to do, really."

"Oh, Dandra, you are amazing," said Marcia. She put her arm around her friend's shoulders. "Milo will watch over Tod," she said. "I'll see you home."

"Don't be long," said Milo.

Down in the Hub, at the foot of the stairs, Dandra and Marcia stepped over the dead Garmin lying folded like a squashed spider in a pool of ink. They both shuddered. "Milo will clear it up in the morning," Marcia said briskly.

Before she left the Hub, Marcia placed a **Seal** on every Way except for VII. And when she returned from taking Dandra back to the Wizard Tower, she **Sealed** Way VII, too.

Upstairs in the Great Chamber, in the red glow cast by the fire, Marcia found Milo waiting beside the sleeping figure of Tod.

"How is she?" Marcia whispered.

"Fine," said Milo. "Sleeping soundly."

"I'll watch her all night," said Marcia. "Just to make sure."

"All night?" asked Milo, dismayed. "But, Marcia, I came back especially."

Marcia reached out and touched Milo's hand. "I am so pleased you did. I was sure you hadn't made it. The mist came in so fast."

"I left *Cerys* on the seaward quay and rowed up," said Milo. "Followed the mist as it rolled in. I had to be here."

Marcia smiled happily. "Well, we can spend the night here by the fire. I'll ask Lucius to do us some supper."

Milo looked downcast. Cooking was not one of a Drummin's finest skills. "You've still not got a cook, then?"

"I don't want my Keep cluttered up with people – especially people who cook. They are nothing but trouble," Marcia said.

"Anyway, Lucius is getting much better. He's very good at omelettes. And gooseberry bake."

"Omelette and gooseberry bake it is, then," said Milo stoutly. "I'll go and tell him, shall I?" He got to his feet.

It was only later, when Milo went down to the Fire Pit to pick up the supper, that he realised he had not made himself clear. In one large dish sat an omelette wrapped around a pile of gooseberries covered with cheesy breadcrumbs. "It's a good thing I also brought some Trading Post chocolates," said Milo, handing Marcia a large, velvet-covered box tied with a big gold ribbon. "Happy anniversary."

GRULA-GRULA

The next morning, Tod felt very nearly human again. She wanted to go back to the Wizard Tower, but Marcia felt Tod's forehead and frowned.

"You are still somewhat cold, Alice," she said. "You need to get warm all the way through. Come and sit in the sun, there is nothing better for getting rid of the lingering chill of **Darkenesse**."

And so Tod spent the morning sitting in Marcia's window alcove, soaking up the sun and watching Milo's ship, the *Cerys*, come in on the high tide. In her hand she held a beautiful silver whistle covered in **Magykal** symbols, which Marcia had given her.

"The Hub is secure and the Drummins will take good care of you," Marcia had said, "but even so, I'd like you to have this. If you need help, just blow. I'll hear."

"But how?" Tod asked. "Aren't you going to the Wizard Tower?"

Marcia held up a twin of the whistle, which she was wearing around her neck. "It's a nice simple way of using **Magyk**," she explained. "You blow your whistle and this one sounds. We'll do a test. I'll go over here and then you whistle." Marcia strode across the room to the stairs. "OK?"

Tod blew her whistle. No sound came out, but Marcia's whistle sounded, thin and sweet on the other side of the room. Marcia smiled. "I won't be long." And with that, she was gone.

Tod listened to the *tippy-tappy* sounds of the purple python shoes disappearing. She leaned back in the sun, the silver whistle warm in her hand, contentedly watching the activity that always accompanies a boat returning to her home port.

Marcia UnSealed Way VII and headed off to the Wizard Tower to speak to Septimus. But she arrived too late. He was already gone. Finding Dandra still occupied in the Sick Bay, Marcia settled down in the Great Hall to await Septimus's return.

Septimus was at Bott's Cloaks with Beetle, Chief Hermetic Scribe and unsuccessful remover of Grula-Grulas. It was Beetle's second day at Bott's Cloaks but this time he had with him an unusual display of force: the ExtraOrdinary Wizard, accompanied by his twin brothers, Senior Apprentices Edd and Erik Heap.

They were met by Miranda Bott – a large, irritable woman who had recently inherited the shop. Although Miranda dutifully continued the family business of selling Magykal cloaks (both *preloved* and *soon-to-be cherished*) she was not very welcoming towards Wizards.

The previous day with Beetle had not been a success – the Grula-Grula had thrown a spectacular temper tantrum and had ruined the last of Miranda's precious ancient cloaks. Finally, with her business in tatters and the stink of old cheese filling the shop, Miranda had agreed to allow the Wizard Tower to be involved. "I'm not having any old Wizard, mind," she had told Beetle. "You can bring the ExtraOrdinary or forget it."

Miranda sniffed disdainfully at the sight of the ExtraOrdinary Wizard in his impressive purple accompanied by what she took to be two bodyguards. Edd and Erik Heap were powerfully built and had a wild air about them, gained from years of living in the Forest. Miranda wasn't keen. "You can leave *them* outside," she said.

There was no way Septimus was going to leave Edd and Erik outside, but since becoming ExtraOrdinary Wizard he had learned a lot about the art of diplomacy. "Miss Bott," he said, "I would *so* much like you to meet my brothers Edd and Erik Heap."

"How do you do, Miss Bott," Edd and Erik murmured politely.

"Humph," harrumphed Miranda.

"And of course, you have already met the Chief Hermetic Scribe, Mr Beetle."

Miranda Bott was not to be mollified. "Of course I've bloomin' met him. He practically moved in here yesterday. Fat lot of good he was too. I hope you are going to do better, ExtraOrdinary."

"We work as a team," Septimus said smoothly. "The Chief Hermetic Scribe performed stage one of the removal yesterday and all went as planned."

Beetle quickly mastered his look of surprise. Sometimes the new, ExtraOrdinary Wizard Septimus took him aback. His old friend had turned out to be a natural politician.

Miranda Bott was less impressed. "Rubbish!" she declared.

"So now, Miss Bott," Septimus was saying, "in stage two we *all* need to attend to your uninvited guest. And I promise we shall do our very best."

The sincere expression in Septimus's clear green eyes and his calm manner began to soothe Miranda Bott's frazzled temper. So she smiled and said, "Thank you, ExtraOrdinary, I do believe you *will* do your best. Please come in."

The Grula-Grula removal party stepped inside and Miranda bolted the door behind them. The smell was atrocious. Even Erik and Edd, who were used to Forest smells, wrinkled their noses in disgust.

"It's the most revolting creature I've ever set eyes on," Miranda declared. "Its personal hygiene is non-existent. Follow me, please." She set off through the shop, past tables sporting piles of neatly folded cloaks of various shades of blue and green. The increasingly queasy group followed Miranda through a succession of interconnecting rooms full of the more expensive cloaks – a forest of green, blue and the very occasional purple hanging neatly on rails suspended from the ceiling.

They emerged from behind the last of the cloaks to find Miranda Bott standing in front of a door marked *Ancient Archive*. "It's in there," she told them. "It's *ruined* them. All those beautiful exhibit pieces – destroyed." She sniffed dramatically and Beetle wondered how she managed to breathe in so deeply.

"At least there is no other harm done," Septimus said. "Remind me, Miss Bott, what form has it taken today?"

"Today?" Miranda sounded flummoxed. "I dunno, I haven't looked. It was a lovely, polite gentleman when it came in. Spent ages trying on all the most interesting cloaks, and he was charming. He even gave me back a five-crown note he found in one of the pockets." She sighed. "You don't get many customers like that."

"Fortunately not," said Septimus briskly, sounding, he thought to himself, rather like Marcia.

"So, when he asked to look at the Ancient Archive I thought that, what with him being such an honest gentleman, I could trust him. I let him in and then a customer came in the shop and I had to go and see to them. And then ..." She gave a shudder. "And then, when I came back, I popped my head around the door all friendly-like, to see how he was getting on, and there was this great orange hairy blob squatting on a pile of the most valuable cloaks. I must have screamed – well, actually, I know I screamed, because my neighbour came around and banged on the door to see if I was all right."

"Why didn't you come and tell us at the Wizard Tower straight away?" Septimus asked.

"Well, I was so shocked I couldn't believe it," said Miranda. "So I counted to ten and looked back inside again, and there was no sign of the blob. I thought I'd imagined it."

"The Grula-Grula had **ShapeShifted** into something else," Septimus said. "Probably a mouse or something you wouldn't notice."

"Are you suggesting I am infested with mice?" Miranda demanded.

"Not you personally, Miss Bott," Septimus replied. "Now, as I am sure you know, there are two ways of getting rid of a Grula-Grula visitation. The first is a little radical and may well lead to some peripheral impairment."

"What?" asked Miranda.

"There may be some damage to the surroundings," explained Septimus.

"I've had enough damage to my surroundings already, thank you very much," Miranda said indignantly.

"So I suggest the second option, which is to persuade the Grula-Grula to exit of its own volition."

"Of its own what?"

"Leave because it wants to," Septimus said.

Miranda Bott looked exasperated. "But it doesn't want to, does it? That is the problem."

"Have you asked it?" Septimus inquired.

"No, of course I haven't bloomin' *asked* it. It's a great fat smelly monster and it's been sitting there pooing over all my most valuable cloaks for days. Why would I want to go and *talk* to it, eh? Sheesh!" Miranda Bott treated Beetle to a conspiratorial look of exasperation, but Beetle did not respond. He was not to be won over.

"So I suggest we ask it," said Septimus. "Nicely." He took a small piece of paper from his pocket and quickly scanned it, making sure he still knew every line. The Grula-Grula sonnet was only effective if proclaimed without breaking eye contact with the creature. "The Chief Hermetic Scribe and I are going in with the sonnet," Septimus said. "I expect to be out with the Grula in two to three minutes. Please make sure we have a clear exit, Miss Bott."

Septimus pushed open the door to the Ancient Archive and stepped inside with Beetle, leaving Edd and Erik on guard. A ten-feet-tall, roughly triangular mass of orange fur with no clear features – apart from what could possibly be two pink eyes at the top point of the triangle – sat in the middle of what was now a virtually empty room. It appeared to have eaten most of the cloaks and furniture and had begun on the walls, where it was, in some places, through to the brick. Taking care not to slip on the slime that pooled across the floor, Septimus and Beetle approached it warily.

The creature watched them equally warily. It recalled its mother telling it that it must never look at anything purple, but it couldn't remember why. And then, as soon as Septimus made eye contact with the two pink, watery circles at the top of its pointy head, it did remember – but too late. The Grula-Grula let out a high-pitched wail of dismay. Septimus launched into the sonnet at once.

> *"What, O Grula, is your substance, whereof are you made,*
> *That millions of strange shadows on you, fair Grula, tend?"*

The Grula-Grula was successfully Transfixed. It stared at Septimus as in a low, steady voice, he spoke the Grula Sonnet. From somewhere underneath its fur, two little pink hands emerged and clasped together in utter delight. As Septimus drew towards the end, the Grula-Grula began to join in, singing softly in an ear-achingly high-pitched voice.

> *"And, O Grula, you in every blessed shape we know.*
> *In all external Grula-grace you have some part,*
> *But, fair Grula, you like none, none you, for constant*
> *   heart."*

Beetle watched in amazement as the creature gazed down at Septimus in adoration. Its little hands wandered up to the point of its head and scraped its greasy hair into a neat parting, revealing a small, flushed face like a tiny pink plate.

Septimus bowed and said, "Fair Grula, come with me, I pray," and when he began to walk towards the door, Beetle had to step smartly out of the way to avoid being mown down by a ton of ecstatic orange fur. They emerged into the sunlight and sweet air of Wizard Way, leaving Miranda Bott to clean up the mess. Septimus stole a quick glance up at the sky to see if Spit Fyre had returned – as he was getting into the habit of doing every time he went outside. But the sky was both cloudless and dragonless.

Slowly, for the Grula-Grula took very tiny steps, they made their way back to the Wizard Tower, to the delight of many onlookers. "What are you going to do with it now?" Beetle asked.

"Stranger Chamber," said Septimus. And then, in case the Grula was listening, he added, "Only the best for our honoured guest." Septimus had long been fascinated by these creatures, which would very occasionally and inexplicably appear in the Castle. Hundreds of years had gone by since the previous confirmed sighting of a Grula-Grula (although recently there had been rumours of one seen drowned in the Moat) and Septimus was determined not to let this one go. Grula-Grulas were superb ShapeShifters, which fascinated Septimus. He wanted to find out more.

Flanked by its escort, the Grula-Grula made its entrance into the Wizard Tower courtyard in a manner that it found highly gratifying. The Wizard Tower was a hotbed of gossip and word had quickly spread. A large group of Wizards and Apprentices were now gathered at the top of the steps to watch the procession. The Grula-Grula was very impressed with its reception, especially when it stepped over the threshold to be greeted by the floor's message: WELCOME, FAIR GRULA, MOST LOVELY OF THEM ALL. However, the Grula-Grula was less impressed when it was suddenly confronted by a figure in a multicoloured cloak, wearing purple pointy shoes that smelled of snake.

"Goodness!" said the snake-shoed figure. "What is that *ghastly* thing?"

"Marcia," snapped the Grula-Grula's purple escort. "Please be quiet."

Marcia was shocked at being spoken to like that. And then she remembered that she was no longer ExtraOrdinary Wizard, that she was only there because Septimus allowed her to be, and if she was not careful he might very well change his mind.

"It is an *honour* and a *privilege* to have such a *glorious* guest," Septimus said very loudly, to make sure the Grula-Grula heard.

Marcia gave Septimus a look of astonishment. She saw the Grula-Grula's little pink eyes peering out – somewhat short-sightedly – from its hair, which hung down like limp, greasy curtains, and the trail of moulted fur it had left behind, sticking to the soft, sand-like multicoloured floor of the Great Hall. She watched the ten-feet-tall hairy triangle being escorted into the Stranger Chamber, saw the Grula-Grula take one look at the deceptively beautiful room – and begin a slow, impressive ShapeShift.

A murmur of appreciation spread through the Wizards who had gathered to watch. The great bulk of fur and flesh began to shimmer and its boundaries grew indistinct. A fuzz of Magyk settled over the creature, there was a loud *whoosh* and the audience jumped back in surprise. In front of them stood a small, neat man in a dark suit. He wore a pair of thick, round spectacles through which peered tiny pink piggy eyes, and his pale-orange greasy hair was parted in the middle. He bowed, turned smartly on his heel and entered the Stranger Chamber.

Marcia waited while Septimus dealt with the usual problems and queries that were always thrown at an ExtraOrdinary Wizard whenever he or she ventured into the Great Hall. When at last people had drifted away, she pounced. "Septimus!"

Septimus looked weary. "Marcia," he said unenthusiastically.

Marcia felt sorry for him. She remembered how many times as ExtraOrdinary Wizard she had longed to be *left alone*. But this could not wait. "Septimus, I am *so* sorry."

The expression of weariness in Septimus's eyes was replaced by shock — what was wrong? Marcia never apologised. But before he could ask what had happened, Marcia had launched into a rapid gabble.

"Septimus, you were right," she was saying.

Septimus looked stunned. "Me? Right?" he said. "About what?"

Marcia sighed. "I'm sure Dandra has told you what happened last night."

"Dandra? Haven't seen her. The Sick Bay's frantic, apparently." Septimus looked at his timepiece. "Look, Marcia, I really must get on. I have an Apprentice Rotation Scheme meeting in a few minutes."

"So you haven't heard?" Marcia said.

"About what?"

"Oh, Septimus. I am so sorry. There was an Incursion. We *must* talk — oh!" A thin, high piping suddenly came from the silver whistle around Marcia's neck. "Oh, goodness!" She put her hand on Septimus's arm. "I have to go. Something's wrong. Septimus, come with me. *Please*."

Septimus knew when Marcia was serious. He left a hasty message with the door duty Wizard and hurried after Marcia as she raced down the steps. He caught up with her outside Way VII, which to his surprise he could actually see. And then he realised why. Racing out of its misty depths was a familiar, slight figure. And as Tod hurtled into the bright morning sunshine, Septimus saw that she had snow on her shoes.

"Blizzard!" Tod gasped. "Horse! Mad girl! Hurry!"

SNOW GLOBE

Tod, Septimus and Marcia ran out of Way VII into the Hub and found themselves in a snowstorm. They stumbled forward, half deafened by a tumult of terrified whinnying and piercing shrieks, and suddenly Marcia found herself nose to nose with a set of tombstone horse teeth. Marcia leaped back, the horse reared up and Septimus lunged for the bridle and grabbed it. Through the blizzard he caught the shimmer of sparkling blue reins and a white, shining figure seated on the horse.

A sudden shout filled the Hub. "Garmin! Garmin!" yelled Tod.

Septimus spun around and briefly, through the blizzard, he saw the unmistakable shape of a Garmin come leaping into the Hub. He saw it stop and crouch down, confused by the swirling snow, and he saw another spring from an arch and join it – then another. A cloud of snow whirled in front of his eyes and Septimus could see no more.

He did the only thing he could. Trusting Marcia's quick reactions, Septimus threw up his arms and yelled, **"Freezer!"** A rush of white crystals tinged with purple streamed from his open palms, swirled around horse and rider and then spiralled out into the rest of the Hub, popping and snapping as they went.

197

Inside the blizzard, Marcia heard Septimus's **Freezer**. She grabbed hold of Tod, held on to her tight and began muttering the **AntiFreeze**. Tod saw the crackling tide of ice rolling towards her, she felt coldness surround her and then the **AntiFreeze** kicked in. A rush of warmth spread through her and the crystal wave rolled harmlessly by.

With the **Freezing** of the horse and rider, the snow began to subside. Across the Hub Tod saw the three Garmin, almost invisible, white against the snow. At the same time, they saw her. There was a long, seemingly endless moment when the Garmin launched themselves towards her and then the river of ice engulfed the creatures and they were frozen in mid-leap. One immediately toppled over. There was the sound of shattering, tinkling glass as it broke into thousands of sparkling crystalline shards, shining like diamonds in the light of the Hub torches. Another Garmin was held upright by one back leg welded into the ice that covered the snow. But as they watched, the ice gave way under the weight of the creature above and the second Garmin fell in another shower of crystals. The third lay **Frozen**, crouched as if to pounce.

"**Stop Freezer!**" Septimus's command echoed around the Hub. He dropped his hands to his side, the light from his palms faded and the crystal wave – which was now heading around the Hub for a second circuit – stopped.

"Goodness, Septimus – that was a bit dramatic," Marcia said, raising her voice above the background crackle of settling ice.

"But necessary," Septimus replied.

"Oh, yes. Totally," Marcia said hurriedly, not wanting Septimus to think she was criticising. A **Freezer** was a rapid-reflex spell – indiscriminate but very effective, it was the kind of spell that was looked down upon by purists. But Marcia was no purist. She knew that when more than one danger must be disabled at once, such a spell was an essential tool. However, like all quick fixes, a **Freezer** has disadvantages – it **Freezes** every living thing in its path and can be dangerous to those who are **Frozen**.

The fizzing and snapping of ice crystals was fading now to a few isolated pops. Tod, Septimus and Marcia stood knee-deep in frozen snow, staring at the bizarre tableau surrounding them.

Tod had once owned a snow globe – a transparent dome filled with fluid in which there was a snowy scene. When she shook the globe, white flakes had swirled up through the fluid to create a snowstorm, which then slowly subsided. Right now Tod felt as though she were inside a big, bizarre snow globe. Captivated, she watched the snow gently subside around the **Frozen** shape of a huge white horse rearing up, its hooves pawing the air and its rider leaning back, trying to stay seated. The rider was striking – a girl not so many years older than she, dressed in a white fur jacket and thick white woollen pantaloons. What struck Tod was her pure white hair, which was braided into scores of thin plaits tied into a horse's tail that hung down her back, all interlaced with blue ribbons that shimmered with ice. The girl's blue eyes were wide open in terror as she stared sightlessly through the film of ice that had **Frozen** her and her horse.

Marcia left Septimus working out how to **DeFrost** the horse and rider and waded through the snow to Way XI, where the useless **Seal** was hanging from the archway like a mist of shredded paper. She gathered the remnants of the **Seal** in her hands, held them close to her face and caught echoes of a wild, untutored **Magyk** and some powerful emotions – fear and anger. Marcia replaced the **Seal**, and this time she added more than a touch of **Darke Magyk**. One of the advantages to no longer being ExtraOrdinary Wizard was that Marcia could now use the **Darke** without compromising the pure **Magyk** of the Wizard Tower.

On her way back to join Septimus and Tod, Marcia aimed a precise, pointy kick at the third Garmin.

Tod watched the Garmin shatter into a thousand shards of ice and she suddenly remembered something. Her hand flew to her mouth. "Oh! The Drummins! They were here. That's what I heard first – the Drummins shouting. Then the horse neighing. Oh no … are they **Frozen** too?"

Marcia stopped dead. "Yes," she said. "They will be."

Anxiously, Marcia surveyed the snow. "I think there's one here," she said, kneeling beside a Drummin-shaped bump. Gingerly she broke through the ice crust on top of the snow and had soon revealed a plaited Drummin beard, ice-hard and glistening white.

"Is it easy to melt things?" Tod asked in a whisper, afraid that any loud sound might make the Drummin fall into a thousand shards of ice, just as the Garmin had.

"Ah, you mean **DeFrost**," Septimus said. "Well, it is relatively easy to do a **DeFrost**, but it is not so easy to do a safe one. **DeFrosting** can be very dangerous for the **Frozen**. However, it is possible to make it safer by using the person's name. Who is this one, Marcia?"

Very gently brushing the snow off the Drummin, Marcia revealed a pair of gingery eyebrows. "It's Fabius," she said.

"Hmm … this is tricky, Septimus. He's **Frozen** mid–stride … standing on only one leg. Horribly easy to knock him over."

Septimus squatted down beside Marcia. He placed both hands on Fabius to steady him and whispered, "Fabius Drummin. **DeFrost**."

Tod saw a warm, reddish glow emanating from Septimus's hands. She could feel the **Magykal** heat in the air as a thin stream of orangey-red mist wrapped itself around Fabius. There was a faint, crackling whisper, like ice on a frozen pond when the sun begins to shine upon it, then Fabius groaned and fell over into the snow. Tod waited for the awful sound of Fabius splintering.

"You can open your eyes, Tod," Septimus said with a smile in his voice. "See the puddle of water beneath him? He's **DeFrosted**."

Fabius Drummin groaned and began to shiver. "I'll take him upstairs to the Fire Pit," Tod offered.

"Good thinking," said Septimus, eyeing a nearby Drummin-shaped mound. "And with any luck, there'll be another one in a minute."

Three **DeFrosted** Drummins were sitting by their kitchen fire wrapped in blankets when Tod hurried back down to the Hub to watch the **DeFrosting** of the horse and rider. She found Septimus and Marcia silently sizing up the problem. Tod could tell that this was going to be tough. Septimus must **DeFrost** both at once, because not only was the horse very delicately balanced on its back legs but the rider looked as though she were about to fall off. And once they were **DeFrosted** Septimus would have to jump out of the way *fast*.

Tod waded through the slush and joined the two Wizards, who were looking thoughtfully up at their project. Suddenly Septimus said, "It's *her*. It must be."

"It's *who*?" asked Marcia.

"The Snow Princess that Jenna and I took all the way home in the Dragon Boat in the summer. The one that Jen still moans about whenever I see her."

Marcia had heard about this from her new stepdaughter. "Oh, *that* Snow Princess," she said with a smile. "How bizarre."

"Yes, it is." Septimus frowned up at the rider, trying to make out her features beneath their glaze of ice.

"You are sure it is her?" Marcia asked. "Because if we use the wrong name …"

"I know, I know," Septimus said snappily. "It's even more dangerous with the wrong name. I am ninety-nine per cent sure." He turned to Marcia. "It's a risk worth taking."

"It's your call, Septimus," said Marcia.

"Yes. I know. I shall use her name. It *is* her. There's something about the expression – kind of annoyed, but charming even so … We'll do this together?"

Marcia nodded.

Septimus placed his hands on the horse's raised hooves. Marcia placed hers on the rider's back to stop her from falling off. Fascinated, Tod watched the two Wizards unfocus their eyes and go somewhere deep inside themselves. In complete synchronisation, she saw them take a long, deep breath in and then slowly let it out. She saw a glow from their hands spread across the ice, melting it as it went, revealing the damp fur of the rider's jacket, the horn of the horse's hooves. The melt travelled fast, the ice crackled and began to fall, then suddenly the white-haired girl tumbled from the horse and landed with a *splat* in the slush below. In a moment she was on her feet. She spun around, saw Marcia staring at her in surprise and snatched a short, shimmering blue stick from a holster on her belt.

Septimus could do nothing – he was still deep in **Magyk**, **DeFrosting** the horse.

"Haii, Magus! Haii, haii!" the girl yelled, advancing on Marcia, stabbing the stick forward like a dagger. Marcia retreated but the stick jabbed her in the shoulder. There was a *hisssss*, a smell of burning wool and she went staggering backwards. Marcia was unwilling to use **Magyk** on someone so recently **DeFrosted**. Hands up, Marcia backed away. *"Denna!"* she said soothingly. *"Denna, Driffa*. Denna."

Surprised to hear her own name and language spoken, the girl stopped and stared at Marcia. Taking advantage of the lull, Tod waded in and grabbed the stick. To her shock it was red-hot. She threw it down, sending it sizzling into the watery slush. Princess Driffa was not pleased. She snatched up her stick, and yelling, *"Haii! Haii!"*, she advanced this time on Tod, stabbing the red-tipped stick at her face. Tod ducked and hurled herself at Driffa's white boots. It was a fine tackle. At the precise moment that Princess Driffa crashed face first into a pile of slush, Septimus finished **DeFrosting** her horse. A wild neigh filled the Hub, two great hooves thudded down to the ground and everyone was covered in gritty, ice-cold water.

A sudden exclamation came from the foot of the stairs. "What the –?" Milo Banda gazed at the inexplicable scene in front of him. "Marcia," he protested. "I can't leave you alone for five minutes."

SNOW PRINCESS DRIFFA,
THE MOST HIGH AND BOUNTIFUL

Up in the big hall of the Keep, in front of the blazing fire, Princess Driffa sat wrapped in blankets. She was shivering uncontrollably – a delayed effect of the **Freezer**. Her translucent white skin had a blue tinge to it and her bright blue eyes were the only natural colour she had. Her blue ribbons laced through her white braided hair hung limp and wet, and her sparkling blue fingernails peeped out from the blankets as she clutched them to her.

Driffa's presence took Marcia right back to being a child. As the daughter of travelling Wizards, Marcia had spent a few years in the Eastern SnowPlains as guests of three princesses who had looked remarkably similar.

Tod looked admiringly at Driffa. She had never seen anyone quite so blue and white before. And now that she knew that Driffa had spent two whole days on the Dragon Boat, she was impressed. She handed Driffa a mug of hot chocolate. "I'm sorry I knocked you over," she said.

Princess Driffa said nothing. She had not got over the affront to her dignity. She sniffed the hot chocolate suspiciously.

"Drink it," said Septimus. "It will warm you up."

Driffa gave Septimus a wan smile and took a sip of the chocolate. It tasted good. The hot drink did its work and soon Driffa's shivering had subsided.

Remembering the formality of the Eastern SnowPlains, Marcia said, "Welcome, Snow Princess of the Eastern Plains. I am Marcia Overstrand, and you are an honoured guest in my house. May you be so for many days yet to come."

Princess Driffa understood formality. She inclined her head in a brief nod and said, "I, Snow Princess Driffa, the Most High and Bountiful, thank you, O wise Sorcerer." Then she looked at Septimus, who had not, Marcia noticed, taken his eyes off Driffa. "ExtraOrdinary Wizard Septimus Heap. I thank you for freeing my horse from its foul Enchantment."

Feeling a little awkward, Septimus bowed his head in acknowledgement. Clearly Driffa did not realise that it was *his* foul Enchantment that had Frozen her horse – and he wasn't about to tell her, either.

Haughtily, Driffa handed her empty cup to Tod. Then she turned to Marcia and said, "I pray you, send the servant boy away. There are important matters I wish to discuss."

Marcia looked puzzled. She didn't have a servant boy. But Tod understood.

"I am not a boy," she told Driffa indignantly. "And I am not a servant, either."

"Ah." Marcia felt bad. She realised she should have introduced Tod properly. She hurried to make amends. "Snow Princess Driffa, the Most High and Bountiful, may I present to you Alice TodHunter Moon. She, too, is an honoured guest in my house."

Driffa inclined her head very slightly in Tod's direction and looked away again. Tod thought she was extremely rude. She sat hugging her knees, feeling chilled and alone. A longing to be home, where she needed no introduction to anyone, came over her. Tod picked up her own mug of hot chocolate and stared into it stonily. She was not going to cry. *She was not.*

While Tod retreated into her own head, the Snow Princess – her thin white hands with their shimmering blue nails fluttering like bird wings – began to speak. At first Tod paid little attention, but as the story unfolded, she found herself listening with increasing interest.

"I, Driffa, am the daughter of the High Emperor of the Great Eastern SnowPlains. We live in the low hills that surround the largest of the SnowPlains. Our people trade and work the precious blue stone, which we take from our Enchanted Blue Pinnacle."

A smile flitted across Marcia's face. She remembered moonlit sleigh rides out to the mysterious tall, conical hill of lapis lazuli, always free of snow, in the middle of a vast plain of white.

Driffa held out her hands to show bracelets made of silver and glittering stones of blue and a ring with a piece of polished lapis as big as Tod's paint-splashed pebble. "This is the stone that the Great Orm has given to us in return for guarding its precious Egg. We are peaceful people. Our pleasure is to build snow towers and polish stones. Our duty is to guard the Egg of the Orm." The Princess bit her lip and her voice trembled. "Which ... we have failed to do."

Tod looked up. *So the Snow Princess is human after all*, she thought.

Driffa continued. "The Egg of the Orm gives us the Enchantment that covers our lands with beautiful snow throughout the year and allows us to live in towers of ice. Far beneath the Blue

Pinnacle is the Chamber of the Egg of the Orm. In the middle of this chamber is the Orm Tube, and at the bottom of the Orm Tube lies the Egg. The Chamber of the Egg of the Orm is a hallowed place, full of silence and sleep. Around it is the Sacred Ice Walk, where we go to contemplate the Egg and give thanks for its Enchantment. Or we did." The Snow Princess blinked back tears. She got out a white handkerchief and blew her nose loudly. "But now ..." she said angrily. "Now all is desecrated. By a fiend called Oraton-Marr."

Tod looked at Driffa with some sympathy. It seemed that the Snow Princess had lost her village too.

Driffa continued. "In our family there is a Time Traveller. She is my great-great-great-grandmother. On my sixteenth birthday I opened a letter from her. It was an invitation to meet her in the House of Foryx."

Marcia gasped.

"You know this place, O Sorcerer?" asked the Snow Princess.

"I do," said Marcia. "It is not somewhere I would invite a granddaughter to."

"I understand what you say, but I did not know what it was then. I thought it was the house where my many-times-great-grandmother lived. When I arrived I found her sitting in the chequered lobby on a chair carved like a dragon. She recognised me at once, but I would never have known her. She was young, no more than ten years older than I am. She took me to her little room high up in one of the octagonal towers and she told me a terrible thing. She said that an evil sorcerer was coming to take away the Egg of the Orm. I asked her how she knew and she said she had seen it."

"If this has happened," Septimus said, "it cannot be changed."

The Princess looked miserable. "That is what I thought too. I asked her why she was taunting me with such terrible news, but all she would say was that some things could be prevented. She did not say what they were. She said it was important for me to do this because we live at the centre of the world, where all roads meet and the evil must not travel further. I laughed at her because we live in a dead end. There is but one pass through the hills that leads into our SnowPlain and we see few travellers. Those who come are usually lost. They walk around the foot-hills looking for a way through to the other side but there is none. We are hospitable people and we offer them shelter and good food and guide them back the way they came. It is hardly the centre of the world.

"My grandmother became cross with me for laughing. She told me to leave. I must wait in the dragon chair for a hand-some, young ExtraOrdinary Wizard – she described him very well – wearing new robes and carrying a Magykal black stone. I must Go Out with him because that would be the right Time. What I did not know was that the right Time for my great-great-great-grandmother was not the right Time for me. When I returned home, my three younger sisters were old women, my parents were dead and our towers of ice were deserted. Almost everyone had run away.

"And Oraton-Marr was already there. My sisters – who, being princesses, were brave and had not run away – had watched the sorcerer arrive. He did not walk the foothills, looking for a way out as others do; he went straight across the plain to our Enchanted Blue Pinnacle and he set up camp. He took the snow and made it into Iglopuks – big, round houses –

leaving the earth bare." She turned around to Tod and Marcia, smiling. "When we are children we do this. We make a snow house, which is fun, and from where we have taken the snow, the rock is bare. Then we watch the Enchantment bringing the snow back. That is even more fun, to see the snow return." She shook her head sadly. "But the snow did not return and my sisters became anxious, because they knew this must mean the sorcerer was destroying our Enchantment.

"My sisters sent our most powerful sorcerer to ask the Darke one to leave, but she did not return. They sent the second most powerful sorcerer and he did not return either. The third most powerful sorcerer pleaded not to be sent, and my sisters told me that there seemed little point in losing him, despite the fact they all found him very annoying. They wished they had sent him first.

"There was nothing my sisters could do but watch. They saw Oraton-Marr dig down into the ice beside our Blue Pinnacle. After some months, they said, people began to appear, although no one saw them come. It was very strange. But these wretched, enslaved people were set to work.

"When I returned everything was being destroyed. Heaps of black and filthy earth were piled up on our beautiful white snow and my sisters told me that Oraton-Marr was digging down to the Chamber of the Egg of the Orm. I had to do something – a princess cannot spend all her life in her tower of ice counting her blue stones. And so early this morning before it was light, I took my best horse, the fair Nona, and I set off to challenge the foul sorcerer.

"I have some snow Magyk – enough to make stupid people think that I am nothing more than a gust of snow. I knew it would not fool Oraton-Marr but I thought it would allow me to get past his guards and get close to him. The **Enchantment** covered Nona's tracks with fresh snow and we made no sound, but as we drew near, the sorcerer's influence came into being, the **Enchantment** weakened and Nona's tracks began to show. But we reached the bare earth unseen and with my small **Magyk**, we moved across the spoil like a gust of Akkilokipok – the soft snow with fat flakes that settles fast. This makes a better disguise than Kanevvluk, the small, sharp snow, which is colder and gives less cover.

"From within our tiny blizzard Nona and I saw that a great pit was being dug down into the ground, towards the Chamber of the Egg of the Orm. Guards with spikes on their heads marched around the top of the pit, each with a Garmin on a leash. Nona and I saw hundreds of people working. Some were pushing barrows of earth up steep paths that led out of the pit. Others were hacking at the rock and ice below. All kinds of people were there; even little children were working and all were dirty, cold and utterly wretched. It was a terrible sight.

"There was a path into the pit that was not being used by the workers and I decided to take a closer look. The path descended, circling deep inside the walls around the pit. Nona is a good horse; she bravely went down the path into the darkness of the rock. Suddenly we came upon Oraton-Marr. I challenged him and asked him what he was doing. He laughed and said that he was 'egg collecting'." Driffa looked disgusted. "He said it with no respect – as though our precious Egg of the Orm were a chicken egg. I pretended not to know what he meant. I told him there was nothing here for him and he should go away and let his poor slaves go free. But he set his guards on us and I am ashamed to say Nona and I fled. Our way back up was blocked by guards by then, so we had no choice but to go down. We found ourselves descending through a circular tunnel of lapis covered in ice, I expected that soon we would be caught, but I was not going to make it easy for them. And then, to my amazement, Nona cantered into the most wonderful place I have ever seen. A huge blue chamber lit with torches with twelve silver arches and a great spiral of blue for the roof."

She was interrupted by a gasp. "The Heart of the Ways," Marcia whispered. "It *must* be."

"No," said Driffa. "It is the long-lost Chamber of the Great Orm itself. This was where the Great Orm came to die after it had laid its last egg – our Egg. But I had no time to look. There were guards in the Chamber waiting at an archway, so Nona and I cantered into the nearest arch and found ourselves in the strangest of places."

"Did the sorcerer follow you?" Marcia asked.

"No, but three of his Garmin did. Nona and I travelled through many strange places. Some were hot, some were cold; in some it was night-time, in others it was day, but always there were twelve arches and always there were Garmin behind us. Nona was fast and brave. She outran them – until we came here, where she cast a shoe. Then I used a blizzard to try to conceal us from the Garmin – and your three fierce creatures with knives."

"I am sorry," said Marcia. "The Drummins meant no harm."

"I understand," said Driffa. She looked at Marcia. "I meant no harm to you, either, but I saw you were a sorcerer. Indeed, you look a little like him."

"I *do*?"

"A little. You are taller, and your hair is longer. But the green eyes are the same. And the purple pointy shoes made of snake."

Marcia was aghast. "He has shoes like mine? Well, that does it, we'll have to get rid of him." She smiled at Tod. "Only one of us can wear these shoes. And that is *me*."

NONA

It was late. Septimus had returned to the Wizard Tower, the Drummins were asleep in the Fire Pit, and down in the Hub Milo was noisily busy with a bucket and a shovel.

A bright purple light emanating from the Seals suffused the Hub. It looked very pretty, Milo thought, but it did not make it easy to search for horse poo. Milo had just found what he hoped was the last shovelful at the foot of the stairs when he heard the *tippy-tap-tap* of Marcia's pointy purple pythons. The pythons were, he could tell, in a hurry.

Marcia rounded the last twist of the spiral stairs, her multi-coloured cloak flying behind her, and ran straight into Milo. "Goodness, Milo, what *are* you doing?" she asked.

"Avoiding the curse of the silent footstep."

"The curse of the silent footstep?" Marcia sounded puzzled, and then a waft of horse dung drifted up to her nose. "Oh, Milo, *thank you*," she said.

Milo put down his bucket and leaned his shovel against the wall. He looked serious. "Marcia, I know we agreed not to interfere with each other's work, but please tell me – what on earth is going on?"

Marcia took Milo's hands. "Milo, Tod and I are going to take the Snow Princess to the Wizard Tower. Septimus wants

213

to understand who this sorcerer, Oraton-Marr, is. He's gone to look a few things up and talk to the older Wizards. I promised we'd follow on."

Milo sighed. "Does this really matter, Marcia? All this stuff is happening on the other side of the world. Why should it bother *us*?"

"Because, Milo, any moment Oraton-Marr could turn up here." Marcia looked anxiously around at the Seals.

Milo had great faith in Marcia's Magykal abilities. "But you've Sealed it all. And I'm not stupid, Marcia. I know you added a whole *ton* of Darke stuff. Nothing can get through those now."

Marcia shook her head. "No Magyk lasts for ever, Milo. And no Magyk is infallible. If Oraton-Marr becomes as powerful as he clearly is determined to be, he will, if he wishes, eventually be standing here, where we are right now. *In this Hub*. And then all he will have to do is take a short stroll into Way VII and he will be in the Wizard Tower. We *have* to stop that from happening."

Milo was not convinced. "Marcia, you worry too much. This sorcerer chap sounds bonkers to me. He's obsessed with some mythical egg. Soon enough he'll find his precious egg doesn't exist, and he will give up and go somewhere else. I can't see him bothering to come here. Why would he?"

Marcia smiled. "To get to the most powerful seat of Magyk in the whole world maybe?" She shook her head. "Anyway, Milo, I think it's possible that this Egg *does* exist. Marwick used to tell me about the legend of the Orm. It was a giant worm, he said, that created the Ancient Ways. It ate through the rock, leaving lapis lazuli behind."

Milo laughed. "Young Marwick always had a few good stories to tell. Better than mine sometimes, I have to admit. But it doesn't mean they are true."

"And it doesn't mean they *aren't* true," Marcia countered. Her hand closed over the silver whistle she wore around her neck. Not so long ago, in its place Marcia had worn the Akhu Amulet. This amulet, a **Magykal** source of power for all ExtraOrdinary Wizards, was made from lapis that – legend had it – came from the belly of the Orm.

Marcia wandered over to Way VII – the one that led to the Wizard Tower. From a space between two stones, she pulled out a tiny piece of pale blue lapis and gave it to Milo. "See? It's sprinkled everywhere. And there is *much* more of it inside a Way. Little bits of lapis folded into the stone. It is very strange."

Milo scraped up the last of the horse poo and set the lid on the bucket with a clang. "Hmm," he said. "But even if there *were* an egg, why would this sorcerer want it?"

Marcia knew exactly why. "For the lapis lazuli. It concentrates **Magyk** like nothing else. The Wizard Tower sits on a huge chunk of the stuff. And think of the Dragon House; that's lined with it. Not to mention the labyrinth that goes to the Great Chamber of Alchemie. That's why the Castle is such a **Magykal** place. With enough lapis even minor **Magyk** can grow powerful. With the right conditions an Orm Egg would hatch and pretty soon the young Orm would begin creating enough lapis lazuli to make even a mediocre Wizard a force to be reckoned with. Not to mention a reasonably powerful **Darke** one." Marcia shuddered. "It doesn't bear thinking about."

Milo sighed. "I suppose not."

There was the sound of footsteps coming down the stairs. "Ah, here they come," said Marcia.

Tod and Driffa stepped into the Hub. Driffa squinted in the purple light, shielding her eyes with her hands. "You have powerful **Magyk**," she said.

"I hope so," replied Marcia solemnly. "Right, let's get going."

Milo picked up his bucket. "And what about the horse?" he asked.

The Snow Princess gazed at Milo with her big blue eyes. "Nona would like to stay with you," she said.

"Nona?" asked Milo, a little too dreamily for Marcia's liking. Clearly Milo thought that the Snow Princess was called Nona.

"The *horse*, Milo," Marcia snapped.

"Of course it's the horse," said Milo, recovering himself. "Who – I mean, what – else could it be?"

Marcia raised her eyebrows. "Milo, I have no idea." She looked at Driffa. "We'll be off now – and see that handsome ExtraOrdinary Wizard of yours."

Driffa blushed pink against the purple-white of her hair. "Oh, he is not mine," she said. "Another Princess has him. A grumpy one with dark hair."

Marcia was puzzled but said nothing. She reminded herself that Septimus's personal life had nothing to do with her.

"Goodbye," Milo said a little sadly. "Stay safe."

"You too." Marcia gave him a quick hug and then, linking arms with Tod and Driffa, strode into Way VII.

Bucket and shovel in hand, Milo watched the trio walk into the depths of the Way. He saw them step into the strange white mist and their dark shapes fade as they went through the **Vanishing Point**. And then they were gone.

Deep in the Way, Tod's hand closed over her little blue lapis box. Inside it she felt the **PathFinder** tap-tap-tapping against the sides, as if it wanted to be set free.

PART
VIII

OSKAR AND FERDIE

Earlier that day, while Tod had been wading through snow, Oskar had been kicking his way through ash.

Three nights had now passed since Tod had sailed away, and Oskar was beginning to realise that not only was Tod not coming back but he didn't even know where she had gone. The Wizard Tower could be anywhere in the world – all Oskar knew for sure was that it was somewhere across the sea. Tod had disappeared as completely as Ferdie had done. *But unlike Ferdie*, Oskar thought angrily, *Tod had* wanted *to.*

Oskar and Ferdie had been helping to clear the site of their old house, and now they were heading back to the place that was, for the moment, home. They were living with their elderly cousins, Marni and Dergal Sarn. Being a little way from the main village and almost hidden behind a dune, Marni and Dergal's house had escaped the blaze. No one wanted to stay in Tod's old house, which was smashed to pieces inside and still smelled of Garmin.

Over a frugal meal, Marni once again tried to console Ferdie. "Ferdie love, your parents didn't want to go, but they had little Torr to think about. All the people with kids went."

"But why did they trust this 'wise woman'?" asked Ferdie. "They had no idea who she was."

Marni shook her head. "Panic, I suppose. Many were facing a night out in the open and the thought of those awful Garmin coming back ... Well, what would you do if someone – especially a big, motherly woman – offered to take you to safety? I would have done the same if I'd had a little one to think of."

Ferdie frowned. "Marni, did you see this wise woman?" she asked.

Marni shook her head. She stuck out a heavily bandaged foot and glared at it. "I was stuck here with my stupid foot and, what with the house being hidden in this hollow in the dunes, I didn't see a thing, except the terrible flames shooting up into the sky. But Dergal saw her. Dergal! Dergal!" Marni called.

Dergal Sarn's head appeared at the top of the ladder. "All right?" he inquired.

"Dergal, you saw the woman come out of the Far, didn't you?" Marni asked.

Dergal heaved himself up the rest of the ladder and plonked himself down in a chair. "Didn't take to her myself," he said.

"What did she look like?" Ferdie asked.

"Well ..." Dergal, a slow-speaking man, considered the matter. "It was the strangest thing. I had to blink to make sure I hadn't imagined it. I saw a light coming out of the Far and then the most bizarre woman emerged, carrying a lantern and looking like she didn't have a care in the world. I mean, there was the village ablaze, flames shooting thirty feet in the air, but she didn't look surprised at all. What really struck me was the smug little smile she had on her face. Not nice." Dergal shook his head. "No, I didn't take to her at all. Not one little bit."

"But what did she look like?" Ferdie asked again.

"Well, she was a big lady, that's for sure. And here's a thing – she looked like she was off to a *very* fancy party. She was wearing a shiny, bright blue billowing dress, silk I would have said, and she had a piece of gold cloth wound all around her head. Very *fancy*." Dergal sounded disapproving.

"Ferdie!" Marni cried out. "Ferdie, whatever is the matter?"

The colour had drained from Ferdie's face. She looked grey. "It's her," she whispered.

"Who, sweetheart?" asked Marni. "Dergal, go and get Ferdie some water, she looks terrible – oh, this *stupid* foot."

"It's the Lady," Ferdie whispered. "From the ship. I was her prisoner. It's *her*!"

Marni stared at Ferdie, shocked. "But ... but it can't be."

"It is her," Ferdie said. "I *know* it is."

"No," Marni said. "No. It must be some other woman in a party dress."

"Marni," Dergal said with an air of exasperation. "And just how many women do you suppose walk around the Far in a fancy blue party dress, eh?"

"There's only one like that," Ferdie said flatly. "She got me. And now she's got Mum and Dad and little Torr."

THIEVES IN THE NIGHT

That night Tod was back in the Junior Girls' Apprentice Dorm, sleeping peacefully. But far away across the sea, Oskar and Ferdie lay wide awake. They were sharing a bedroom, just as they used to before Torr was born and, as ever, they were talking late into the night. But they were no longer whispering about Oskar's plans for what he called "contraptions" or Ferdie's ideas for a new kite. Now their conversation was serious – because Oskar and Ferdie had decided to track down the Lady.

When everyone had gone to bed, Ferdie crept downstairs. She put as much dried food as she felt was fair to take into her backpack, filled up the water bag and took two light sticks from the cupboard. Ferdie knew it was not good to be raiding Marni and Dergal's store cupboard. She felt like a thief in the night, but she hoped they would understand.

Meanwhile, Oskar was writing a letter, and finding it difficult. When Ferdie returned with the backpack he showed it to her.

Dear Marni and Dergal and Jerra and Annar,
 Ferdie and me are going into the Far to find Mum and Dad and Torr. And everyone. I know you will be worried, but we will be all right.
 Love from Oskar and

Ferdie looked at the letter. It was a typical Oskie letter, she thought, short and to the point, but she didn't think she could do any better. She signed her name beside his.

They slept for a few hours. Oskar woke just before dawn and shook Ferdie awake. In minutes they were easing open the outside door and climbing stealthily down the ladder. The first rays of the sun were creeping over the dunes as Oskar and Ferdie stepped into the Far.

Far away across the water, in the Wizard Tower, Tod slept on. At the foot of her bed, Dan's fishing jacket was neatly folded. And under her pillow was her blue lapis box, where the Path-Finder, like Tod, now slept. But unlike Tod, the PathFinder slept peacefully. It had no nightmares of dark forests and prison cells.

THE FAR

The early morning sun shone through the pale green leaves of the beech trees as Oskar and Ferdie walked briskly along. It felt like the beginning of so many family picnics they had enjoyed over the years, and neither of them could quite believe that this expedition into the Far was going to be any different.

They had no trouble following the path that people had taken. Oskar was in his element. "Look, Ferd," he said. "You can see all those snapped twigs, the leaves broken off and brushed on to the ground, the trodden grass. You can tell that *loads* of people have been this way. It will be easy to follow them."

After a few hours of steady walking they reached the usual Sarn picnic spot – a bright clearing with a small stream bubbling through on its way to the sea. Oskar paced the clearing, looking for clues in the sunlight. He felt that if he looked carefully enough he would surely see traces of his parents and little brother. There were indeed signs of children – a few small footprints in the mud beside the stream – but nothing that could tell Oskar to whom they belonged. But as Oskar walked slowly along the stream he came across something that he did not want to see.

"Ferd." The tension in Oskar's voice had Ferdie running to his side.

"Oskie, what is it?"

"Come here."

Ferdie peered at the patch of mud that Oskar was squatting beside. "What?" she asked anxiously.

"Garmin."

"*Garmin?* But … but how can you tell?"

Oskar pointed to what looked like a huge, dog-like paw print scuffed into the mud.

Ferdie didn't want to believe it. "It could be any kind of animal, Oskie."

Oskar shook his head. "No, Ferd. Look at this … See here? That's the front paw. Like a monkey's hand. See, where it's leaned down to drink?" He looked up at his sister. "It's a Garmin, Ferd. There's no way around it."

Ferdie picked up a stone and hurled it angrily into the stream. "I hate her," she said. *"I hate her."*

Oskar knew exactly who Ferdie was talking about. "Yeah," he said.

"Mum and Dad and Torr. They must have been so *scared*."

"Yeah," said Oskar.

Ferdie kicked the Garmin tracks in disgust. Then she looked up at Oskar and said, "We're going to get her, Oskie. She's going to regret she ever messed with us."

"Yeah," said Oskar. But he didn't sound convinced.

They sat down miserably on the well-trodden grassy bank and Ferdie fished out two large biscuits, a handful of dried raisins and an apple. "Breakfast," she said.

"Not hungry," muttered Oskar.

"Oskie, *eat*," Ferdie instructed. "We have to keep strong."

They had lapsed into silence, picking at the raisins, when Ferdie said, "I wonder what Tod is doing right now?"

"Who cares?" Oskar said crossly. He picked up a small stone and hurled it into the stream. "But you can bet she won't be thinking about us, that's for sure."

But right then, thinking about Ferdie and Oskar was precisely what Tod was doing. She was in a stuffy conference room in the Wizard Tower, listening to long and complex discussions about Ancient Ways. The meeting was slow, technical and full of words she did not understand. Tod gazed out of the hazy, purple window and longed to be outside in the sun. She ached for the smell of the sea and the feel of sand beneath her bare feet once again. And she wanted to see Ferdie and Oskar so much that it hurt. As the meeting droned on and the hands on the clock hardly seemed to move, Tod made a decision. She would go to see Nicko and Snorri on the *Adventurer* as soon as she could. And then she would beg them to take her home. She could not bear being parted from Ferdie and Oskar a moment longer.

"Argh!" A sudden yell from Ferdie put an end to Oskar's angry thoughts. She leaped to her feet, kicking out at the dead leaves, shouting, "Get off! *Get off*!"

Ferdie hopped around clutching her ankle, and Oskar caught sight of a small and very furry rodent scurrying for cover. "It's a wood vole!" he exclaimed. "Oh, wow, I've never seen one before. Wasn't it sweet?"

"Sweet? It bit me!" Ferdie said, rubbing her ankle. "You have a funny idea of *sweet*, Oskar Sarn."

Ten minutes later, having put both wood voles and Tod firmly out of their thoughts, Ferdie and Oskar set off from the clearing and took the path that the PathFinder villagers had been driven along. They were now in new territory. Soon they noticed that the trees were getting closer together and the light was growing dimmer; by midday the air felt cold. They pressed on through the afternoon, following the trail.

"It's such a long way," said Ferdie. "Torr must have been so tired. So scared …"

Oskar didn't reply. He didn't want to think about it.

The Far was getting very dense now and Oskar could tell that people had been split up into smaller groups in order to move through the trees. He imagined the Lady with her lamp striding up ahead, the terrified villagers staggering after her, herded by the Garmin, their yellow eyes flashing in the dark. Maybe some people had tried to make a break for it. Maybe a few villagers had got free and were now wandering, adrift in the depths of the Far. Maybe little Torr was one of them and now he was lost and alone and … Oskar shook the thoughts away. He must concentrate. He must follow the trail.

By late afternoon Ferdie and Oskar were very tired. The light was so dim that Oskar was using a light stick to follow the tracks. The trees felt oppressive and uncomfortably close, as though they were leaning over and watching them, and as Oskar and Ferdie pressed on, they began to hear strange howls and whoops from creatures that sounded a lot larger than wood voles.

"Oskie, we'd better stop before it gets really dark," Ferdie said in a half-whisper.

They had planned, if they were still in the Far by sundown,

to spend the night up a tree. Oskar had prepared for this. He'd brought a weighted rope to throw over a branch and get them up a tree, a hammock for them to share, plus a thick blanket. But what Oskar hadn't prepared for were the sounds of large creatures moving through the treetops. A sudden *crack*, then the crash of something heavy falling through the trees made them both freeze.

"What was *that*?" whispered Ferdie.

"Big," said Oskar. He stared up, trying to see into the dark green canopy above, but all he could see was a swaying branch and a drift of leaves falling to the ground. The trees no longer felt so safe.

"Perhaps we should keep going," said Ferdie.

"Yeah," said Oskar. "Perhaps we should."

The trail had the look of chaos about it now. It wound drunkenly through the trees and Oskar could see places where people had sat down, where they had stumbled and signs of a struggle where it looked like someone had put up a fight. He wondered what had happened to them. Some ten minutes later, Oskar stopped. "I can't see the trail any more, Ferd. It's too dark."

Ferdie did not reply.

"Ferd?" asked Oskar.

Ferdie was staring intently ahead. "Shh," she hissed.

"What?" whispered Oskar.

"Look, Oskie." Ferdie pointed through the trees. "Lights. I can see lights up ahead."

Oskar waited a few seconds to allow his eyes to adjust from the glow of the light stick, and then looked. He saw them too: small white lights in the distance, unmoving, forming a regular pattern, with the occasional flash of a small, very bright, red light, which *did* move.

"I think it's some kind of building," Ferdie whispered.

"Yeah," said Oskar. "It's *massive*."

Ferdie looked at Oskar excitedly, her skin and long red hair shimmering in the dark, her eyes shining with excitement. "That's where they are, Oskie. I'm sure of it. *That's where they are!*"

"But I can't see the trail, Ferd," said Oskar. "We don't know for sure."

"*I* know for sure," Ferdie declared. "Come on, Oskie, we're going to find them!"

THE FAR FORTRESS

Oskar led the way. "Try to tread and move *exactly* as I do," he whispered to Ferdie. "Then no one will see us coming. OK?"

They put on their night gloves and pulled up their hoods, then Oskar moved forward, as silently and sinuously as a snake. Ferdie followed, not quite as silently but doing the best she could. The lights grew closer and very soon they reached the last of the trees. In front of them was an open patch of grass, in the middle of which squatted a short, round tower topped with battlements from which a brilliant red pinpoint of light could be seen moving slowly along. The tower stood out dark against a bright background of floodlights shining down from the battlements, illuminating the clearing in which it sat. Below the battlements was a single line of brightly lit slit windows. On either side of the tower stretching out like pale arms were two single-storey stone buildings with no visible windows at all.

"It's like a fortress," Oskar whispered.

"It's horrible," said Ferdie.

"There are guards," Oskar whispered. "Look. On the battlements." He pointed to a figure, tall and bristling with spikes, holding a long lance that sent a needle-thin beam of red light up into the sky.

"We have to get in there, Oskie." Ferdie sounded desperate. "They are there, I can feel it."

Oskar frowned. "How can you possibly *feel* that, Ferd? You can wish they were there. You can think that it's very likely they are there, but you can't *feel* that they are there."

Ferdie returned Oskar's frown with an added scowl. "Well, I can. *So there.*"

"Huh," muttered Oskar, unimpressed. Ferdie stood up. "They'll see you. Sit *down*," Oskar hissed.

"No," Ferdie told him crossly. She stared intently across the open ground to the long, low arm of the fortress that stretched towards them. "Oskie," she said excitedly. "I can see a door at the end. That's where we can get in!"

Oskar cast a knowledgeable eye across the open space. The wide, undulating patch of turf was lit by floodlights on the top of the towers and was frighteningly exposed. But Oskar could see that the lights were not well aligned and there were some deep shadows between the beams. The dips in the ground could, he thought, also lend cover. But it was a huge risk and Oskar didn't give much for their chances of getting across unobserved. "Ferd," he said, "you're crazy. Suppose the trail doesn't stop here? Maybe it carries on through the Far – and what happens then? We get into this place, they catch us and that's it. We'll never find Mum and Dad and Torr, will we?"

"Don't be silly, Oskie," said Ferdie. "Mum and Dad and Torr are in there. Everyone from the village is in there. I *told* you. I can *feel* it."

Oskar was struggling to keep his temper. "Look, Ferd," he said. "*Feeling* is no more than wishful thinking. But we will

233

know for sure tomorrow as soon as it gets light and I can see the trail."

"And then it will be light enough for those guards up there to see us, won't it? And a fat lot of use that will be."

Oskar and Ferdie were dangerously close to having a serious row. Oskar did what he usually did at that point: he stopped talking. Ferdie also did what she usually did: she pushed things too far.

"Oskar Sarn, you are a *wuss*," she hissed.

"And you are an *idiot*. Hey, Ferd. *Come back*." But Ferdie was up and running. Horrified, Oskar watched her heading towards the fortress, zigzagging through the shadows like a rabbit escaping a fox. Oskar broke cover. Dodging into the shadows, he raced across the exposed turf, following Ferdie's dark shape.

Craaaack!

A shot from the tower echoed across the clearing. A flock of large birds fluttered up from the trees and a warning *whoop-whoop* came from a creature somewhere deep in the Far. Ferdie threw herself into a dip in the ground and in a moment Oskar had landed beside her feet.

Craaack! Craaack!

There was a crashing through the branches, the thud of a heavy body falling from a tree and then a triumphant boom of a voice from the top of the tower. "Got 'im!"

"They've shot something," Ferdie whispered, a little unnecessarily.

The booming voice continued. "Go and pick 'im up, pie-face. There's some good meat on that one."

"You shot him; you pick him up," was the response.

There was a loud thump from the battlements and then, "Ouch! That hurt!"

"Good. So do as yer told."

"All right, all right. I'm going."

There was silence while, Oskar and Ferdie guessed, one of the guards was coming down from his post.

"Hurry," whispered Oskar. "Before he gets down here."

Crawling like snakes, they made their way across the grass as fast and efficient as any python. At the precise moment the thud of boots hit what sounded like hollow ground, they reached the door safely. Crouching in the shadows, they watched the guard tramp off towards the trees where so recently they had been hiding.

"See?" whispered Ferdie. "It's a good thing we didn't stay there."

"Yeah, yeah," said Oskar, still annoyed.

"Can you open it?" Ferdie pointed up at the door.

Close up it looked formidable – a thick slab of iron peppered with rivets – but Oskar knew that the metal of the door would make it easy to listen to the telltale click of levers inside the lock.

"Yeah," he whispered. "I think I can." Oskar pushed up the rusty plate covering the lock to reveal a small keyhole. He selected a large pin with a bend in it from his lock-pick kit and set to work, while Ferdie kept watch.

Suddenly from the trees there was a yell. "Hey!"

Oskar froze – *they'd been seen*.

"Hey you, fatso!" the yell continued. "Yes, you up there. If you want tree-leopard steak tonight, you can come down and give me a hand. I'm not doing my back in, thank you very much."

From the top of the tower came a very rude word.

Oskar put his ear to the door once more. He gave the pick a sharp twist and as the second set of heavy boots hit the ground, he felt the lock move. As the guard's heavy footsteps headed towards them, Oskar pushed against the door. It moved silently open and in a moment they were inside the fortress.

They knew at once that they were in a cellblock. A wide, straight corridor lit by a line of white, hissing lanterns hanging from the ceiling ran to another iron door at the far, misty end. On both sides of the corridor were cell doors with tiny barred windows set in them at eye level.

"They were in those cells," Ferdie whispered.

"But they're not there now," said Oskar.

Ferdie concentrated hard. "No. But they are here somewhere."

"OK. We'll keep looking." The sight of the cells had shocked Oskar. He was beginning to take Ferdie seriously.

They moved stealthily along the passageway. Oskar checked a few cells, but he saw nothing but bare sleeping shelves. At the iron door at the far end of the corridor he carefully pushed the plate covering the lock to one side. Something moved – it was the door. "It's open!" he whispered.

They slipped through the gap and walked straight into something pink and squashy.

MY LADY'S CHAMBER

A huge sofa, lavishly upholstered in pink velvet and awash with a sea of tiny blue silk cushions, had been placed a few feet in front of the door. It took Ferdie and Oskar some seconds to understand that they were actually in someone's bedroom. It was a very large, round room clad in dark wooden panelling above which were painted vibrant blue and pink stripes with a row of tiny windows far too high up to look out of. A big four-poster bed hung with shining blue silk stood opposite them. There were two large painted wardrobes on either side of the bed, and the rest of the room was taken up with tiny chairs with bendy legs painted in gold leaf. Ferdie shuddered; there was no doubt in her mind as to whom this room belonged.

Oskar hardly noticed the contents of the room – to him it was just a stuffy old room full of weird furniture. However, he did notice a metal door identical to the one they had just come through, leading off from the other side of the room. He had no doubt that it, too, led to a cellblock. Oskar was about to suggest they check it out when Ferdie grabbed him and pulled him down behind the sofa. *"There's someone coming,"* she hissed.

They heard a sharp *click* of a concealed door opening in the panelling beside the bed, and then Ferdie heard something that made her go cold – the trilling voice she had grown to loathe during her time aboard the *Tristan*.

"How many more does he want, for goodness' sake?" the Lady was demanding.

Ferdie and Oskar heard the rustle of silk as the Lady swept across the room. They heard footsteps hurrying behind her and a voice said, "My Lady, he has asked for twenty."

The voice was shockingly familiar. *Aunt Mitza*, Oskar mouthed to Ferdie.

Ferdie opened her eyes wide in astonishment.

"And we are sending him *thirty-five*," said the Lady. "So what is his problem?"

Aunt Mitza sounded unusually conciliatory. "My Lady, as you know, these thirty-five are not regular workers. They have other … er, skills. Well, maybe three or four of them do – if we are lucky."

"So he can use the other thirty-one." There was a crackle of silk, the sigh of overstuffed upholstery and Oskar and Ferdie felt the joints of the sofa sag as the Lady sat down. The sickly sweet smell of powder took Ferdie right back to the *Tristan*. She felt panic beginning to rise. Oskar looked at Ferdie in alarm; he knew she wanted to run. He gave her the PathFinder "OK?" sign with his left hand. Ferdie gave Oskar a strained smile and returned his sign using her right hand.

Aunt Mitza was a changed woman. Her grating, impatient tones had been replaced by a conciliatory wheedle. "But my Lady," she said, "by the time we discover which three or four are the useful ones, the other thirty-one may not be very, er … *employable*. Ha-ha."

"Humph." Oskar and Ferdie felt the Lady give an irritated

wiggle on the sofa. "Then send the creatures out to get some more. There are settlements on the other side of the Far."

"With the waxing of the moon, every night becomes brighter, my Lady," Aunt Mitza replied uneasily.

"I know what the moon does," came the snappy response.

"Indeed, my Lady. You are an accomplished observer of the heavens. But it is not advantageous to use Garmin past half-moon. Their paleness gives them away."

There was a sudden movement and the sofa upholstery groaned in relief. The Lady had got to her feet. "Tell me something I *don't* know, Mitza," she snapped.

"Er. I cannot, my Lady. Your immense knowledge far exceeds my own small sum of learning." Oskar rolled his eyes at Ferdie. *What a creep*, he mouthed.

They heard the Lady sigh. "How I wish my little pet had not left me."

"Your pet, my Lady? Did you have a little dog?"

"No, Mitza. The girl from the test run on the village. The girl who sewed so nicely and was too good to send to that awful pit. *She* spoke plain and simple. *She* looked me in the eye, unlike you, Mitza. Or anyone else, for that matter. I am surrounded by a tribe of sycophants."

Aunt Mitza did not know what a sycophant was, but suspected it to be related to an elephant. "We do our best, my Lady," she murmured. "And like those magnificently determined, great grey beasts, we, too, will get there in the end."

"What a lot of tosh you do talk, Mitza. Perhaps I should send *you* along to make up the numbers."

"No, no, my Lady! I beg you!"

"Oh, give it a rest; you're safe for the moment." The Lady sighed wistfully. "But my little pet, she would have stared me down and dared me to send her. She had such spirit. And she never *did* tell me her name."

Suddenly Oskar and Ferdie heard a swift, light footfall approaching. They looked at each other in panic – anyone coming through the door would see them at once. They crawled very carefully towards the end of the sofa, hoping they could take cover behind its overstuffed arm. They didn't make it. The door from the cellblock swung open and a young woman hurried in. She had long, brown hair worn in two plaits tied together; she wore a tired-looking dress with the remains of a few ribbons woven through the cuffs of her sleeves and a pair of scuffed but sturdy brown boots. Her face was thin and there were deep, dark circles beneath her eyes. Ferdie thought she looked haunted.

The young woman gave a quick curtsy and began to speak. "Those in Block One have gone through, my Lady, but there is some trouble with Block Two. The guards ask for permission to get reinforcements from the tower."

"No. The tower must be kept secure. Trouble? I'll give them trouble. I will be down directly."

"Yes, my Lady." The young woman did not move.

"Well, go on, girl. Go and tell them."

"Oh, my Lady …"

"What?"

"It – it is so harsh to send a whole village. The little ones are so upset. Can't you let the children go free?"

Ferdie and Oskar exchanged glances.

The Lady's reply was not a surprise. "No."

"But *surely* —"

"Madam, you forget yourself. We had a deal. If you want your boy back you will do as you are told."

"But I never thought that I'd be doing *this*."

The Lady laughed. "What did you think you'd be doing — making fairy cakes? Wise up, girl. Come, Mitza. We will go below and sort out the troublemakers."

Oskar and Ferdie froze. They saw the Lady sweep out of the door, with Aunt Mitza scurrying behind. The young woman stared after them and burst into tears.

"Madam!" came the Lady's shout.

The young woman rubbed the tears from her eyes and hurried to the door. As she was about to go through, something caught her eye. She stopped and stared.

Ferdie and Oskar froze. They had been discovered.

MADAM

"How did you escape?" the young woman hissed, glancing around to check the room was empty.

Ferdie sized up their opponent. The young woman's brown eyes were friendly and she was nervously twisting one of her long plaits through her bitten-to-the-quick fingers. Ferdie liked her.

"We haven't escaped," Ferdie whispered. "We've broken in. We're trying to find our parents and our little brother. *Please* don't say anything."

The young woman sighed. "It's OK, I won't tell on you. But take my advice: get out of here while you can. She'll get you, too. Like she gets *everyone*."

"But we *have* to find them," Ferdie said stubbornly.

The young woman shrugged. She seemed defeated. "OK. If they are from that shiny-hair village, then they're here."

Oskar looked amazed. "Really?"

"They're downstairs. Where I have to go." With that, the young woman hurried out.

Ferdie and Oskar scooted after her just in time to see her push open a door on the left and disappear inside. They quickly followed and found themselves at the top of a flight of spiral steps, lit by lanterns that gave out a dull red light. Halfway down the young woman realised they were following.

She waited for them to catch up. "You're crazy," she said in a low, urgent voice. "There's nothing you can do to help them, got that? Just go. *Get out of here.*"

"Madam! Where are you?" The Lady's accusing voice flew up the spirals of the stairs.

"I am coming, my Lady!" The young woman hurried down, flapping her hands at Oskar and Ferdie in shooing-away movements.

But Oskar and Ferdie were too close to give up now. They tiptoed down the steps, picking their way carefully. The air was cold and damp, and smelled of fear. They heard barked commands of the guards: *"Move! Move! Move!"* Then a sudden scream … someone sobbing … the frightened wailing of a child. Oskar looked at Ferdie in dismay. The child was too young to be Torr, but the sobbing could so easily be their mother.

They reached the last twist of the stairs and a shaft of white light glanced up from below. Oskar and Ferdie wrapped their night cloaks around them, pulled their hoods further down over their faces, then peered gingerly around the last twist of the stairs. They saw a large, round chamber, with twelve archways leading off from it. They saw the sheen of PathFinder hair and the shining steel of the spikes on the guards' helmets and elbows as, prodding with long red-tipped sticks, they herded the villagers into one of the archways.

Ferdie peered around the last spiral, straining to see. She could name every person there, but she could not see her parents and little Torr. A wave of desolation ran through her – *she was too late*. Suddenly a guard who had been obscuring her view stepped to one side and Ferdie saw her mother.

Ferdie didn't care any more. She took off down the steps, yelling, "Mum, it's me, Ferdie. I'm OK! Mum, Mum! I love you, Mum!"

Rosie Sarn whirled around, and Ferdie saw that she had Torr clasped tightly to her. *"Ferdieeeeee!"* Rosie screamed.

Feeling as though he were in a nightmare, Oskar crept down a few more steps, watching in horror as the scene unfolded before him.

"Mum!" Ferdie was in the Hub now, running headlong towards the guards. Her sudden appearance confused them, and Ferdie was able to plunge into the throng unhindered. Desperately Rosie Sarn tried to push her way back towards her daughter.

A piercing shriek came from the shadows on the far side of the Hub. "My pet! My pet!"

Oskar saw a flash of shimmering blue, like a giant kingfisher diving for its favourite fish, and the Lady plunged after Ferdie.

It was pandemonium. The guards stood, uncertain what to do. They were unwilling to act without orders and their commander was running amok. The chamber echoed with competing shouts.

"Mum, Mum!"

"My pet! My pet!"

"Ferdie, Ferdie!"

And then, suddenly they were together – Ferdie, her mother and Torr hugging one another as though the world were about to end. And then it very nearly did. A pair of soft white hands with an iron grip wrenched Ferdie from her mother's arms. Her mother landed a punch on the Lady's nose and Torr began to scream.

But the Lady screamed louder. "Guards! Guards!" she yelled. "Get them off me!"

The guards waded into the group, which scattered before the fearsome red-tipped sticks. Some villagers ran voluntarily into the arch to escape; others were pushed. With the Lady's long nails digging into her arms, Ferdie watched her mother and little brother being herded through the archway, and then suddenly, as if a switch had been thrown, Torr's cries stopped.

Sticking to her resolution never to cry in front of the Lady, Ferdie bit her lip. She gave a quick glance at the stairs but all she could see was the young woman with the faded ribbons dangling from her sleeves standing on the bottom step. She had her hands over her face and her big brown eyes were staring through her fingers in shock.

The Lady dismissed the guards and turned her attention to her new prisoner. "You were so naughty to leave me," she told Ferdie. Her face dimpled into a frown and her fat, white fingers tightened around Ferdie's wrist.

Ferdie was thinking fast. The tears in the Lady's eyes told her that all was not lost. If only, she thought, Oskar had enough sense to go back up the stairs and get out, she could talk the Lady round, if she played it right. Ferdie hated lying, but she forced herself to speak. "I'm really sorry," she said. "I've come back because ... I missed you."

The Lady's expression melted. She let go of Ferdie's wrist. "Did you really?" she asked. A movement on the stairs made the Lady look up, and Ferdie was spared having to answer by the Lady's shout of, "You, Madam! Come here!"

The young woman came reluctantly, like a dog pulled across

an invisible lead. She caught Ferdie's eye and a
of sympathy passed between them.

"Yes, my Lady?"

The Lady launched into a torrent of abuse. "You, you trumped-up piece of *nothing*, are a sulky little madam and no use to me at all. You were meant to get those people away hours ago, and instead I find myself dragged into a *sordid* fight." She put a handkerchief to her throbbing nose. "It's disgraceful!"

Ferdie saw fear jump into the young woman's eyes. "I – I did my best, my Lady," she stammered.

"Your best is not good enough, *Madam*. You have one last chance to prove yourself and then you can forget about your precious son for ever. Understand?"

Ferdie saw the young woman press her lips together to try to stay in control.

"One last chance," the Lady steamrollered on. "Our quota this month is twenty short. And you, Madam, will provide the shortfall."

The young woman looked horrified. *"Me?"*

"*You*, Madam. You live in a well-populated Castle, do you not? They will not miss twenty fools from there, I am sure."

"No! Oh no ... please, *no*."

The Lady shrugged, as if bored with the conversation. "Well, Madam. I hear your boy is still alive. However, I cannot guarantee he will stay that way."

The young woman was as white as a sheet of paper. "I ... I'll do it," she whispered. "I just need to ... to work out how ... to get them."

"You have until this time tomorrow."

"No!" the young woman gasped.

"Yes! If I do not have twenty people right *here* by then, I promise you will never see your son again." The Lady smiled. "Because, Madam, there will be nothing left of him to see."

The young woman turned grey.

"You have a choice," the Lady said coldly. "I leave it up to you." Another movement on the stairs caught the Lady's eye. "A boy! There's a boy left behind!"

Ferdie stared in horror. Unnoticed by Oskar, the hood of his cloak had fallen back and his red hair was shimmering in the dimness of the stairs. Ferdie saw Oskar's eyes wide and dark, staring out from his pale face, like a rabbit caught in a beam of light. *"Run, Oskie. Run,"* she muttered under her breath.

But Oskar knew he couldn't leave Ferdie. There was only one thing to do – he ran straight at the Lady. In a moment he was at Ferdie's side. The Lady went to grab him, and Oskar, truly his mother's son, landed another punch.

The Lady's hands flew up to her nose and blood began dripping between her fingers, soaking into the silk of her dress in angry, dark patches. Oskar looked shocked at the effect – he'd never punched anyone before.

"Quick! This way," the young woman whispered urgently. To Ferdie and Oskar's surprise, she turned and hurried into one of the archways with the letters *VII* carved into it. Ferdie grabbed Oskar's hand and they ran.

"Dop!" the Lady screamed out from beneath a rapidly reddening handkerchief. "Dop!"

Inside Way VII, Ferdie and Oskar ran along a tunnel,

following the young woman towards a shimmering white mist. And when she disappeared into it, they hurled themselves after her, no longer caring what lay beyond. Whatever it was, it had to be better.

ORDERS

The Lady stared into Way VII in dismay. She dared not follow. The last time she had **Gone Through** there she had fallen straight over a precipice and very nearly drowned. She hoped that the little madam would fall in tonight, just as she had. She swore and tugged violently on a bellpull.

In her tiny room – known as the kennel – at the far end of the Garmin cages in Cell Block Two, Mitza Draddenmora Draa was summoned by the screeching of a bell. A few minutes later she arrived breathless into the Hub to find the Lady holding a bloody handkerchief to her nose.

"You rang, my Lady?" Mitza's voice trembled.

"Send Garbin into Way Sebben!" the Lady yelled through her dripping handkerchief.

"How many, my Lady?" Mitza asked anxiously. The Garmin terrified her.

"All."

"All?" Mitza asked faintly.

"All. I'll show that Madam and her precious Castle. They'll be sorry!"

PART
IX

THE OUTSIDE PATH

In a tall, ancient castle wall some twenty feet above a dark, slow-flowing moat, the outline of an archway began to glow with a dim purple light. If anyone had been standing on the far side of the water they would have seen the eerie sight of the archway appearing out of seemingly solid stone, and a strange white mist swirling within its depths. But it was late in the evening, the Castle drawbridge was raised and no one was foolish enough to walk the Forest edges at night.

Suddenly, from out of the mist, a wild-eyed young woman came running. Just in time she grabbed hold of the edge of the arch to stop herself from falling headlong into the Moat below. She turned and shouted a warning: "Slow down! There's a steep drop!" She stood in the entrance while two smaller figures appeared from the depths. They stopped dead – breathless and confused.

"It's really narrow," the young woman whispered. "I'll move along a bit. You must lean back against the wall, OK?"

"OK," said Ferdie. She didn't care how narrow it was. She was free of the Lady once more. She took a deep breath of unfamiliar, damp air. Above was the night sky, scattered with stars; ahead, the darkness of trees; and far below, dark reflections in water, slowly moving. Shuffling sideways, Ferdie made room for Oskar.

Oskar could smell the earthiness of land, the wet woodiness of trees and the sharpness of water – but not seawater. This was fresh, but muddy. He knew at once they were far away from home.

"Come on, you two, let's get going." Oskar recognised the voice of the young woman. "Be careful," she said. "There's only a ledge here and the stones are loose. Hold on to the wall, OK?"

"OK."

"OK."

"And don't look down. By the way, I'm Lucy. Lucy Heap."

"Ferdie," said Ferdie.

"Oskar," said Oskar.

"Sarn," they both said together.

The path was precarious. At times it was so narrow that all they could do was to edge along crab-wise; at other times it would widen but be covered with slippery gravel. Oskar was last and he kept glancing back to see who – or what – was following. To his relief, he saw and heard nothing. He hurried along, following Ferdie and Lucy Heap by the dim light of the moon, which was sinking towards the treetops on the far side of the water.

After a frighteningly narrow section of the path, Ferdie and Oskar saw a light ahead. Lucy sped up and soon they were picking their way down some precarious steps, which took them down to a slipway where dark water gently lapped. Here was the light that Ferdie had seen – a lantern illuminating a sign that read: *Rupert's Paddleboat Hire*.

Lucy looked anxiously back along the path. "Not far now," she whispered, hurrying them up the slipway.

The slipway led into a street with tall, thin houses on the left-hand side and lower, smaller houses on the right. After the dark of the pathway it was bright and cheerful – many of the houses had lights in the windows, and one had a blaze of candles burning at every window. It was to a little house opposite this that the young woman took Oskar and Ferdie. She opened the front door and they followed her inside to a narrow passageway cluttered with boxes and bags.

"Simon," Lucy called out softly. "Si, are you there?"

A door at the end opened and a young man dressed in black appeared. He looked, thought Ferdie, both anxious and relieved at the same time.

"Lu!" he said, hurrying towards them. And then, suddenly noticing the shimmer from Ferdie's and Oskar's hair, he stopped. "Who are they?" he said suspiciously.

"It's …" Lucy hurled herself into Simon's arms. "Oh, it's awful. Just *awful*."

WILLIAM

Ferdie and Oskar were sitting beside the fire in a small front room lined with books. While Simon placed some mugs full of something hot on the table in front of them and Lucy put down a plate of biscuits with trembling hands, Ferdie looked at the books. They were an odd mixture of knitting patterns, **Magyk**, building construction manuals and Alchemie texts. The lower shelves were full of brightly coloured children's books and some well-worn toys.

The mugs contained herbal tea, which smelled like old straw. But Ferdie and Oskar were glad of the warmth, and they sat cradling their mugs, listening to the story of how the Lady had invaded the lives of Simon and Lucy Heap.

Lucy began. "Two months ago our little boy, William, disappeared."

Ferdie and Oskar exchanged glances – so it wasn't happening only to them.

"William … he was – I mean, he *is* – only six." Lucy stopped for a moment, took a deep breath and continued. "William loved to sail his toy boat in the Moat. One day after school I let him go to the slipway with his friends to play with their boats. It was a lovely, warm evening and it was still light, and he was perfectly safe – well, I thought he was – because his uncle, my brother Rupert, has a boathouse there and he was working outside, keeping an eye on them. Well ... oh, it was *all* my fault ... I just didn't notice how late it was getting – I was busy working on a design for a stupid tower thingy. Suddenly I realised it was nearly dark and William wasn't home. I ran out of the house and there was no one at the end of the slipway – no little boys and no Rupert. It was deserted. I raced down to the water and shouted for William. Rupert came out and said he thought that William had gone home when all his friends did. I yelled at Rupert for being so *stupid* and then I saw William's favourite toy – a little white knitted sheep his granny made him – up on the Outside Path – you know, where we just walked along." Lucy gulped. "I knew then that something terrible had happened. I ran along the Outside Path so fast you wouldn't believe it. It curves around with the Castle walls, so you can never see very far ahead, and it was really dark by then because there was no moon that night, but as I got around the bend I saw something." Lucy shuddered. "A huge animal, white and horrible, with a head like a snake. Standing up on two legs. *And then I saw it go through the wall.*"

Simon sighed. He looked wretched and Ferdie felt sorry for him. She could tell he did not believe Lucy – but Ferdie believed her, all right. And so did Oskar.

Lucy continued with her story. "I raced towards where the white thing had disappeared but there was no sign of anything. The wall was ... well, it was just a wall. And it was dark by then too."

"We searched all night," Simon said quietly.

Lucy nodded dismally. "People were wonderful. So many came to look for him. The next day Rupert found William's toy boat floating in the Moat, and everyone began to say he must have fallen in the water and drowned. They went out searching for his ... well, you know, for *him*, but I knew he hadn't drowned. *I just knew.* The next day Simon and I walked along the Outside Path looking for clues. But we found nothing." Lucy looked down at the crumb-covered rug in front of the fire. "Simon, there's something I haven't told you."

Simon leaned forward, his green eyes fixed on Lucy. "Lu – what haven't you told me?"

"Er. Well. Every day, while you were at work –" Lucy broke off and said to Ferdie and Oskar proudly, "Simon's the Deputy Castle Alchemist, you know. Every day I walked the Outside Path to where I'd seen the white things. I would stare at the wall for hours – I was so sure that something had to be there. And then, one day, I saw it: the outline of a filled-in archway with some faint letters carved into the keystone: 'IV'. I was so excited – I'd found it! I *knew* that was where the Garmin had taken William."

"Garmin?" said Simon dismissively. "That's a mythical creature. Garmin don't exist."

Ferdie took a deep breath. Simon scared her a little, but she had to speak up. "But Garmin do exist. And they *do* take people away. People like me."

Lucy shot Ferdie a look of surprise.

Aware that Simon's intense, piercingly green eyes were on her, Ferdie said, "Garmin took me one night at the dark of the moon. They took me from my house."

Lucy took a deep breath. "Si, Garmin took William away. And I've been trying to get him back."

"What?" Simon looked dumbstruck.

"You remember one month after William disappeared I went missing?"

"All night," said Simon. "I'm hardly going to forget that, Lu."

"Well, I reckoned that William had gone at the dark of the moon, and maybe that meant something. I thought that maybe if I went back to that place at the next dark of the moon I would see something. I didn't tell you because I knew you thought I was crazy to think like that. But that's what I did. I went back to the filled-in archway."

"You went on the Outside Path at the dark of the moon?" Simon was aghast. "Lu, why didn't you tell me?"

"Because you would have stopped me. Or made me think I was silly. Or something. Anyway, I had marked the archway with white chalk so I found it easily in the dark. I leaned back against the stones that filled it in and waited." Lucy shivered. "I was *so* scared. And then ... and then it happened." She stopped and took a deep breath. The atmosphere in the little room was tense.

"Suddenly there was nothing behind me and I fell back into an empty space. I picked myself up and realised I was in a tunnel – a tunnel that would lead me to William. I ran into it and all at once I felt like I was falling down and down and down. It seemed to go on for ever – well, long enough for me to think that at least now I knew what had happened to William. He had fallen through some kind of hole and now I had too. Just as I understood that I wasn't actually falling – it felt more like something was pulling me along – I was out, hurtling into a big, round cellar with lots more arches, and I ran straight into something big, blue and squashy."

"The Lady!" said Ferdie.

"Yes. And I was *so* pleased to see her. You see, I thought that she was looking after our William. I thought that he had somehow fallen through to this place and that now I would see him again and I could bring him home and I ..." Lucy choked back a sob. "How *stupid* can you be?" she asked bitterly.

Simon was staring at his wife in amazement. "Why?" he asked. "Why is that stupid?"

"Because, Si, this spiteful, vicious, cruel person has stolen our William, just like she has stolen others. She uses children to get hold of their parents, sometimes their whole *village*. She uses Garmin to collect people and then she sends them away to serve some tyrant in some horrible place somewhere, I have no idea where. And she doesn't care about *anyone*." Lucy turned to Ferdie. "Except she quite likes you, I think."

"I *hate* her," Ferdie growled, not wanting to be seen as having anything to do with the Lady.

Simon was on his feet again. "Take me through that archway, Lu. I'll show her she can't mess with us. I'll —"

"Sit down, Si. It's not that simple."

Simon sat down. Lucy was in charge now.

"Si, this is the bit I am not proud of. You see, the Lady told me that she would get William back if ... if I helped her."

"Help her do what, Lu?" Simon looked like he dreaded the answer.

"Well. Um. You see ... the place I fell into is like some kind of transit post. She calls it a Hub. It's somewhere in a fortress in the middle of a forest, I have no idea where. The Lady uses the Garmin to snatch people who live in out-of-the-way places so that no one notices they've gone for a while. Then she sends the people away through these arches. It's awful."

Simon was staring at Lucy in horror. "And you were *helping* her?"

"I was trying *not* to, Si. I helped quite a few people escape too, but yes, I suppose I *was* helping her. Si, I *had* to. It was our only hope of seeing William again." Lucy hid her head in her hands and her voice shook. She looked up, her eyes full of tears. "Last night the Lady sent a whole village away – *a whole village*, Si. But it still wasn't enough for her. She had twenty more people to find, she said. And she told me I had to get them for her. From here, from our Castle. And if I didn't, then William would be …" Lucy was unable to finish.

"What did you say?" Simon asked quietly.

"I told her I would do it, but I needed time," Lucy whispered. "But she didn't give me any time."

"How long did she give you?" Simon asked.

"One day." Lucy burst into tears. "One measly day."

SLEEPLESS

In the attic of Lucy and Simon's house, Ferdie and Oskar could not sleep. They gazed out of the little window into the night, amazed at the place they had come to. An autumn mist had rolled in, but they could still see the gap in the ancient Castle Wall where the slipway ran down to the Moat – wide, still and dark. On the other side of the street was a row of tall, narrow houses – the one directly in front still had its windows ablaze with lighted candles – and beyond that they saw rooftops disappearing into the mist, with lights in people's windows flickering through the darkness.

Ferdie and Oskar were fascinated. They had never seen so many houses before, never dreamed that they could be crammed so close together. They watched the lights glistening in the night-time mist and tried to imagine all the thousands of people so close by. But one thing they did not imagine was that no more than half a mile away was Tod, lying in her bunk on the *Adventurer*, also finding it hard to sleep – because the *Adventurer* was catching the early morning tide and Nicko and Snorri were taking her home.

The mist grew thicker and a chill began to seep through the window. Ferdie and Oskar were about to retreat to the warmth of the quilts piled on to the beds that Lucy had made up for them, when they heard a door open and close on the landing below and heavy footsteps going down the stairs. A few seconds later came the muffled thud of the front door slamming, and their windowpanes shook. They peered down into the street below. Simon Heap was standing outside, and surrounding him was a faint purple glow.

"Look, Oskie," Ferdie whispered excitedly. "He's doing **Magyk!**" But before Oskar could see anything, Simon was striding away, his short dark cloak wrapped around him, heading rapidly up the street and into the mist.

Ferdie and Oskar were burrowed deep beneath their quilts, when ten minutes later, a group of Garmin came loping up from the slipway, their white, flat heads turning from side to side. They did not hear the *click-clicker-click*s as the creatures walked along the street, heading straight for Simon and Lucy's front door. They did not see them stop and sniff the air, their yellow eyes glinting in the light from the house opposite. And they did not feel them nudge the front door and then go staggering back as Simon's **Magykal Armed Bar** sent a shock wave of terror through them.

As the Garmin ran off, heading into the Castle, somewhere in the house Oskar and Ferdie heard the soft sound of Lucy Heap sobbing.

THE RAT OFFICE

One of the lights that Oskar and Ferdie had seen beyond the rooftops belonged to the East Gate Lookout Tower, home to the Castle's Message Rat service. Behind a scruffy wooden door with a brass plate declaring it to be the *Official Confidential Registered Rat Office* were three rats, two of whom were working late to the background music of snoring from the third. One rat was writing out a list of messages to be sent the next day. Most of these were birthday or anniversary messages, which the rat found extremely tedious. She transcribed the very last message – *Happy Birthday Binkie-Boo Twenty-One Again Ha-Ha From Guess Who* – and slammed it down on to a tall pile of message cards, colour-coded green for Castle delivery.

"Done!" she said.

Mo – or Morris, to give the other rat his full name – threw down his pen with relief. He had been adding up the message money, which he hated. "What a day, Flo," he said.

"Florence," the other rat said severely. "I am Florence at work."

"Well, we're not at work, are we?" Morris pointed out. "You just said we were done."

"We are still in the office, Morris, and that means we are on duty."

A loud snort came from the third rat in the office, a rotund elderly rat asleep in a rocking chair. "See?" said Florence. "Da agrees with me." She raised her voice. "Don't you, Da?"

Another snort came in reply. Florence and Morris looked at the elderly rat in amused affection. He was slumped back in his rocking chair, his hands folded over his plump tummy, his mouth open in a little whistling O with his two long front teeth just touching his lower lip.

"It seems a shame to wake him," said Florence.

Morris nodded. "Yeah. I'll get his rug and cover him up."

"And his pillow," said Florence.

They tucked the old rat into his chair, propped his head up against his favourite pillow and headed for the stairs to the living quarters above the office.

Tiiiiiiiiiiiing! Tiiiiiiiiiiiing! Tiiiiiiiiiiiing!

"Argh!" yelled Florence. She stared in dismay at a line of bells behind the desk, one of which was swinging wildly.

"Crumbs," gasped Morris, reading the lighted square above the bell. "It's the Palace."

Tiiiiiiiiiiiing! Tiiiiiiiiiiiing! Tiiiiiiiiiiiiiiiiiiiiiiiiiiiiiing!

"Waassermarrer?" The old rat sat bolt upright in his chair. He looked puzzled for a few moments while he worked out where he was and then he threw off his rug. "Answer it, Florence," he said. "Immediate dispatch. We mustn't keep Her Majesty waiting."

"Yes, Da." Florence hurried across to a panel of different-coloured buttons below the bells and quickly pressed the green one. A panel below the button lit up. It said: *Message received. Rat dispatched immediately. ETA three minutes.*

"Right," the old rat said. "I'm off."

265

Both Florence and Morris looked aghast. "But you *can't*," they choroused.

"Yes, I can," said the rat. "As senior rat I *must* go. The Queen will expect *me* to, due to the fact *I* am a friend of royalty."

Florence and Morris exchanged exasperated glances. "But what about your Bumblefoot?" said Morris.

"Bother the Bumblefoot," said the old rat. "Florence, press the twenty-minute delay."

Florence pressed an orange button. The panel below shone with the message, *Apologies. Rat delayed due to unforeseen circumstances. ETA twenty minutes.*

From the little window in the room above the office, Florence and Morris watched their adoptive father, Stanley, scuttle off.

"Perhaps I ought to go after him," said Morris. "And check he's OK."

"I think," said Florence, "that would be a really good idea."

Morris hurried off into the misty night and soon saw the old rat's bulky shape lolloping along in front of him. Stanley suffered from Bumblefoot in both feet, and after a fast start to show off to the watchers in the window, he had slowed to a painful hobble as soon as he thought he was out of sight. Morris slowed his pace to match that of the old rat, and set about shadowing him. All he wanted to do was see Stanley to the Palace and back safely.

Morris followed Stanley along the path on the top of the Castle Wall, which was the quickest way for a rat – or anyone else with a good head for heights – to get to the Palace, and before long they came to the steps that led down to Snake Slipway. Morris waited for the old rat to ease his way down and quickly followed after him. Stanley weaved through the upturned paddleboats on the hard standing on the front of Rupert Gringe's boatyard and headed up Snake Slipway into the brightly lit street beyond.

It was here that Morris, a sensitive rat, began to feel uneasy. The glowing purple **Armed Bar** on the door of the Deputy Alchemist's house spooked him, but it wasn't just that. Morris could smell something vile – a foul mixture of snake, slime and dead dog. It made the young rat want to throw up. But in front of him Stanley, who had almost lost his sense of smell, carried on regardless.

The old rat was now tottering towards the mouth of the rat-run – an ancient drainpipe – that ran beneath the Palace gardens and would take him directly into the Palace itself. He was very nearly there when Morris saw a nightmare ahead. Coming out of the darkness were three white shapes, even bigger than a human, walking almost upright on long, horse-like legs, with wide, white snakeheads. Morris's little rat heart began to beat even faster than usual as he watched Stanley hobbling towards the creatures, clearly not having seen them. If only Stanley would speed up just a little, Morris thought. All he had to do was get inside the rat-run and he would be safe.

The lead Garmin stopped and looked down at Stanley. Morris held his breath – surely a fat, elderly rat pottering along the street was not worth bothering about? He watched the Garmin's bright yellow eyes follow Stanley's unsteady progress, its head to one side as if deciding what to do.

Morris could watch no longer. He broke cover. Hurtling towards Stanley across the street, he saw the yellow eyes of the three Garmin latch on to him. "Run, Dadso, *run!*" Morris

267

squealed high and shrill in rat-squeak. Stanley looked around, puzzled. He saw Morris racing towards him and then, at last, he saw the terrifying white shapes above. He saw the red open mouth of the nearest snakehead; he saw its long black tongue flick out, dripping thick saliva on to Morris's shiny young coat, and then he saw its head dart down to snap up its victim.

Stanley forgot his Bumblefoot, forgot his creaking joints and his aching back and he leaped into the air, squealing, biting, kicking, punching out at the monstrous snakehead that was heading for his son. And somehow, Stanley got it right. His clenched paw hit the pale spot between the Garmin's slit-like nostrils and the creature reeled back in silent pain. Stanley grabbed hold of the scruff of Morris's neck, pushed him into the mouth of the drainpipe and kept right on pushing (much helped by the slime covering Morris's coat) until he was certain they were out of reach of any questing snake tongue or stabbing claws.

The two rats lay exhausted and trembling in the drainpipe. After some minutes Morris croaked, "Thanks, Dadso."

"'S'all right, son," mumbled Stanley. He got to his feet with a groan. "Right," he said. "Let's get going. Mustn't keep Her Maj waiting. What is it I always say?"

"I dunno. Er … Pass the biscuits?"

"No, son. *Nothing stops a Message Rat.*"

MESSAGE RECEIVED

Stanley and Morris emerged from beneath the washbasin in one of the Palace cloakrooms off the Long Walk. With some difficulty, Stanley squeezed out through a hole gnawed in the bottom of the door and Morris easily followed. Stanley hobbled and Morris walked alongside him, and together they progressed down the Long Walk, Morris wide-eyed, staring at all the treasures glittering in the light of fat candles placed in the alcoves. The young rat had never been inside the Palace and he felt quite overawed. Eventually Stanley took a left turn and Morris followed him into a tall entrance hall with a grand staircase winding up to a gallery above. To their left was a line of little red and gold chairs ranged along the wall beside the old wooden Palace doors, and Stanley limped across to these. Above the chair nearest the doors was a brass sign, which read: *Reserved for Message Rat*. Beside it was a small set of steps. Wearily, Stanley climbed the steps and plonked himself down on the chair.

"Ring the bell, Morris," Stanley said, pointing to a long red-cord bellpull beside the chair. "Just to let Her Maj know we're here."

Morris saw the Queen come hurrying around the corner, red robes flying. With her came a young man, who the rat recognised as Simon Heap, the Deputy Castle Alchemist. Morris scuttled under the chair. He watched the Queen's sensible brown boots run across the chequered floor and stop right beside him, the heavy gold hem of her dress brushing against his tail.

On the chair above, Stanley struggled to sit up. "Message Rat reporting for duty, Your Majesty," he wheezed.

"About time," Jenna said crossly. "Stanley, where have you been?"

"So sorry, Your Maj. Had a bit of trouble," Stanley replied weakly.

Jenna's expression softened. "Stanley, you don't look well," she said. "Not well at all."

"Possibly not," Stanley agreed. Now he had got to his destination, he felt like a wet rag.

From beneath the chair Morris was shocked at how weak his father sounded. He knew what he had to do. He scampered up the steps – much to Jenna's surprise – and jumped on to the Message Rat chair. Then he stood up on his hind legs, took a deep breath and began to squeak, "Your Majesty, I am the Deputy Message Rat on this mission. I am a Chartered Confidential Rat and I am at your service. Please state your message, its destination and recipient."

Jenna and Simon scrutinised the young rat. Despite its strange appearance – it was covered in strings of sticky white stuff – they could tell that it was squeaking in a purposeful way.

"Tell it the **Speeke**," said Simon.

Jenna nodded. She looked Morris in the eye and said, **"Speeke, Rattus Rattus."**

At the sound of the **Speeke**, a swarm of goosebumps ran over

Morris, sending the hairs on the scruff of his neck standing up on end. He took a big breath and repeated what he had squeaked. This time the Queen understood.

"Your destination is the Wizard Tower," she told him. "The recipient of your message is the ExtraOrdinary Wizard, Septimus Heap. Message begins: Septimus, **Activate** the Castle **Alert**. Extreme danger. Please be present for Queen's Crisis Council at the Palace at six tomorrow morning. Jenna."

Morris's jaw dropped. He caught Stanley's disapproving glance and shut his mouth at once – a Message Rat must show no reaction to a message, whatever its content. He waited until he was sure the Queen had finished and then said, "Message received and understood, Your Majesty."

Stanley watched Morris hop down and scurry away into the Long Walk. He felt proud of his ratlet – but frightened for him too. He struggled to his painful feet and the next thing he knew, he had been scooped up and cradled in the Queen's arms. "But you, Stanley," she told him firmly, "are not going anywhere. I will make you up a bed by the fire." Stanley closed his eyes in utter bliss. If he died now, he thought, he would be happy.

"I'll be off now," Simon said.

"It's dangerous out there, Si." Jenna sounded worried. "Stay here the night."

"Thank you, Jen," Simon said, "but I must get back to Lucy." He lowered his voice. "Don't worry, I'll be fine. There are a few **Darke** tricks I have up my sleeve."

"Simon!" Jenna sounded shocked.

"Needs must," said Simon. Careful not to squash the rat, he gave her a hug. "I'll see you first thing in the morning."

"Give Lucy my love," Jenna said. "Tell her we're going to get William back."

"I will." Simon headed for the Palace doors, where the ghost of a one-armed knight who guarded the door saluted smartly. "Good luck, Heap," he said.

"Thank you, Sir Hereward," Simon replied as he let himself out into the night. "I'm going to need it."

MORRIS

Of all Stanley's four foster ratlets, Morris knew the Castle the best. As soon as the ratlets had been old enough to go off on their own, Stanley had given each one a map and told them to run the Castle until they knew the place with their eyes closed. Morris had been the only one to do this literally. It had earned him a few bumps and bruises, but now his hard work had paid off. Scurrying through pipes, over rooftops, along the tops of walls and even, at one point, hurtling down a playground helter-skelter, Morris made his way steadily towards the Wizard Tower. The rat-runs kept him safe, but not all of them joined up, and every now and then Morris was forced out into the open. He was crossing the mouth of Measel's Ope, which, like all alleys that led off Wizard Way, was lit at its entrance by two large lanterns, and was running through the pool of light when he smelled snake and dead dog.

Morris was so scared that he didn't know where his feet were. He stared at the huge white shape that loomed out of the mist above him. He saw the flat snakehead dart down and as the cavern of the mouth loomed over him, Morris let out a high-pitched rat scream. The Garmin flinched – the creatures had sensitive ears – and its mouth snapped shut and Morris felt a terrible pain. And then he was free, running, running,

running across the alley, diving into the pipe in the wall that went through to the Wizard Tower courtyard. Morris felt light-headed with excitement as he realised he had escaped, that he would be able to deliver his first, and probably his most important, message ever. He reached the foot of one of the massive buttresses of the Wizard Tower and scrambled into the rat tube. The tube was steep and winding and as he clambered up it, Morris began to feel oddly tired. He forced himself on and at last pushed open the rat flap and fell out into the fuzz of night-time lights of the Great Hall. Morris was far too dizzy to notice that the floor of the Wizard Tower was flashing on and off with the words: *MESSAGE RAT! MESSAGE RAT! MESSAGE RAT!* He got to his feet and leaned against the wall, his head spinning.

In the distance Morris saw blurry figures in blue looming above. He heard a voice say, "Yuck – look at the blood."

Another said, "Quick, pick it up and get the message. Before it's too late."

"*You* pick it up," was the reply.

Someone grabbed his scruff between finger and thumb and Morris found himself being lifted dizzyingly high into an achingly bright light. A face not bothering to conceal an expression of disgust loomed in at him and a booming voice filled his ears. **"Speeke, Rattus Rattus."**

With a huge effort, Morris **Spoke**. "First, I have to ask, are you Septimus Heap, ExtraOrdinary Wizard?"

The person holding him turned around and Morris felt the world spin out of control. "Get the EOW!" his holder yelled. "Fast, before the rat pegs it."

Morris was floating. Sparkling lights spun around his head, fuzzy noise filled his ears and then, after what seemed to him to be many hours later, something purple filled the space in front of him. A voice from far, far away said, "I am Septimus Heap: ExtraOrdinary Wizard. What is your message?"

Gathering all his remaining strength, Morris **Spoke**. Then, message delivered, Morris collapsed.

In a lonely window in the Rat Office, three young rats stared out into the night. The distant tinny chimes of the Drapers Yard Clock drifted through the still night air. *Ting ... Ting ... Ting*.

"Something awful has happened," said Florence. "I just know it."

FLORENCE

Tod was woken just before dawn by an upside-down rat banging outside on the porthole. She thought she was still dreaming, but Nicko's voice told her otherwise.

"Morning, Tod! Welcome to the Castle communication system," he said. "You've got a Message Rat. Come up on deck."

Tod tumbled out of her bunk and scrambled up the ladder. A small brown rat was shivering and looking anxiously at the Night Ullr, who was sitting on guard in the prow.

"You have to say, **'Speeke, Rattus Rattus'**," Nicko told Tod. "Then it will tell you the message."

"It *talks*?" Tod was amazed.

"Message Rats do, yes. In fact, some Message Rats never *stop* talking," Nicko said with a smile.

Tod was intrigued. **"Speeke, Rattus Rattus,"** she said.

The rat spoke in a thin, high voice. "First, I have to ask, are you Alice TodHunter Moon?"

"Yes, I am."

"Ask it what the message is," said Nicko.

"What is your message, please?" said Tod.

"Message begins: Alice, there is a Queen's Crisis Council meeting at the Palace at six this morning. I know you want to go home, but because of your knowledge of the Garmin, the Queen wishes you to be there. Alice, please do go. Ask Nicko and Snorri to take you. And, oh, Alice, I would be so happy if you would reconsider your decision to leave. Your homesickness will pass and there is so much for you here. You have great **Magykal** potential. And I will miss you very much. Love, Dandra. Message ends."

Tod was more than a little relieved at the message. After her bad attack of homesickness the previous day in the Wizard Tower, she had been surprised when Nicko and Snorri had agreed to take her home so soon. She had then spent the evening on the *Adventurer* feeling sad about leaving Dandra Draa. Tod had hardly slept that night, she had felt so wretched. It seemed that wherever she lived now she would be missing people she loved. By the early hours of the morning, Tod had realised that she wanted to stay with Dandra – all she had needed to know was that she could go home if she wanted to. "Thank you very much," she happily told the rat.

"You're welcome," the rat replied. It lingered uncertainly. "Excuse me," it squeaked. "I hope you don't mind. This is not part of the message and I know that I shouldn't really use the **Speeke** for anything else but ... oh *dear*." The rat sat down and put its paws over its face.

Tod kneeled down beside it. "What's the matter?" she asked.

"Something awful has happened to my brother. And my dad. They went to the Palace on a message last night and they never came back. Please, please, could you ask the Palace people if they know what happened?"

"Of course I will," Tod promised.

"Oh, thank you," said the rat. "Thank you so much. I'm

Florence. If you find anything out, please get a message to the Rat Office. I ... oh, I'd be so grateful." With that, the rat jumped off the boat and Tod watched it scuttle away through the boatyard.

The sun rose over the Castle rooftops, and in the prow of the *Adventurer*, the Night Ullr Transformed into the Day Ullr. A few minutes later, Tod, Nicko, Snorri and a small orange cat walked down Wizard Way, heading quickly for the Palace. At the entrance to Measel's Ope, Tod stopped. She recognised the dead-dog scent of Garmin.

"What is it, Tod?" Snorri asked.

"Garmin," Tod said. "They've been here."

"Here?" Nicko looked shocked.

As they walked towards the Palace, bathed pink in the light of the rising sun, everything seemed so quiet and peaceful. But Tod remembered the burning remains of her village, the wreck of her house stinking of Garmin, and she felt suddenly afraid. Suppose it was *her* who had led the Garmin to the Castle?

PART
X

TOGETHER AGAIN

Tod was the first to arrive for the Queen's Council. Nicko and Snorri left her sitting in a quiet corner of the Palace ballroom, talking to Queen Jenna. The Queen asked her to tell her all she knew about the Ancient Ways and Garmin. Tod knew little about the Ways and there was not a lot she wanted to say about the Garmin. Jenna made notes as she talked, although Tod noticed that when she began to talk about what had happened to her village, Jenna's pen stopped moving and she kept glancing up at the ballroom doors. Soon the Queen excused herself. She left Tod eating toasted sweet Palace buns while she joined the Chief Hermetic Scribe – an impressive sight in his dark-blue-and-gold robes – and waited for new arrivals.

The early morning sun began to stream through the tall windows of the ballroom, sprinkling squares of colour from tiny pieces of stained glass across the polished wooden floor, and through the ancient wavy panes Tod could see the dew-covered Palace lawns sweeping down to the misty river. Her fear of the Garmin evaporated in the beauty of the morning and Tod was thankful that she was not now on her way home. She looked at the opulent surroundings – the long, white-clothed table piled high with anything one could possibly wish for breakfast; the delicate little red-and-gold chairs scattered around the room in groups; the deeply luxurious red velvet armchairs – and began to appreciate what a big and varied world it was outside the PathFinder village. A buzz of excitement came over her, which was swiftly followed by a wave of guilt – where were Oskar and Ferdie now? Certainly not anywhere as comfortable as this. She had deserted her friends just when they needed her most. What was it her father used to call people who behaved like that? A "fair-weather friend", that was it. The sweet Palace bun turned sour in her mouth and Tod put down her plate. She felt sick.

Tod watched Marcia and Alther come in. They exchanged a few words with Jenna and wandered over to join her. To Tod's relief they sat and chatted like the old friends they were, leaving her to her thoughts. Occasionally Tod sneaked a look at Alther just to see him floating a few inches above the arm of the chair. Once he caught her eye and winked.

The white-and-gold double doors to the ballroom opened once again and Tod saw the ExtraOrdinary Wizard walk in with the Snow Princess hanging on his arm. Behind them followed a neat little man with orange hair and thick spectacles. Tod watched the Queen greet them.

"We meet again," Jenna said. She held out her hand to the Snow Princess, who took it with a limp, cool grasp.

"So we do," Princess Driffa replied, her gaze flicking away from Jenna and travelling around the ballroom. "You have a pleasant little Palace here, Queen Jenna. Tiny, yet quite *charming*. In its own way."

Falling back on her Queen training, Jenna managed a smile through gritted teeth. "How kind," she replied. Then she greeted Septimus with a formal "Good morning, Extra-Ordinary Wizard".

Septimus returned it in kind. "Good morning, Your Grace," he replied. "Good morning, Chief Hermetic Scribe. May I introduce to you Mr Benhira-Benhara Grula-Grula?"

Jenna raised her eyebrows at Septimus. "Oh?" she said.

"I will explain," Septimus said apologetically.

Mr Benhira-Benhara Grula-Grula held out his hand to Jenna, who took it gracefully and then found that the Grula-Grula was unwilling to let go. At last, after some interminable small talk, Jenna managed to excuse herself, leaving Beetle to carry on the conversation. It took her five long minutes in the bathroom to scrub away the stickiness.

Jenna returned to her business of talking to people and making notes. Every now and then she cast an irritated glance at the huge gold-and-blue clock at the end of the ballroom – affectionately known as the Pumpkin Clock for as long as anyone could remember. Now, due to Jenna's repairing and refurbishment of the Palace, the clock no longer always pointed to twelve but told the correct time: twenty-seven minutes past six. Jenna began to pace impatiently.

"Who do you think Jenna's waiting for?" Alther whispered to Marcia.

"Don't ask me, Alther," muttered Marcia. "No one tells me anything now. Mind you, that's no different. Aha, this must be whoever-it-is now."

The big white-and-gold doors opened.

"Gosh," said Marcia. "I wonder what Lucy Heap has to do with all this? And Simon, too. And who are those children – Tod, whatever is the matter?"

283

Tod had leaped up with a yell. And then, before Marcia could stop her – for it was not the thing to interrupt the Queen when she was welcoming visitors – Tod had broken into a run and was shouting out, "Oskie! Ferdie! Oh, it's you. It's *you!*" And a moment later a huddle of young PathFinders were hugging one another and jumping up and down as if they were on springs.

QUEEN'S COUNCIL

The Queen's Council Room was a small, dark panelled chamber upstairs near the Throne Room. It contained an old round table with twelve ancient oak stools — uncomfortable enough to encourage quick decisions. All the places were taken, and as Queen Jenna took the last seat, she surveyed the strange mixture of humans, ghost and ShapeShifter gathered that morning. Sitting on her right was the ExtraOrdinary Wizard and next to him was the annoying Snow Princess, who was inspecting her long blue nails and already looking bored. Next to her was the sticky Mr Grula-Grula, then Simon and Lucy, both hollow-eyed and pale. Then came the two PathFinder kids who had turned up with Simon and Lucy, then Tod, Marcia, Alther and back to Beetle, seated on her left.

Jenna was nervous. She had been Queen for seven years and had never had anything particularly important to do. But now the Castle was in peril and this was a huge test. She dared not fail. Jenna coughed a little anxiously and began to speak. "Welcome to you all. Last night my brother Simon came to tell me some shocking things. The Castle is under a grave threat and one of our Castle people, William Heap, is in imminent danger. From my conversations both last night and this morning, I understand that our troubles stem from a sorcerer named Oraton-Marr." Jenna glanced over at Marcia. "That is his name?"

"It is," Marcia confirmed.

"Many months ago," Jenna continued, "this Oraton-Marr arrived in Princess Driffa's homeland – the Eastern SnowPlains – and began to desecrate a sacred site by digging for, the Princess believes, an … er … *egg*."

Some amused glances were exchanged around the table.

"A mythical sacred egg from a mythical worm that makes lapis lazuli."

"The Egg of the Orm is not mythical," Driffa said indignantly. "It is real."

"Princess Driffa," Jenna said icily, "please keep your comments until after I have finished." Princess Driffa raised her delicate white eyebrows in exasperation and Jenna continued. "Mythical or not, Oraton-Marr has been abducting people – sometimes whole villages – to use as labour to dig for this egg. This would not affect us but for the fact that through the system of Ancient Ways, our Castle is linked to the very place where he is digging. I heard last night that William Heap, who we feared had drowned, has in fact been taken by those serving Oraton-Marr. And I also heard that two nights ago Garmin abducted our guest here, Alice TodHunter Moon, from the Wizard Tower courtyard."

"No!" gasped Ferdie. All eyes turned to Tod, and she stared stonily down at the table. She didn't want to think about that night ever again.

"Luckily, they were intercepted," Jenna said. She looked at Septimus disapprovingly. "Although, ExtraOrdinary Wizard, no one thought to tell me."

Septimus looked nettled. "It was Wizard Tower business, Jenna. I mean, Queen Jenna. What happens in the Wizard Tower stays in the Wizard Tower."

"Not when it affects the well-being of the Castle," Jenna said severely. She turned to Lucy. "Unfortunately the ExtraOrdinary Wizard is not the only person here who has been keeping secret matters of threat to the Castle. Is he, Lucy Heap?"

"I had no choice," Lucy said, her voice trembling.

"We all have a choice," said Jenna. "You could have come to me and told me what was happening but you chose not to. Instead you deceived us all – including your husband – and went running off to help this servant of Oraton-Marr."

Everyone looked at Lucy in shock.

"No!" Lucy was aghast. "No, it wasn't like that. Please, it *wasn't*."

"That's enough, Jenna," said Simon, angrily getting to his feet.

"Sit down, Simon," Jenna said. "I will not be interrupted. Our ex-ExtraOrdinary Wizard, Madam Marcia Overstrand, has access to the recently discovered Ancient Ways. *She* has kept me informed about these at every stage." Jenna smiled at her new stepmother – Marcia had been unexpectedly considerate in the past year.

"Now, Lucy tells me that she has been given a choice by this servant of Oraton-Marr. She must provide twenty people from the Castle to dig for this egg or her son will die."

Lucy began to sob.

"I'm sorry to be so blunt," Jenna said. "But I have to make things clear. How long do we have until this threat is carried out?"

"Seventeen hours," Lucy replied bleakly.

"So." Jenna stopped and looked around the table, aware that all eyes were upon her. "I believe our only chance of saving William and indeed keeping the Castle safe from future invasions of Garmin, and whatever other creatures this Oraton-Marr has at his disposal, is to beard the lion in his den. We must go into the Ancient Ways and, with the help of our talented team of Wizards, we must, er … remove him. I see no other option. We must act at once. Today. If we do not, William Heap will die."

Simon clutched Lucy's hand so tightly that his knuckles were white.

"If we do not do this," Jenna said sombrely, "we, too, will become slaves to this evil Wizard. We have no choice. Does anyone disagree?"

There was silence around the table. No one disagreed.

"Any questions?"

"There is one big problem," said Marcia. "We know that Oraton-Marr is at the Heart of the Ways, but we do not know how to get there. We could end up anywhere in the world at all."

"Forgive me, Marcia, for leaving this until last," Jenna said. "I wanted to make sure I had all the facts before I asked Mr Grula-Grula to speak." She turned to the little man with spectacles, who was gazing at her in admiration. "Fair Grula-Grula, I pray you tell us your wisdom."

The Grula-Grula gave an apologetic cough and launched into a high, rapid monotone. "I, Benhira-Benhara Grula-Grula, greet you. I wish you nothing but well, my friends, for you have treated me most respectfully. I fled to your great Castle when our Heart of the Ways was overrun by Garmin. This was a day of despair for all Grulas, for many were hunted and killed by the Garmin as sport. We Grula understand the Ways. We know how to switch and change, how to twist and turn, duck and dive; we know the Ways of the World. And so I came to safety in your beautiful Castle. I found myself on a perilous ledge beside some water and I fell in. But just in time I **Shape-Shifted** into a small duck. After swimming for a while my feathers became itchy, and I came on to the land and **Shape-Shifted** into human form. In this guise I entered an establishment selling cloaks. Unfortunately I became trapped by some kind of ancient **Magyk** in one of the cloaks and was rendered help-less. I lay among these ancient cloaks becoming ever more desperate until Mr O. Beetle —" here, the Grula-Grula bowed his head and Beetle returned the compliment — "tried to assist me in my sad predicament. But even his wisdom was not enough for the ancient **Magyk** in which I found myself ensnared. But when this most *ExtraOrdinary* of Wizards" — the Grula-Grula bowed to Septimus, who bowed in return — "attended me, the **Magyk** was vanquished and I was able to return to my desired state. I was treated with such hospitality and such politeness. It is my great pleasure to place myself at your disposal as a guide through the Ways in your time of trouble. I, Benhira-Benhara Grula-Grula, will take you to the Sorcerer Oraton-Marr." The little man closed his mouth tightly shut in an oddly mechanical fashion and bowed his head.

"Benhira-Benhara Grula-Grula, we thank you and accept your most benevolent and generous offer." Jenna turned to the rest of the table. "Thank you, everyone. Does anyone have anything they wish to add?"

Marcia spoke. "I suggest we all **Go Through** to my Keep at once. We need to make a detailed plan on how we are going to confront Oraton-Marr. And there are a few points of **Magyk** I would like to clarify before Mr Grula-Grula kindly leads us through to the Heart of the Ways."

"Thank you, Marcia," Jenna said. She got to her feet. "This meeting is ended. There is not a moment to lose."

Everyone stood up and began to file out of the room. Tod, Ferdie and Oskar stayed sitting at the table.

"But no one said *anything* about our village," Ferdie said in a low voice.

"It was all about this Castle," said Oskar. "It was all about *them*."

"I don't think they meant it to be," said Tod.

"How do you know?" Oskar demanded.

"Well … I think it just sounded like that. They are really nice here." Tod trailed off, realising she was convincing neither Ferdie nor Oskar.

"The Queen wasn't very nice to Lucy," Ferdie said.

Tod felt sad, sensing that a gulf had opened up between them. "I'm sure they really care about our village too."

"Are you?" asked Oskar. "Why?"

Tod didn't have an answer.

ULLR

Nicko and Snorri were waiting for Tod in the Palace Entrance Hall. When at last, after everyone had come down, they saw her appear at the top of the stairs, there were two familiar figures beside her. "It is Ferdie!" Snorri gasped. "And Oskar!"

"It can't be," said Nicko. And then, "Great Neptune, it is! How did *they* get here?"

As the group from the Queen's Council – minus Alther and the Queen herself – hurried back along Wizard Way, Tod, Ferdie and Oskar lagged behind with Nicko and Snorri. Ferdie and Oskar were gazing in amazement at the wide, paved street with its silver torch posts glinting in the early morning sunlight. They had never seen so many different shops before. They were entranced by every single one, but each time they stopped, Tod chivvied them on, much to their annoyance. As Tod caught up with Nicko and Snorri from yet another Ferdie and Oskar retrieval, Nicko inquired with a smile, "So you're not wanting a berth home today?"

Tod smiled sheepishly. "Oh, Nicko. Snorri. Thank you. It was so wonderful to know that I could go home if I wanted to. But now that Ferdie and Oskar are here it feels so different.

And besides, we have to go and rescue everyone from that horrible sorcerer."

Snorri did not think Tod was taking the "horrible sorcerer" seriously enough. "Tod," she said. "This is dangerous work. I am surprised that Septimus is allowing you to go."

"But we *have* to go," Tod said. "He has kidnapped our village." She caught sight of Oskar staring into a shop window full of automata. "'Scuse me," she said, and she ran off to drag the unwilling Oskar back to the fold.

Snorri and Nicko exchanged anxious looks. "They are too young for this," Snorri said. "It is very dangerous."

"It is," Nicko agreed. "But I don't think you should worry. Tod didn't actually say that Septimus *was* allowing them to go. Frankly, I can't see him letting them walk into this kind of danger. Septimus has become surprisingly sensible now that he's ExtraOrdinary Wizard."

Snorri grinned. "Septimus always *was* sensible, Nicko. Unlike you."

"Me? I am just about the most sensible person here," Nicko said with a grin. He put his arm around Snorri. "Apart from you, of course."

Tod was the last to **Go Through** Way VII. As she waited with Nicko and Snorri, Tod suddenly remembered Florence.

"Snorri, could you please take a message to that little rat? I asked Queen Jenna and she said that Florence's father is safe at the Palace, but her brother was injured – he lost his arm. Or I suppose it's a foreleg with a rat. Anyway, he's being cared for in the Wizard Tower Sick Bay."

Snorri picked up Ullr and scratched behind his ears. Ullr

purred. "First I will take Ullr back to the boat and *then* I will go to the Rat Office," she said. "That will save a lot of fuss, I think."

The Way VII arch began to glow purple, and a moment later, Marcia came striding out to collect Tod. Tod felt sad to be leaving Snorri and Nicko. "Goodbye," she said. "And thank you ... for *everything*."

Snorri gulped. The way Tod had spoken made it sound like a final farewell. Snorri had become very fond of Tod; there was something about her that reminded Snorri of herself at that age. As Tod turned to go, Snorri called out, "Tod! Wait a moment." She hurried over to her and pushed the little orange cat into Tod's arms. "Take Ullr. He will look after you. Tell him, '*Komme*, Ullr,' and he will follow you. Anywhere."

"Oh!" Tod gasped. "Oh ... I ... oh, thank you!" And then she turned and ran into Way VII.

"Tod!" Marcia yelled, hurrying after her. "Wait! Wait for me!"

As the purple glow faded and the arch of Way VII blended back into the white marble, Nicko looked at Snorri. "You gave her Ullr," he murmured, a little stunned.

"I had to give her some help, Nicko," Snorri said. "Because I think she will go and rescue her people, whatever Septimus says."

"Yes. I think you may be right," said Nicko. He linked his arm through Snorri's and together they walked slowly over to the Rat Office.

BREAK AWAY

An hour later in Marcia's Keep, Tod – with a small, orange cat in her arms – was perched on a high stool in a book-lined room set inside the thick walls. Tod was amazed to have been asked to sit in on such a **Magykal** and serious conversation. Septimus and Marcia were having a last-minute strategy discussion. Fast and full of **Magykal** shorthand, their talk was breathtaking to listen to. It was exhilarating, and any other time, Tod would have been thrilled to be there. But right then it was bittersweet, because Tod had seen Oskar's expression as she had followed Marcia and Septimus up the tiny stairs that led to the study. And she knew exactly what the look had meant: *You've gone over to the other side, Tod.*

Marcia and Septimus were discussing Oraton-Marr's possible weak points – of which there seemed to be very few. Marcia sighed. "We could do with Alther." She looked at her time-piece. "He should be here soon. It's only about half an hour at the rate he flies. I've never seen a ghost whizz along so fast." She turned to Tod and asked, "Would you mind going down and waiting for Alther? And bring him up here as soon as he arrives?"

Tod tucked Ullr under her arm and slipped out of the room. She hurried down the stairs to the main hall, where Ferdie and

Oskar were sitting by the fire, and gave them a smile. Ferdie responded but Oskar looked away. Suddenly, from the Fire Pit below, an argument erupted between Lucy and Simon.

"Of *course* I'm coming," Lucy was yelling. "I'm his mother, for goodness' sake!"

There were some low, soothing rumblings from both Milo and Simon followed by Lucy yelling, "No *way*!"

More calming noises followed and then Lucy yelled, "Just you try and stop me. Just you try!" There was the sound of boots pounding up the stairs and Lucy appeared in the doorway, her face streaked with tears, her eyes wild. Ferdie pushed past Tod and hurried over to Lucy.

"Won't they let you go to find William?" Ferdie asked.

"They are being so *stupid*," Lucy said furiously. "Milo and Simon are saying only the men are going. They're planning some kind of battle. It's *ridiculous*."

"But Marcia's going," Tod said.

"Oh yes, they'll *allow* Marcia to come," Lucy said, "because of her **Magyk**. But this is 'a *serious* expedition' and she's not going to be allowed to wear her shoes."

"Well, *that's* not going to happen," said Tod.

"It's like they've taken over everything," said Lucy. "And they are spending so long *talk-talk-talking* about strategy and equipment, and every minute that goes by is another minute we won't get back. And neither will William. And Marcia's just as bad; she's up there with Septimus doing the same thing, I'll bet: *talk, talk, talk*." Lucy threw herself down into one of the chairs beside the fire. "Oh," she wailed, "I don't know what to *doooo*."

"I know what to do," said Ferdie.

Lucy looked up in surprise. Ferdie sounded so sure. So calm.

"We'll go anyway," said Ferdie. "We'll go right now. We'll go and we will find your William, and Mum and Dad and Torr and all our friends."

Oskar grinned. "And I'll bet we'll bring them back before anyone has even a chance to notice we've gone."

"Oh, Ferdie, Oskar," Lucy said sadly. "It's not that simple. Nothing ever is, believe me."

Tod stepped in. "It doesn't matter whether it's simple or not. Sometimes you have to do what you feel is right." She looked at Ferdie and Oskar. "Even if no one else understands."

Oskar looked surprised.

Lucy frowned at the fire, thinking hard. "But there's one big problem," she said. "How do we get to the right place?"

"With the Grula-Grula," said Oskar. "He knows the way. All you have to do is ask him nicely."

"But he's downstairs with Simon and Milo," Lucy said glumly. "And he thinks they are *wonderful*."

Tod remembered how the PathFinder always tapped inside its lapis box when she went through Way VII. She remembered what Dan had said at the Circle. And suddenly she understood. "I can find the Way," she said.

"How?" asked Lucy and Ferdie together.

Tod took the lapis box from her pocket. She opened it and brought out the PathFinder. "With this," she said.

Lucy frowned. The arrow looked more like a piece of jewellery than a compass. "Are you sure?" she asked.

"Yes," said Tod. "I am. I'm sure."

There was something about Tod's steady gaze, about the way she considered her reply, that made Lucy say, "OK. Let's go."

On the way down, Lucy stopped off at the kitchen, where the Grula-Grula was contentedly eating his way through a pile of little iced cakes. She grabbed a fur jacket. William was not going to be cold a moment longer than she could help it.

"Hey, Lu!" Simon protested.

Lucy blew him a kiss. "Sorry!" she said with a gulp, then she turned and raced down the steps to the Hub.

Simon and Milo looked at each other, puzzled. Simon shrugged. "It's this thing with William. It's getting to her. Poor Lu." He looked at the pile of baggage arranged along the wall, bristling with swords, knives, bows and arrows and not a few cooking pots. "Milo, do you think we'll be able to carry all that?" he asked.

"We'll put it all on the Princess's horse," said Milo. "It's about time that animal did something to earn its keep."

The Princess's horse was not the kind of horse *anyone* put baggage on. Pure white, with wicked blue eyes, the horse had attitude. It was a Royal Horse and expected to be treated as such. Horses of such status did not get left in a smelly underground chamber for days on end with a servant who had the cheek to complain about cleaning up after them. It was an honour to wield the Royal Horse shovel. There was no doubt in the Royal Horse's mind that it was slumming it. Its owner, who was grooming the Royal Horse, felt much the same. Princess Driffa had expected to be welcomed at the Palace with great ceremony, but all she had got was a buffet breakfast with a group of common people, a boring meeting and some snide remarks from the Queen. Even the handsome ExtraOrdinary Wizard was turning out to be a bit of a disappointment, she thought as she vigorously brushed the Royal Horse's mane. She had expected to be included in the high-powered discussion going on in the study and instead she had been dismissed as if she were an annoying child. Her angry brush caught a snarl in the Royal Horse's pure white mane and the Royal Horse threw its head back. Driffa was sent flying into the straw, which the servant of the Royal Horse had neglected to renew that morning.

Lucy arrived in the Hub just in time to help Driffa to her feet. She brushed the straw off Driffa's now somewhat grubby white pantaloons. "There," Lucy said soothingly. "That's the worst of it off. You'll be wanting a bath, though."

The Princess looked shocked. No one spoke to her like that. *No one.* She was about to tell Lucy to keep to her place when she realised no one was listening. They had gathered around Tod and were looking at something. Driffa was not someone who liked secrets being kept from her, and this looked suspiciously like one. She pushed Oskar aside and saw Tod holding the PathFinder arrow, which was gently turning on its sphere.

"A PathFinder compass!" she cried. "Where did you steal that from?"

Tod's eyes blazed with anger. "This belongs to me. *This* is my inheritance. My father gave it to me. It was his father's before him." She remembered Dan's words in the Circle and decided that she would have to tell a little bit of the secret. But not the big, important part about the gills – *that* she would never tell. "My people have great skills navigating what were called the Ancient Ways," she said. "For this we are revered and called PathFinders."

Princess Driffa stepped back, astonished. "You are from the mythical PathFinder tribe?"

"I am a PathFinder," Tod said coldly. "And we are not mythical." She turned away from Driffa. "Ready?" she asked Lucy, Ferdie and Oskar.

Ferdie and Oskar looked dumbstruck – how did Tod know this stuff?

"Ready, Tod," they said meekly.

But Lucy shook her head. "Tod, how do you know where to go?"

"This will show me," said Tod.

"OK, I get that. But what I mean is, does the PathFinder thingy know you want to go to the Eastern SnowPlains?"

The confidence drained from Tod. She hadn't thought of that. She was about to admit defeat, when Driffa stepped in.

"That," Princess Driffa told Lucy snappily, "is a very stupid question. It doesn't *know*. You have to *show* it where you want to go."

"How?" Lucy retorted. With some difficulty, she resisted adding *Miss Princess Fancy-Pants Know-It-All*.

It seemed to Tod that Driffa knew something useful about the PathFinder. "Princess Driffa –" Tod said quickly, before Lucy could annoy Driffa any more – "please, do you know how to show the PathFinder where to go?"

Driffa turned her back on Lucy and addressed Tod. "I do. I know this because we have a PathFinder in the Ancient Artefact room in my palace. It is so precious that it lives beneath a glass dome and we are not allowed to touch it. We learn about these ancient Magykal Charms when we are children. We were told that you must touch the PathFinder to something from the earth of the place you wish to go."

Tod looked at her in despair. "But I don't have anything."

Princess Driffa smiled. "But I do." She held out her hand to show her big blue stone ring. "This is lapis from our **Enchanted** Blue Pinnacle. It will guide you to the Heart of the Ways."

Tod looked at the beautiful lapis streaked with gold and she knew that Driffa spoke the truth. "Thank you," she said.

The Princess put her hands behind her back. "*If* you let me come with you," she said.

Tod knew she had no choice. "All right," she said.

"And my horse," said Driffa.

Tod sighed. "OK. *And* your horse."

Princess Driffa took off her lapis ring and handed it to Tod. Tod touched the tip of the PathFinder arrow to it and the arrow swung around and pointed to the arch with *XI* inscribed into the keystone.

"It's right so far," said Tod, remembering the broken **Seal** hanging down from Way XI after Driffa had smashed through it. She turned to Ferdie, Oskar and Lucy. "We should hold on to each other," she said. "So we stay together." They formed a chain of hands and Driffa took hold of the Royal Horse's bridle. Tod knew that she was going to have to trust what Snorri had told her – that Ullr would follow her anywhere. She placed the little cat on to the floor and said, "*Komme*, Ullr." Then, holding the **PathFinder** in her right hand and Oskar's hand in her left, Tod took a deep breath and stepped into Way XI.

PART
XI

PathFinding

As Lucy walked through arch XI, she remembered how a ribbon had led Tod and Oskar to Ferdie. She let go of Ferdie's hand for a moment, pulled a ribbon from her sleeve and dropped it at the entrance to the Way so that Simon would see where she had gone.

"OK?" Tod called from the front.

"Yes. Sorry!" said Lucy. She took hold of Ferdie's hand and once more they set off into the tunnel.

Tod went forward, feeling the pull of everyone behind her. She had never had so many people depending on her before – but it felt right. Tod, who hated the cramped earthen burrows beneath her village, realised that these beautiful tunnels with their flashes of blue and gold veined through the stone were somewhere she felt at home. Confidently, she held the Path-Finder out before her and walked slowly towards the Vanishing Point. When she reached the swirling, eerie white mist Tod halted and looked back at the chain of people – and one horse – behind her. "OK?" she asked.

There were nervous murmurs of assent and the Royal Horse gave a snort.

"Let's go." Tod took a deep breath and stepped into the mist. With a suddenness that made her jump, a stream of light poured from the **PathFinder**. It enveloped her in a silver bubble and as each person walked through the **Vanishing Point**, the bubble expanded to encase them, too. Another step ... another ... Tod went ever deeper into the mist, which swirled outside the silvery skin of light that surrounded her. She wondered how she would know when everyone was through the **Vanishing Point**, but she dared not look around – her eyes were fixed on the **PathFinder**, which sat steadily on its sphere of lapis, pointing forward. But there was no mistaking the moment when at last the bubble of light closed over the tip of the Royal Horse's tail and they were all encased within. Suddenly a sensation of travelling at breakneck speed kicked in. Tod was still walking slowly and steadily, but she felt as though the world were rushing past. This was very different from the quick trips through Way VII with Marcia – it made her head spin. Concentrating hard on the **PathFinder**, Tod watched the lapis dome shimmer in the light and the silver pointer move sedately on its gimbal: up and down, a little to the left, a little to the right – as the Way took them.

Before long Tod realised she could see the dark shape of an archway ahead. A moment later she was walking out of the **Vanishing Point**, leaving the silver bubble behind. When the Royal Horse's tail cleared the last of the mist, the bubble disappeared with a tiny *pop* and they were plunged into darkness.

"Argh!" A loud squeal came from Lucy.

Tod knew she must stay calm. "Oskie," she said, "have you got a light stick?"

"Yes. Can I let go of your hand?" Oskar whispered.

"Yeah, we're out now."

Oskar broke open his last light stick. The glow illuminated the archway before them and they walked out of the Way into a Hub full of dim greenness.

"Oh no!" cried Lucy. "This isn't what it's supposed to look like!" Lucy felt like a coiled spring; she could take no more setbacks. She rounded on Tod. "You've taken us to the wrong Hub! Oh, what are we going to *doooo*?"

Lucy's certainty that she had led them through the wrong Way threw Tod. Once again, Driffa came to her rescue.

"Lucy Heap, stop fussing," Driffa said severely. "To reach the Heart of the Ways we must pass through many different Hubs. You must trust the PathFinder."

Lucy said no more; she stared around at the Hub, an expression of dismay set firmly in her face – the more Hubs they had to go through, the longer it would take to reach William.

The Hub was the same size as the one they had just left, but it was utterly derelict. Where Marcia's scrubbed white stairs would have been was a pile of rubble. Rivulets of water ran across the earthen floor, which was scattered with small animal skeletons, probably rats. The roof was falling in, held together only by thick strands of a dark green creeper that had covered most of the stone inside. The place smelled dank and dead. It felt, Lucy thought, like a tomb.

The PathFinder swung around and pointed to a creeper-covered arch. While everyone pulled the vines away from the entrance to reveal the number II, Oskar checked the number of the arch they had just come out of – it was VII – and began a memory map. He wanted to be sure of getting home again, with or without the PathFinder.

As they walked into the next Way, Lucy pulled another ribbon from her sleeve and dropped it at the entrance. At the Vanishing Point, the silver light enclosed them and they set off once more in their bubble of speed.

The next Hub was very different. They were greeted by a blast of heat, and as they walked along the tunnel to the oddly small but brilliantly bright archway, sand crunched under their feet. As they reached the arch they saw why it looked so small – it was half blocked with drifting sand.

Ullr leaped lightly up on to the gap at the top of the sand and mewed encouragingly, but it took them a long half-hour to dig their way out – although it would have been much less had it not been for having to get the Royal Horse out. When they eventually emerged – hot, sticky and all, bar Driffa, annoyed with the horse – the heat hit them like a hammer. They stumbled into the open and were greeted by the scorching sun high in a brilliant blue sky. The bleached white stone of the Hub intensified the light and heat so it was almost unbearable. They waded through the drifts of sand, following the PathFinder to the next Way. Oskar looked at the arch they had come out of and added XI to his mind map, then he helped to dig their way into the welcome cool of the next Way and its tunnel beyond.

As they traversed the Ancient Ways, a feeling of awe descended upon Tod. She began to understand that she was leading Oskar, Ferdie, Lucy and Driffa – not to mention Ullr and Nona – on a long and complex journey. She was a true PathFinder. The sense of speed within the PathFinder's silver bubble was exhilarating, and each time Tod walked into another Hub, the world had changed.

Tod led them through a Hub full of small, writhing green snakes, through a Hub deep in a cave, through one covered in snow and ice, through one used as an aviary for exotic birds and one that was, to their shock, a busy market. Each was different. As were the smells: spicy, rank, fragrant, earthy. And the background sounds: sibilant whispering, distant shouts, raucous screams of birds and once, the clash of a battle not so very far away. The temperature ran from unbearably hot and humid to piercingly dry cold. Some were light, some dark, but each Hub gave Tod the thrilling sensation that she had taken another giant stride across the world. Strangely, except for the market, all were empty of humans bar the last one, where a lone old woman sat knitting and followed the sound of hooves with wide, sightless eyes. As they went past they bade the woman hello and followed the PathFinder as it led them to yet another Way. Some minutes later, Tod and a small orange cat stepped into the Heart of the Ways.

THE HEART OF THE WAYS

A sudden blaze of torches bursting into flame greeted Tod and Ullr as they walked into their destination. Both human and cat stopped and gazed in wonder.

The Heart of the Ways was magnificent.

Although it was recognisably a Hub – the typical circular chamber with the twelve Ways – it was huge. About, Tod reckoned, twelve times bigger than a normal Hub. Every detail outshone all Hubs they had seen before. The entire space was carved from deep-blue lapis stone with brilliant streaks of gold. The arches that led to the Ways were built from great blocks of pale blue lapis edged with silver. The numbers incised in their keystones were inlaid with gold, and in between each Way was a burning torch set into a silver holder. These were **Magykally** primed to light whenever a **PathFinder** was brought into the Heart of the Ways.

As Tod carefully placed the **PathFinder** back into its lapis box and murmured her thanks to it for guiding them safely, she heard the *ooh*s, *aah*s and *wow*s of those emerging behind her. A *clip-clop* of hooves told Tod that the Royal Horse was out. She turned to Driffa and gave back her ring. "Thank you," Tod said, her voice echoing eerily in the chamber.

Lucy was gazing around edgily. "So how do we get out?" she whispered.

Driffa sighed. "Lucy Heap, you fuss too much."

Lucy turned on Driffa angrily. "My William has …" She looked at her timepiece. "Three more hours left of his life. *That* is why I fuss."

Driffa coloured. "Forgive me, Lucy Heap."

Lucy nodded curtly, biting back the tears.

"The prisoners are working their way down to the Chamber of the Great Orm," Driffa said. "Far above here." She pointed upwards to the roof, which was made from thick spirals of lapis curled up like a snake coiled asleep, and gasped in shock. "Oh! This must be the palimpsest of the Great Orm," Driffa whispered. "I never dreamed that one day I would see this."

"Yes, very nice," Lucy said impatiently. "Can we get going now?"

Driffa led her horse across the chamber towards a perfectly circular hole in the lapis wall between Way I and Way XII. Oskar ran and caught up with her. "What," he asked, "is a palimpsest?"

Excited to be home, Driffa was happy to talk. "It is the imprint of the Orm – like a fossil. The Great Orm made the Heart of the Ways and then it came up to our SnowPlain. It rested a while, then ate its way back down through the rock, transforming it to lapis lazuli as it went, leaving us our Enchanted Blue Pinnacle. It hollowed out a great chamber and then burrowed down once more to make the Orm Tube. At the bottom of the Orm Tube the Great Orm laid its egg, then curled up beneath it and died. The lapis inside it became the roof of the Heart of the Ways."

Now Oskar understood. There were worms like that in the sand at home. "Worm poo," he said.

"Oskar, don't be rude," Ferdie chided, but to her surprise, Driffa agreed.

"Yes. It is the last cast of the Orm. It is very precious."

"Where are its bones?" Oskar wanted to know.

"An Orm has no bones," said Driffa. "An Orm is no more than a fragile tube of gold, eating its way through rock. The little flecks of gold in the blue are all that is left of it."

As they hurried across the chamber Lucy, too, was gazing up at the coils of the Orm. But only Ferdie understood what she was thinking. "They are so close now," she whispered.

"But so far away," Lucy said.

As they reached the centre a long, low rumble shook the walls. A sudden crack snaked along the spirals of the Orm cast and a fall of blue dust drifted down.

"Run!" Driffa cried. Tod snatched up Ullr and as they ran for cover, two dead, golden eyes looked down from the head of the Orm.

They reached the pile of blue rubble and raced past it into the passageway down which Driffa had fled the day before. As they gathered together, Driffa whispered, "This is how the Great Orm left the Heart of the Ways; it is a beautiful, curving tunnel —" She stopped. A flash of fear came into her eyes. "There's someone coming," she whispered.

Everyone fell silent — apart from the Royal Horse, which suddenly became spooked. It skittered its hooves and jerked its head up against the reins. Driffa turned very, very pale. "It is *him*. It is Oraton-Marr. I know his pinky-ponky steps."

"*Pinky-ponky?*" whispered Tod.

"Yes," hissed Driffa. "The sound of the spring blades on the bottom of his stupid shoes. We have to get out of here. *Move, you silly horse.*" Driffa gave Nona a shove, but the animal would not budge.

"My William's up there," Lucy said. "I'm not going anywhere."

"Neither are we," said Ferdie.

The strange metallic sound was getting ever nearer: *pink-ponk, pink-ponk.*

With a loud neigh, Driffa's horse kicked out and cantered into the Hub.

"Nona!" Driffa yelled. "Come back!"

But the Royal Horse was off, galloping across the lapis floor. Driffa wheeled around to give chase, and suddenly there was a loud *clang* and a metal grid came crashing down like a portcullis in front of her, nearly crushing her toes. She leaped back with a scream.

Their way back to the Hub was barred. There was no escape now.

Pink-ponk, pink-ponk.

"OK," whispered Lucy. "We run at him and knock him off his feet. I mean his spring things."

"He won't be alone," muttered Driffa.

"So?" hissed Lucy. "Do you have any better ideas?"

Pink-ponk, pink-ponk.

"Let's do it," whispered Tod. "We'll all go together. One … two … three!"

They ran up the gently curving incline of the Great Orm's exit. They had travelled the first full spiral when they cannoned into another metal grid. They were trapped like rats in a cage.

Pink-ponk, pink-ponk.

ERMINTRUDE

A bright light lit up the lapis tube and suddenly, there was Oraton-Marr walking towards them. He stopped just out of arm's reach of the grille and, leaning on two long black staves, regarded his catch with satisfaction. Oraton-Marr was a slight man – physically no taller than Tod – but he towered over his captives, the reason being the pair of long spring blades he wore fixed to the soles of his pointed, purple shoes. He was resplendent in silk, and his shimmering blue cloak lined with white fur swept down to the ground, hiding the blades on his purple, pointy shoes. His steel-grey hair was cut short and his green eyes were amused as he surveyed his captives.

Behind the sorcerer stood his sword carrier, a thin bald man in black, with a servant's white ruff around his neck that gave him the look of a vulture. His job was to carry Oraton-Marr's sword and laugh at his jokes.

"Well, well. We have netted ourselves some fish," Oraton-Marr said in a high, oddly accented voice. "If I am not mistaken by the sheen on their hair, the small ones will be worth throwing in. Ha-ha."

The sword carrier laughed. "Little fish to catch the worm," he said. And then he closed his mouth in panic. He had been too clever.

Oraton-Marr's eyes narrowed. Very deliberately he said, "Give … me … my … sword … Drone." Trembling, his servant unsheathed the sword and, with a small bow, presented the hilt to his master. Oraton-Marr let go of his staves – leaving them floating unsupported in the air – and grasped the sword. Drone stood to attention and closed his eyes. He knew that whatever was going to happen next was going to be bad.

"Stop!" Driffa's voice came, strong and authoritative.

Oraton-Marr shifted his grip. "Stop what?" he inquired.

"Terrorising your servant," said Driffa.

The sorcerer smiled as though amused by a child. "Is that not what servants are for?"

Drone, amazed to be still in one piece, dared to open an eye. He saw his master's attention was now on the stunningly white-haired captive who had spoken out. Drone allowed himself to breathe again.

"I know you," Oraton-Marr was saying. "You are the Snow Princess with the horse. The one who came to surrender. Well, well. I accept."

Driffa looked indignant. "I did *not* come to surrender."

"Why else would you have come? You've got cold feet, but what else does one expect from a Snow Princess? Ha-ha!"

"Oh, ha-ha! Oh, ha-ha-ha! Ha-ha, *ha-ha-ha*!" Drone laughed, desperately trying to make up for his previous error.

"Shut up, Drone," snapped Oraton-Marr, his eyes still focused on Driffa. "I am *so* looking forward to moving into your lovely Snow Palace and to walking the fabled lantern walkways of ice. Such a wise decision of yours. A surrender does save so much bloodstaining of the snow, do you not think?"

Driffa stared at the sorcerer in dismay.

With a sudden squeak from his blades, Oraton-Marr spun around and threw his sword to Drone. The servant caught it awkwardly and cut his hand. He smothered a cry, clenched his fist to stop the blood and slid the sword back into the scabbard, praying that not a speck of blood had stained the blade.

Oraton-Marr grabbed hold of his sticks. "Open the gate, Drone," he ordered.

Drone undid the lock and a small door in the grille swung open.

"Princess Driffa," said Oraton-Marr. "We have the terms of your surrender to discuss. Perhaps you would care to accompany me. No? Well, maybe I can tempt you with a little show that I have arranged. All is turning out very well indeed; the roof to your Orm Chamber has just collapsed."

"No!" cried Driffa.

The Sorcerer gave a wolfish smile. "*Yes*. We gave it some encouragement, of course, but it has been most obliging. The serfs are clearing the rubble and soon the entertainment will begin. Come." Oraton-Marr offered his hand to Driffa, but she spat on the ground.

Oraton-Marr's expression of amused tolerance changed into something nastier. "You will come *now*. You may bring your serving woman."

Driffa looked puzzled but Lucy understood. She was desperate to get out of the cage and have a chance of finding William, and if she had to go out as a serving woman, then so be it. She curtsied to Driffa, who stared at her in amazement.

"Ma'am, I would be honoured to accompany you, Your … er … Bountifulness," Lucy murmured.

"What?" said Driffa.

"Please forgive me for saying, ma'am, for I am but a mere *serving woman*, but we have no choice. We *must go*," Lucy said, hoping that Driffa would understand.

Suddenly, Driffa got it. "Oh! Very well ... er ... Ermintrude," she said.

Lucy opened her mouth to exclaim, *Ermintrude! Are you trying to be funny?* But Tod nudged her hard.

"What?" Lucy said crossly.

Tod put her finger to her lips. She knew that Driffa was protecting Lucy, because to give a **Darke** sorcerer a person's real name was to give him tremendous power over her.

"Come, Ermintrude," said Driffa.

Drone bowed to Driffa as she stepped out.

"No need to bow. She is nothing now," Oraton-Marr snapped.

Lucy followed, trying her best to look like a demure serving woman. It did not come easily.

"Lock the cage," Oraton-Marr instructed Drone. "Tell the guards to collect the fish. And their cat." The sorcerer frowned. Fish ... cat ... There was a joke there somewhere, but he couldn't quite think of it.

Drone laughed anyway, just to be on the safe side. "The cat! And its fish! Oh yes, indeed. Ha-ha-ha!" With blood dripping from the deep cut across his palm, the sword carrier fumbled with the lock until it clicked home.

Clutching the bars of the cage, Tod, Oskar and Ferdie watched the figures trudge up the walkway – Oraton-Marr escorting Driffa, followed by Lucy and then Drone, who left bright red spots of blood seeping into the trodden snow. The purple light disappeared around the next spiral and they were gone.

Ullr was restless. He slipped through the bars and mewed.

"Ullr," Tod whispered. "Ullr, come back." Ullr mewed again. The little cat crouched down and Tod suddenly understood. Far above them, the sun was setting and Ullr was about to **Transform**.

Thirty seconds later, a sleek, big black cat lay free on the other side of the bars of the cage, and Tod had a thought. "Ullr," she said. "Go and find William Heap. Keep him safe."

Ullr's green eyes looked at Tod, but she had no way of telling if he understood or was able to do what she had asked. She watched the panther pad away up the blood-spattered incline and wondered if she had let go their only protector.

CAGED

"Sheesh," Oskar hissed. "Just stop asking me stuff, OK? Let me *think*."

Oskar was kneeling beside the lock, methodically twisting and pushing his lockpick, listening for the telltale click, feeling for a shift in the mechanism. The lock was complicated. Oskar had to pick through a section at a time, keeping each one open as he went – it was the most difficult thing he had ever done. Ferdie was helpfully holding a light stick for him, but she was also breathing in his ear and anxiously asking him how he was doing.

"I don't need the light. I just need someone to stop breathing down my neck," Oskar said snappily.

Rebuffed, Ferdie stepped back.

Ker-lunk!

"Woo-hoo!" Oskar leaped to his feet. "I've done it!"

"Hey, Oskie, that is *amazing*," said Tod.

Oskar gave the door a tentative push and it swung open.

"Clever boy," Ferdie said, forgiving Oskar his grumpiness.

"Phew," breathed Oskar. "I thought I wasn't going to get that one."

They hurried up the passage, following the trail of blood. At every twist the air grew colder, and soon the blue lapis walls had become covered in a frosting of ice. Around and around they went, climbing ever upwards, afraid that they would meet the guards coming down to get them. After more turns than they could count, the blood trail left the walkway and went up some steps carved into a wall of ice.

They stopped, wondering which way to go.

Thud-thud … thud-thud.

The sound of heavy boots marching above decided for them. They raced up the steps, along a short tunnel carved through the ice, and came to a small, circular space. This was the lobby where people would rest before visiting the Chamber of the Great Orm. The ice passage led out of the opposite side of the chamber, but the blood trail disappeared through a curtained doorway to their left. This had once been a tunnel to the Snow Palace, but Driffa's sisters had blocked it when Oraton–Marr arrived and it was now a short blind alley, where the sorcerer had made his underground headquarters. From behind the curtain some distance away, they could hear Driffa's voice, low and angry.

The little lobby had once been beautiful. Swirling patterns were carved into the ice walls, in which lay touches of gold and silver; these rose up to a high, conical ceiling glittering with a mosaic of blue and gold stones. Ebony benches were set into the walls and two fur cloaks hung from a line of lapis pegs driven into the ice. On the right hung a long blue silk curtain. From behind it came the dull thud of rocks being shifted and the hushed groans of effort.

Ferdie stared at the curtain – something on the other side of it felt very bad. She felt so scared that her whole body seemed to be made of jelly. "They're here," she whispered, pointing at the curtain. "Through there. I can *feel* them."

After Ferdie had been right about the cells in the Far Fortress, Oskar was no longer scathing about what she felt. He caught his twin's fear, and Tod saw Oskar turn as white as ice. Tod knew *someone* was going to have to look, so very gingerly, she drew back the curtain, just a little. "Oh!" she gasped.

It was a dramatic scene. The curtain concealed a hole that had been smashed through the wall. Beyond it was a roughly made balcony, which looked out over a huge cavern. The cavern was open to the night sky far above and was lit by a bright ball of light that hovered **Magykally** in the air, illuminating clouds of dust and shining its light on to the floor below. There, men, women and children in tattered rags, dirty and exhausted, were working to clear the remains of a lapis roof that had recently fallen in. Slowly and painfully they were piling up lumps of rubble at the sides of the cavern. They had already cleared the dusty circle of ice in the very centre, which a guard – dressed in chain mail and spikes – was sweeping clean. Tod searched the workers for a telltale sheen of PathFinder skin but saw nothing. And then, in the shadows, she caught the glint of light on bars. A huge cage was placed at the back of the cavern directly opposite the balcony. In this cage were people packed tightly together, and some of the less dusty had a sheen to their skin. Tod gasped. At the very front, illuminated by small globes of light fixed to the bars, were Rosie and Jonas Sarn, staring out with expressions of dread.

Tod let the curtain drop back. "Ferdie, you're right," she whispered. "They're down there. In a cage."

"Oh!" Ferdie gasped. She went to look but Oskar, afraid that Ferdie might once again shout out, stopped her. "No, Ferd. They might see us."

"We have to get them out," whispered Tod. "They know that something horrible is about to happen to them. I can see it on their faces."

Suddenly, they heard Driffa's voice raised in anger. Then the sound of a slap and a shriek. Then silence.

"Let's go," said Tod.

ICE AND RUBBLE

Tod led the way out of the little lobby. They went down a small flight of steps and found themselves in a broad gallery dug from the walls of ice. Tod guessed this was the Sacred Ice Walk that Driffa had talked of.

They moved slowly along the Walk as it curved gently within the walls of the Great Chamber of the Orm. Despite the destruction and sudden shouts of *"Move! Move!"* from the guards below, the Sacred Ice Walk still had a peaceful atmosphere. Every ten yards or so an ebony bench was set into the wall opposite a small, circular opening that looked down into what had once been the beautiful Chamber of the Great Orm with its **Magykal** frozen Orm Tube. Tod could easily imagine Driffa's people sitting quietly in contemplation.

At the sixth opening, Tod stopped. She reckoned they were now above the cage of PathFinders. Unable to resist a look, Oskar leaned out.

"Careful, Oskie!" hissed Tod, pulling him back. "Someone will see you."

"No, they won't," said Oskar. "We're in shadow here. And they're all too busy moving rocks. Look."

Tentatively, Tod looked down. Through the dust she saw a muddle of people. Some of the guards were herding them to the edges of the cavern while others swept away the dust so that the perfect circle of ice now glittered and sparkled in the light of the sphere above. Tod got the feeling that time was running out.

"Move it! Move it!" came more shouts from the guards below.

"I'm going to climb down and unlock the cage," Oskar said. "There's a rock pile that reaches almost up to here."

"No, Oskie," whispered Ferdie. "It's dangerous."

Oskar looked annoyed. "Of course it's dangerous," he said. "Everything's dangerous now. Do you have any better ideas?"

"No," said Tod. "We don't. But we're *all* going. OK?"

One by one, they slipped out of the opening and dropped on to the rubble. A few stones skittered to the ground but went unnoticed in the activity below. Cautiously, Tod, Oskar and Ferdie moved down the rubble pile, through the deep shadows thrown by the bright sphere of light above, which was focused precisely on the circle of ice at the top of the Orm Tube.

At the foot of the rubble things began to get tricky. They became caught up in a group of workers who were being herded towards the cavern wall by a guard, his long stave with its red end prodding them like cattle. Tod, Oskar and Ferdie had no choice but to go with the flow. They ended up pressed against the sides of the Orm Chamber, wedged behind people so weary that no one gave them a second glance. Oskar began checking through his lockpicks. "I'm going to get the cage open," he whispered.

A sudden movement behind the balcony curtain caught Tod's eye, and when she looked back Oskar was gone, slipping away like a sand snake and melting into the shadows.

It was then that something happened to Ferdie, which she would remember for ever – she felt a small, warm, gritty hand grasp hers. She looked down and saw a face encrusted with dirt, with streaks of pink revealed by smudged tracks of tears. Gazing up at her were the big blue eyes of her little brother, Torr. Ferdie snatched up Torr and held the little boy so tight that he had to struggle to breathe.

"Look," Ferdie whispered, swinging around to Tod. "Look what I've found!"

TORR

So many strange things had happened to Torr that seeing Ferdie again did not surprise him at all. "Ma and Pa are in a cage," he whispered.

"I know, sweetheart," Ferdie whispered back. "But Oskie is going to get them out."

"Hurry, Oskie," said Torr, with tears welling up in his eyes. "Before they make them jump in."

Ferdie felt sick. "Make them jump into what?" she whispered.

"The ice," Torr whispered, his voice hiccupping with sobs. "The ice on that pond thing. It's really, really deep and they're going to melt it and make people from our village jump in."

Ferdie and Tod exchanged horrified looks.

"Why?" asked Ferdie.

"To find something at the bottom," whispered Torr.

"How can they possibly find anything?" Ferdie said to Tod. "It must be fifty feet deep at least. They'll drown. I don't understand."

But suddenly, Tod did understand. She understood now why Aunt Mitza had been hiding, listening to the MidSummer Circle, hearing their secret. She understood that now their secret was known it would destroy most of them. One by one the PathFinders would be thrown in until the guards found a useful one with gills. Even if they had to throw in nine people who couldn't breathe underwater before they came to one who could, what would that matter? There were plenty to spare.

But Ferdie – who had yet to go to the Summer Circle and hear the secret – still could not understand. "Torr," she said, "are you *sure* about this?"

"Yes," said Torr. "Me and my friend, we've been listening to the guards. They can't see us; we've been hiding up there." Torr pointed to a hollow in the rubble behind them, and Tod and Ferdie saw a thin, grubby little boy with long, wavy fair hair crouched like a monkey. They exchanged excited glances – the boy's arm was casually draped over the broad shoulders of a large black panther.

"He's Willum," Torr whispered, and William Heap flashed them a white-toothed smile. "Willum put dirt on my hair and my face so they didn't know I should go in the cage. And now he's found a panther. I want one too. If we had lots of panthers we could attack the guards and – oh! Look!" Torr pointed up to the balcony.

Two torches on either side had suddenly burst into flames.

LUCY

Ever since Lucy had lost her William, she felt she was living a long, slow nightmare – and now it had reached the part where you wake up screaming. Except Lucy knew she wasn't going to wake up.

When they had been marched into Oraton-Marr's headquarters, Lucy had been horrified to see the Lady sitting at a silver table at the end of the long ice passage. The Lady had coolly checked her timepiece and said, "So, Madam. Your boy's time is very nearly up."

Driffa had caught Lucy as she began to sway. "It will be all right," Driffa murmured. "Do not fear."

But Lucy *did* fear. And now, as she and Driffa walked behind Oraton-Marr and the Lady, heading for the long blue silk curtain in the little gilded chamber, the Lady's orders to Drone played over and over in Lucy's head. "Find the boy called William Heap. Bring him to the Orm Tube. We shall see how he swims."

As the curtain was drawn back and Oraton-Marr and the Lady stepped through it, Lucy knew she was going towards something terrible from which there was no escape.

THE MELT

The blue curtains at the back of the balcony were suddenly opened and Oraton-Marr sprang out like a jack-in-the-box. A suppressed gasp went through the Chamber of the Orm below, followed by silence as a sense of dread took hold. All eyes were on the balcony. They watched the Lady bustle eagerly out and then saw two young women quickly follow, clearly shoved through the curtains by an officious guard.

Tod and Ferdie watched Lucy and Driffa blinking into the light, trying to work out what was happening. They saw Lucy squint down at the scene below, and they knew who she was searching for. They longed to be able to tell Lucy that William was with them. That he was safe – or as safe as any of them were.

Up on the balcony Lucy could see very little. Dust hung in the air like a fine mist and the harsh glare of the overhead ball of light cast deep shadows around the sides where people were gathered. All she could see was the blind white circle of ice on top of the Orm Tube staring up at her.

But William Heap had no such trouble. The balcony was ablaze with light and he could see everyone up there perfectly. And one of the people he could see was *his mother*. He leaped up, at once realised his mistake and stopped dead. But he was too late. The Lady had seen him. She turned to the guard behind her. "There is a boy loose on the rubble. Get him."

Oraton-Marr was annoyed. The Lady, who was his younger, endlessly annoying sister, was always trying to take over. "Leave the boy," he snarled. "We have more important things to think about."

Behind the Lady, Lucy saw her William for the first time in two long months. She managed to stifle a gasp but her heart began to thud so loudly she was sure the Lady would hear it and realise who the boy was. Her mind began to race, thinking of ways to get to him. She watched him greedily, his blond hair standing out against the dark walls, and soon she saw in the shadows William's companions. Lucy's spirits soared. Tod and Ferdie had escaped from the cage, *and now they had found William*. Lucy's eyes did not leave her son for a moment, and whenever he dared, William Heap popped his head up just to check that his mother was still there. And she was. William felt safe now. Because unlike Torr, who had seen his parents rendered powerless, William Heap had complete faith that his mother would make everything all right.

With a *pinky-ponk* squeak, Oraton-Marr stepped forward to the edge of the balcony. He clapped his hands, and from them came a stream of dark sparkles, which spun into a circle to form a small, black ball. With a powerful overarm throw, Oraton-Marr sent it flying from his hands. All eyes – except for Lucy's – followed the sphere as it whizzed around the chamber, buzzing like a demented black hornet, and finally came to rest a few feet above the ice of the Orm Tube.

Oraton-Marr raised his hands and, holding his index fingers at eye level, he pointed them at the hovering sphere. Deep inside a dull orange light began to glow, brightening rapidly so that within no more than ten seconds the sphere looked like a miniature sun, shining an incandescent, dazzling white. Those close could feel waves of heat coming from it. The sorcerer stabbed his fingers downwards and the white-hot sphere dropped on to the ice with a great *hissssss* and began to whizz around in a tight circle. Faster and faster it went, with the ice fizzing and sizzling as it turned into water. Soon all that could be seen was a stream of brilliant light, glimpsed within billows of rising steam.

From the balcony above came a desperate cry from Driffa.

"Stop! Please! Stop!" Her voice echoed desolately around the Chamber of the Orm and faded away. Nothing was going to stop now.

The top of the Orm Tube was now water, but ice was continuing to rise to the surface, sending small waves out across the lapis floor and washing over the feet of those in the cage. Dusty with blue scum, the water bubbled and frothed as the sphere heated its way down through the pillar of ice inside the Orm Tube. It took ten long minutes for the ice to melt, and when the last sliver had vanished in a hiss of steam, Oraton-Marr set the sphere free, sending it shooting up into the night sky to join the stars.

The sorcerer leaned over the balcony. He gazed eagerly down into the depths of the Orm Tube for a few moments, then turned his attention to the cage full of PathFinders below. He saw the people in it staring up at him, their faces white with fear, and he smiled.

"Let the diving begin!"

THE DIVE

Oskar was still looking for a lock to pick. He had managed to creep behind the guards only to discover that the PathFinders' cage had no door. It was open at the back and led straight to a roughly hewn tunnel, which was heavily guarded by the spiky guards he had seen in the Far. As he crouched in the shadows wondering what to do, Oraton-Marr's order rang through the Chamber of the Orm. Oskar felt the bars shudder and heard a harsh clattering sound – he realised that the whole front section was being raised. In the darkness at the back of the cage, someone began to push his way forward.

The bars were up, the cage open at the front. Torches on either side flared alight, illuminating a huddle of frightened people looking down at the water, knowing that whatever was about to happen was not going to be good. A terrified silence descended.

Oraton-Marr leaned out over the balcony and addressed the PathFinders. "Before you is the last burrow made by the Magykal Great Orm. It was frozen by the Enchantment of some misguided people –" There was a scuffle behind him. Drone grabbed Driffa mid-lunge at Oraton-Marr and forced her into an arm lock.

"Please let her go," Lucy begged the guard. "My mistress is distressed. I will make sure she does not do it again."

Drone, who did not like what was going on any more than Lucy, nodded and released Driffa.

Oraton-Marr continued his address. "At the bottom of the Orm Tube lies the lapis Egg of the Great Orm. My **Magyk** has now released it from its **Frozen** imprisonment and soon it will be free to fulfil its destiny and become a beautiful Orm. But first it must be retrieved."

Oraton-Marr looked down at the huddle of PathFinders. His voice acquired an edge of menace. "The Orm Tube is about fifty feet deep. One by one, you will dive down to the bottom. And do not fear, ha-ha –" he chuckled at what he thought was a good joke coming up – "do not fear that this will be difficult. It will be easy to reach the bottom, for you will each have a belt of lead around your waist. And you will each in turn have a chance to find the Egg of the Orm and bring it to the surface. Anyone who returns without the egg will be thrown back in until they have it. Or do not return at all. The choice is yours."

At last Ferdie understood that what Torr had said was really true. She looked at Tod, horrified. "No one can go that deep and survive. *No one.*"

"Some can," whispered Tod.

Ferdie stared at Tod as though she were mad. "No, they *can't*," she said.

Tod shook her head. "Some can," she repeated. "But most can't."

"Send the first one in!" shouted Oraton-Marr.

The guard prodded Jonas Sarn forward but Rosie came too,

331

clutching Jonas's hand. The guard understood that Rosie wanted to jump with her husband, and he did not stop her. He would have wanted his wife to do the same, he thought – though he doubted she would. The guard fastened the weight belt around Jonas's waist, muttering his apologies as he did so. Then he unclipped one of the light globes dangling from the cage and pressed it into Jonas's unwilling free hand.

As Jonas and Rosie looked into each other's eyes to say goodbye, a shout came from inside the cage. "Stop! I will jump! *I* will get you what you want."

Tod's heart did a weird, happy-sad flip and she found she had forgotten how to breathe. She watched a tall figure step forward and she no longer knew if she was awake or dreaming. He was here. Alive. Her father. *Dan Moon.*

Dan's natural authority was such that the guard did not object when he unclipped Jonas's weight belt and placed it around his own waist. As Jonas stood dumbstruck, Dan confidently took the light from his hand. And then, before Tod had a chance to call out, Dan Moon had launched himself into the water in a perfect dive.

Too late, Tod found her voice. "No!" Her shout cut through the sound of the neat splash. "No, *no!*"

"Who is that brat?" Oraton-Marr asked, peering into the dimness below.

"There's a whole pack of them down there," the Lady said grumpily. "I told you before. Like rats."

"Dad!" screamed Tod. "Dad, Dad!" She pushed her way forward and people in front stepped aside to allow her through. Tod stood on the edge of the Orm Tube and stared down into its black depths: Dan Moon and his light were gone.

"Get rid of that brat," snarled Oraton-Marr. "Shove it in too." But there was no need. Copying her father's graceful dive, Tod put her hands above her head and dived into the deep, dark blue.

GILLS

The cold made Tod gasp with shock. She coughed, spluttered and a sharp stab shot into her eyes – it was the pain of ice-cold water filling up the spaces behind her nose, awakening her gills. Tod coughed once more, she gulped again for air and took in yet more water. The back of her throat closed up and she spat the water out. Tod felt the water swirling into her sinuses, filling her head and making it heavy. She felt her face grow numb with the cold and instinctively closed her mouth and took a deep breath through her nose. The pain of the cold stayed but her head cleared; she felt water moving through; she breathed out, pushing the precious warmth away, and took another draught of icy water. It stung the back of her eyes, it made her jaw ache with the cold, but Tod did not care – she could breathe underwater. *She had gills!*

Controlling her breath so she sank as quickly as possible, Tod pushed her way down the smooth sides of the rock, always looking down, hoping to see Dan's light. But the weight belt had taken him down fast and Tod could see nothing below but blackness.

A sudden *clunk* came up through the water. *Something* had hit the bottom. Tod was sinking rapidly, and through the blackness she now saw a dim white glow far below, showing the dark shape of a figure lying on the bottom of the Orm Tube.

Tod landed in the light of the sphere and Dan Moon looked up. His face, bluish-white, stared as though he had seen a ghost. He reached out to Tod, his long white fingers like tendrils, hardly daring to touch her.

Dad! mouthed Tod. *Dad!* And she threw her arms around him.

Suddenly, the PathFinder sign language made sense. *OK?* Dan signed.

OK, Tod signed in return. And then, *What to do?*

Even through the distortions of the water, Tod could see the anger in her father's eyes. *Take egg up*, he signed. *Knock sorcerer off perch. Like coconut. With egg.*

Where egg? Tod signed.

Don pointed down and Tod saw beneath his foot a huge, oval shape.

Big, signed Tod. *Heavy?*

Dan nodded and then he smiled. *OK for two*, he signed.

And very good for hitting coconut, Tod signed.

Dan laughed and Tod saw bubbles of air coming from his mouth like tiny silver fish. He joined his thumb and forefinger to make the PathFinder *OK* sign once more.

Tod grinned. *OK*, she signed.

PART
XII

LAPIS LAZULI

No more than a few feet below Tod and Dan lay the Heart of the Ways. As Dan let go of his weight belt and he and Tod struggled to grasp hold of the slippery, ice-cold egg, the torches in the Heart of the Ways sprung alight once more.

Like a bottlebrush coming out of a bottle, Benhira-Benhara Grula-Grula emerged from Way VI. Behind him came Marcia, Septimus and Simon. Milo – much to his disgust – had been left behind with his stash of weapons to guard Marcia's Hub.

"Welcome to my home," said the Grula-Grula. He stood tall and proud, his orange fur tinged with blue dust of the lapis, his pink eyes shining with joy at having guided such eminent Wizards through what all Grula-Grulas considered to be *their* Ancient Ways.

Marcia and Simon looked around in amazement, but Septimus remembered his manners. "We thank you for your guidance, O wise Grula," he said.

Benhira-Benhara Grula-Grula bowed, and a sprinkling of blue fell lazily from his fur.

Marcia was awestruck. Lapis was a **Magykal** stone and the Castle was reputed to contain the largest amount of lapis lazuli in the world, but even she had never seen so much lapis in one place. It looked as though Driffa's story of the Egg of the Orm was true. Marcia began to grow very concerned. If Oraton-Marr did indeed get the egg – and, of course, manage to hatch it – then he, too, could produce vast amounts of lapis lazuli. The Castle could soon find itself in thrall to a very powerful sorcerer indeed.

Septimus was equally stunned. "This is a powerful place," he said, his voice echoing in the empty chamber as an icy drop of water landed on his hair and ran down the back of his neck. "Fair Grula, I pray you tell us," Septimus said. "Where is the Egg of the Orm?"

The Grula-Grula began to hum a high-pitched tune, which he had a tendency to do when worried, then he raised a long, hairy arm and pointed to the dome of lapis above. "It is up there," he said. "Wrapped in ice for its sleep." A sudden deluge of water landed on the Grula-Grula, soaking his fur.

"Doesn't look like it's ice any more," Marcia muttered.

Clutching a handful of Lucy's ribbons, Simon cared nothing for the Egg of the Orm. All he could think of was his wife and son. "But where *are* they?" he muttered, looking around. "How do we get out of here?"

Grula-Grulas tended to be shortsighted and Benhira-Benhara was no exception. He screwed up his eyes and squinted at the round hole between Way I and Way XII, puzzled by the shine of metal across it. "Through there," he said. "But now there are bars."

Simon strode off across the smooth lapis floor, slippery with water, oblivious to the icy drips, which were falling fast now. At the barred exit he saw, just beyond the portcullis, the last of Lucy's ribbons. "They're here!" he shouted, shaking the bars impatiently. A trickle of stones fell from the roof.

"Leave it be, Simon," Marcia said, hurrying after him. "There's an easier way to get through bars than that. I'll do a Flux."

Simon gave the portcullis another angry pull and a serious shower of gravel and stone fell, covering them in blue grit. "I've got it!" he shouted. "It's coming away." But it was not the portcullis shifting; it was the stone above it. With the sound of rolling thunder, the roof of the passage collapsed, blocking their way out and covering Lucy's ribbon with rock. Simon swung around, his eyes desperate. "I don't care what I have to do," he said in a low voice. "But I have to get to them. Now."

Marcia put her hand on Simon's arm. "Simon, please. We need to calm down and think this through."

Simon, however, had no need to think – he knew what he must do. He dropped to his knees and began scrabbling through the stones that had skittered out from the rockfall.

Marcia was afraid that Simon had gone crazy. "Please, Simon, stop," she said. "We will get to Lucy and William, I promise you. We just need a little time to work out how."

"*William* doesn't have any time," Simon said tersely, stabbing a finger at his timepiece. Then he resumed his frantic clawing through the stones, picking up the larger ones, inspecting them and throwing them away in disgust.

Septimus knew his brother well enough to see that there was some method in what he was doing. He dropped to his knees beside Simon and said gently, "Si, what are you looking for?"

"Lapis," he muttered. "I need a good, smooth piece big enough to fill my palm."

Septimus rocked back on his heels. He suddenly realised what Simon was going to do. "Not a Blind Transport?" he said.

"Yep," muttered Simon.

"But that's *suicide*."

Simon looked up, and Septimus saw the determination in his brother's eyes and the power behind it. "Not necessarily," Simon said. "Not if I **Go Through** with **Like-for-Like**. Not if I find the right piece of lapis." He swore. "But I can't find one. I *can't*."

Even though Simon was now an Alchemist, his first love had been **Magyk**, and some of his **Magykal** skills would put the everyday Ordinary Wizard in the Wizard Tower to shame. Simon possessed a fair amount of **Darke** skills too – he had once been an assistant to the bones of a **Darke** Wizard.

Septimus knew his brother was deadly serious. His hand went to the **Magykal** lapis lazuli amulet that he, like all Extra-Ordinary Wizards before him, wore around his neck. Known as the Akhu Amulet, it was imbued not only with power from the Wizard Tower, but upon accepting it, Septimus had – as was traditional – transferred most of his own personal **Magyk** into its core. Without the Akhu Amulet, Septimus was scarcely more **Magykal** than Miranda Bott. But despite this, he knew what he must do. Septimus pulled the amulet over his head and held it out to Simon.

"No!" both Marcia and Simon exclaimed together.

"Yes," Septimus said calmly. "This is ancient Orm lapis. The best **Like-for-Like** you can get. But more important than that, it will protect you. Take it, Simon. Please, *take it*."

Simon stared at the beautiful teardrop stone bounded by a gold band with the delicate lines of a dragon scribed into it. Never, not even in his most fevered dreams, had it ever crossed his mind that one day his youngest (and once-hated) brother would be holding out the Akhu Amulet to him, begging him to take it.

Marcia said nothing. Septimus was ExtraOrdinary Wizard now. If he wished to risk giving the symbol of his office to Simon, then that was for him to do. She did not think she would have done the same, however.

"Thank you," Simon murmured. "I will return it, I promise you on my life."

Septimus pushed the amulet into Simon's hands and felt an emptiness come over him. Simon clutched the warm lump of lapis in his palms and felt the power of thousands of years of Magyk coursing through him. Exhilarated, he raced to the centre of the Heart of the Ways and stood exactly beneath the head of the Great Orm. Looking up at the coils of lapis roof, Simon raised his arms like a diver and began to murmur the Blind Transport Incantation.

Septimus lip-read the Darke words: *ekat em, Nomis, sipal nihtiw sipal.* There was a flash of what Septimus called Darke light, and Simon Heap and the Akhu Amulet were gone, drawn up into the rock above, Like joining with Like. A sudden downpour of ice-cold water from the very spot that Simon had Gone Through drenched them all.

"Umbrella?" asked Marcia.

"Yes, please," Septimus said rather faintly.

"Umbrella!" Marcia commanded. A rounded purple canopy spread over their heads and the water stopped pouring on to them. The Grula-Grula, which now looked not unlike an enormous, upright drowned cat – and just as miserable – shuffled underneath the Umbrella apologetically. He smelled of wet and very old dog.

The water hammered down on their purple canopy and Marcia shepherded Septimus out of the deluge and took shelter in the entrance of one of the Ways. Septimus looked shocked and pale. Marcia reached up, took off Septimus's purple wool beanie, which Sarah had knitted for him and he had taken to wearing — much to Marcia's disapproval. She wrung out the hat, did a quick **Dry** spell and put it back on Septimus's head.

"Now, Septimus," she said. "Give me your dragon ring."

Septimus looked down at the ring he wore on his right index finger, a beautiful gold dragon with an emerald eye, biting its tail. "Why?" he asked, sounding as though he had little interest in the answer.

Marcia put her arm around his shoulders. "You remember many years ago, when I was prisoner on the *Vengeance*? When I no longer had the amulet and was sick from the loss of my **Magyk**?"

Septimus gave Marcia a small smile. He remembered. He had been only ten years old; a Young Army Expendible known as Boy 412. It felt like another lifetime.

Marcia continued. "Septimus, you gave me this Dragon Ring to help me. And it did. Do you know how?"

Septimus shook his head.

"You had natural **Magyk** even then, and some of it had flowed into the ring. So when you gave me your Dragon Ring, that **Magyk** came to me. So I know this ring can be a conduit for **Magyk**. If you give it to me again, just for a few minutes, I will transfer as much **Magyk** as I can into it. And then, Septimus, when you are up and running, I have a plan to get us out of here and back on the trail of Oraton–Marr."

"You do?"

"I do. But I need a few quiet minutes to remember my time here as a child. I need to visualise a safe space to **Transport** to. And then we will go together."

Septimus shook his head. "A **Transport** is a personal spell, Marcia. You can't take me with you."

"Quite right," Marcia said briskly. "So when you've got some **Magyk** back you can do a **MindScreen** on me and I will show you the space. I will show you all the information you need to get there. It won't be easy, I admit, but it is the very least I would expect from my ex-Apprentice. Now hand over that ring."

Septimus did as he was told. "You know, Marcia," he said ruefully, "I knew being ExtraOrdinary Wizard was going to be … well, extraordinary. But I never expected to be giving the Akhu Amulet to Simon while I waited in a cavern in a rainstorm with a sodden hearth rug treading on my toes – get *off*, will you?" This last was addressed to the Grula-Grula, which had moved in very close.

Marcia looked down sadly at her shoes, from which the purple python skin was peeling away. "Well, Septimus, if I learned anything when I was ExtraOrdinary Wizard, it was this."

"What?"

"Expect the unexpected."

THE ORM TUBE

Time slowed for Simon as the Enchantment took him up through the lapis lazuli and the echo of an ancient creature deep within. A mineral chill entered his bones, and in his right eye, where he had long ago placed a Darke compress over a deep cut, Simon felt a stab of pain and the sensation of stone entering his eye socket. Fear struck deep into him, knowing that his whole body could be turned to lapis. But there was no going back. Like a worm burrowing through rock, Simon laboriously progressed through the palimpsest of the Great Orm.

At the bottom of the Orm Tube, Dan and Tod began to swim slowly upwards, holding the Egg of the Orm. It was heavy and glassy-smooth, and muscles aching, they held it tight, afraid that it would slip from their grasp and tumble to the depths.

Dan risked some quick signs. *Faster. Or someone else will be thrown in.*

Suddenly a pressure wave from below sent them rocketing up.

Far below at the bottom of the Orm Tube, Simon emerged through the coldness of stone into the darkness of water.

Immediately his once much practised **Darke Art** of Suspension Underwater kicked in and Simon, feeling as though he were still full of rock, forced himself to ascend through the icy chill.

Tod and Dan burst out from the Orm Tube in a spume of dusty blue water, clutching a huge blue egg. A soft sound of wonder ran through the chamber. *"Aaaaoooooh …"*

The guard who had apologised to Jonas ran to help Dan and Tod out. "Your good health, sir, miss," he muttered as he took the heavy egg from their trembling arms and laid it carefully on the lapis floor.

Oraton-Marr stared greedily down at the Egg of the Orm, which lay shining a brilliant blue streaked with gold. "Bring it, bring it! It is mine! I want it *now*!" he screamed down from the balcony.

"No!" Driffa shouted. "The Egg is sacred. It belongs here. With us!"

An angry murmur of agreement began to spread through the Chamber of the Orm.

Spooked by the unrest surrounding them, some of the guards slunk out of the chamber. However, there were still a few eager to be in their Master's good books. Two of them picked up the Egg of the Orm and staggered away. Tod and Dan watched it go, too exhausted to even protest. Eagerly, Oraton-Marr followed the egg's shimmering blue progress past the necklace of openings of the Sacred Walk, watching his treasure draw ever closer.

The realisation that the PathFinders were now safe spread through the Chamber of the Orm. An air of celebration began to take hold. Torr leaped up and down, yelling, "Dad! Mum!"

William jumped up too. "Mum! Mum!" he shouted, waving madly.

In the excitement, Lucy could keep quiet no longer. "William! Oh, *William*!" she called out and then clapped her hands over her mouth in horror, realising too late what she had done.

The Lady worked it out at once. "So that brat is yours," she spat. "I have not forgotten, Madam, that you have reneged on your contract. And his time is now *up*." She leaned over the balcony, her short, fat finger pointing down at William Heap. "Throw that boy in!" she yelled at the guards below. "*Throw him in!* Yes, him, with the yellow hair!"

All eyes turned to William. Terrified, he skittered away down the rubble and slipped – straight into the arms of a guard. The man lifted his struggling, yelling victim up triumphantly, only to be hurled to the ground by a huge black cat that came flying out of the shadows. William squirmed his way free and hid behind Ullr, who stood with teeth bared, snarling.

Two more guards now approached, one carrying a flaming torch grabbed from the wall. Ullr shrank away – fire was the only thing he feared. While the big cat cowered, growling at the flames, the other guard cornered William and grabbed him. He carried the boy kicking and screaming to the edge of the dark, deep circle of water – and threw him in.

"*Noooooooooooo!*" A wild, animal scream came from Lucy Heap.

On the surface of the Orm Tube there was nothing but a few ripples and a smear of rocky dust.

Lucy ran at the Lady and landed a wild punch that knocked her off her feet. The balcony gave an ominous crack as she hit the floor. Drone watched impassively and when Lucy and

Driffa turned to run, he stepped politely aside and bowed. He did not like what had happened to William Heap.

Down in the Orm Chamber, Dan and Tod struggled to their feet, intending to dive in after William. But an intense shivering had set in, leaving them weak, and when guards roughly pushed them away, they staggered back helplessly.

"Ullr!" yelled Tod. "Ullr!" There was no response.

In the PathFinder cage, anger was spreading. People at the back were pressing forward and those in the front were daring to venture out. The guards could feel the rage coming through the bars.

"Leg it," one muttered under his breath.

"Yeah. Before they get us," growled his neighbour.

They broke ranks and ran – and were followed by several others. On their way up they met Lucy hurtling towards them. They stood back respectfully and allowed her to pass.

"It's not right what they did to her boy," said one.

"We should have stopped it," said the other.

"I would have if you had," said his friend.

"You never said."

"Neither did you."

"Well, we can all go home now," said another.

"*If* we've got a home to go to. *If* that sorcerer hasn't set fire to it like he said he would," said his friend.

Oraton-Marr was the last one standing on the balcony. He looked down with disdain at his sister, lying on her back like a stranded beetle. She was always *so* undignified. He saw the unrest in the Orm Chamber below, the guards deserting their posts, the angry fists shaking at him, the wagging fingers pointing and then, in the depths of the water of the Orm Tube, he saw a dark shape moving towards the surface – a shape far too big to be a boy. A sudden fear came over Oraton-Marr. Maybe the Great Orm had not died. Maybe it was a *living* Orm curled up on the roof of the Heart of the Ways. And maybe the living Orm had come to reclaim its egg. He sprang out through the curtain, grabbed the waiting egg from the guards and wrapped it in his cloak. Then he swung it over his shoulder like a huge sack of potatoes and leaped away in great bounds, heading for the Heart of the Ways. At that, the last of the guards quietly left the Chamber of the Orm.

On the balcony, the Lady struggled to her feet. A jeer rose up from below. "Get her!" one of the PathFinders yelled, and the shout was taken up. "Get her! Get her! *Get her!*" The Lady turned and fled, a roar of triumph following in her wake.

But the triumph was not for the Lady's departure – it was for an unexpected arrival. In a cascade of black water, Simon Heap burst out of the Orm Tube with his son in his arms.

Halfway down the passage leading to the Heart of the Ways, the Lady bumped into her brother bounding back up. "Blocked!" he gasped. "Rockfall."

"Oh no! What shall we do, Orrie?" his sister wailed.

"Clear it!" snapped Oraton-Marr. "Then meet me at the rendezvous."

The Lady watched her brother spring away. It wasn't fair, she thought. She always had to do the dirty work. Why was he **Magykal** and she wasn't? Everyone seemed to have something special about them, even those grubby PathFinders. So why didn't she? *It just wasn't fair.*

350

EXTRAORDINARIES

On the SnowPlain above, a shimmer of purple light appeared at the foot of a tall spire of lapis lazuli and within it two figures – one in a purple fur cloak and matching beanie, the other in a shimmering multicoloured cloak and some rather ratty purple python shoes – began to materialise. Marcia and Septimus had successfully managed their **Transport**.

The last flickers of purple evaporated and they took stock of where they were. Above them the magnificent Blue Pinnacle of the Eastern SnowPlain rose up, dark against the star-dusted sky, but all around them was destruction. The snow had become mud littered with huge piles of spoil, in the middle of which was a gaping hole in the ground from which a column of light blazed up into the sky. As the disconnection of the **Transport** slowly left Marcia and Septimus, they saw a tall yet hunched shape come springing up from the light. It bounded away into the night in high, bouncing leaps.

"That's *him*," Marcia whispered. "That's Oraton-Marr. Look at the way he's moving. But I didn't realise he was so hunched."

"That's not a hunch," said Septimus, whose eyesight was much better than Marcia's at night. "That's the Orm Egg!"

"But *how*?" Even as she spoke, Marcia saw that Septimus was right.

"He's not getting away with it," Septimus said. "I'm going after him."

Marcia stopped him. "No, Septimus. *I'll* go. It's too dangerous for you. You don't have enough **Magyk**."

Far below in the Chamber of the Orm, William Heap lay lifeless in his mother's arms. Desperately, Simon tried to revive his son, but William's lips were dark blue; his face was ice-cold and beginning to set like stone. Everyone looked on in horror. There was nothing they could do.

It was then that Tod remembered the whistle that Marcia had given her. She guessed that Marcia was still in her Keep, on the other side of the world, but there was nothing to be lost in calling her. And so Tod took out her silver whistle and blew.

A faint whistle came from beneath Marcia's layers of fur under her cloak. She looked down in surprise.

"No, *I'm* going," Septimus was telling Marcia impatiently. "Listen to you, you're in no state to do anything – you're wheezing with the cold. I'm going to get him." And he was gone, racing across the snow, following the long, thin tracks of the spring blades. Another faint sound drifted up from beneath her cloak and Marcia at last remembered the silver whistle. With a jolt of fear, she realised that Tod was in trouble somewhere. But *where*? Marcia closed her eyes and tried to **Feel** where Tod might be.

And so it was that Marcia did not see Oraton-Marr stop and take a small **Darke Dart** from a holster he wore on his belt. She did not see him raise his hand and take aim at the young man in purple running towards him. Nor did she see Septimus stop, aware that something **Darke** had him in its sights.

But Marcia did feel something nudge her leg. Her eyes snapped open and she saw a panther, black as the night, crouched beside her. Its green eyes looked deep into hers and Marcia understood.

"Ullr," she said. "Take me to Tod."

Down in the Chamber of the Orm, Lucy was pleading. "Si, please … you *have* to do something. I don't care what it is. **Darke** stuff or anything. But please, please do *something*."

Simon was numb. He felt like his head was full of rock. He couldn't think of anything at all.

Tod pushed through the crowd gathered around William. "Lucy, Lucy! Marcia can help!"

"But Marcia's not here, is she?" Lucy said bitterly.

"On the contrary, Marcia *is* here," a familiar voice said. "Stuck at the back of a crowd of nosy gawpers. Now get out of the way and let me through." The anxious crowd around William parted and Marcia strode forward. She kneeled beside Lucy, placed her hand on William's forehead and said quietly, "All will be well."

Lucy looked at Marcia in disbelief – William lay heavy and cold in her arms, no longer part of the Living world.

But Tod understood what Marcia could do. She – along with everyone in the hushed Chamber of the Orm – watched as Marcia took a deep breath in, one that seemed to go on for ever. She saw Marcia lean over William Heap's ice-blue face and begin to breathe out a stream of pinkish air. It came, tumbling and curling around William, surrounding him in a soft, warm cloud. Slowly the pallor left William's face, the stony set of his features relaxed and then, suddenly, William sat up. He coughed, spat out a mouthful of water and was promptly sick all down Lucy's front.

Lucy looked up at Marcia with tears in her eyes. "Thank you," she whispered. "Thank you, Marcia. Thank you *for ever*."

Marcia stood up. "He'll be fine now. But excuse me. I have to go back and help Septimus."

Simon sprang to his feet. "Is he in trouble?" he asked.

"Possibly," said Marcia.

"I'll come with you," Simon said.

A Darke Dart

They found Septimus lying in the snow, hands outstretched. A red dart with black flights was stuck into the soft part of his right hand – the web between thumb and forefinger. His hand was black and swollen but the Dragon Ring on his finger glowed bright, keeping the **Darke** at bay as best it could. Around Septimus's wrist was a tight purple band where the black stopped – he had used his old Senior Apprentice ribbon as a tourniquet.

"Marcia," Septimus whispered. "It's a **Darke Dart**. Take it out. I … can't."

Marcia looked at Septimus's hand in dismay – streaks of black were already snaking beneath the purple band and flowing up his arm. Marcia knew it was not easy to remove a **Darke Dart**. The flights were razor-sharp and the point had a venomous barb on the end that would tear Septimus's hand as it came out and spread the poison still further. But Marcia also knew that Simon knew more about the **Darke** than she ever would. "Simon," she asked, "can you do this?"

"Yeah," said Simon. "I think I can." He kneeled down beside Septimus. "Sep," he said. "You must keep totally still. OK?"

"OK," Septimus whispered.

From his Alchemie belt, Simon took out a tiny pair of wire cutters. "Marcia, I need you to hold the Dart steady. But be very careful. You know the flights are often poison-tipped?"

Marcia nodded. She cautiously closed her fingers around the body of the dart, well below the flights. Simon lay flat on the snow, squinting at Septimus's hand. Very gingerly he placed the wire cutters around the point of the dart where it joined the body. Then, muttering something that neither Marcia nor Septimus recognised, he closed the wire cutters and cut through the point. Marcia threw the top of the Dart into the snow. The point of the Dart now stuck up through Septimus's hand like a black spike.

"Right, Sep," said Simon. "I'm going to hang on to the barb and Marcia will pull your hand straight up. Fast. OK?"

"Yep," said Septimus.

Concentrating hard, Simon took hold of the poisonous barb. Marcia gripped Septimus's hand.

"Pull!" said Simon.

"Aaaargh!"

It was done. All that was left in the snow was the point of the Darke Dart surrounded by a pool of red. Septimus sat up blearily, clutching his hand. "I can't see," he groaned.

"Your hat's slipped down, Sep," said Simon, gently pulling up Septimus's beanie. "And this belongs to you, little bro." Simon slipped the Akhu Amulet over Septimus's head so it lay around his brother's neck once again. "Thank you, Sep. I will never forget. Never, *ever*."

Septimus smiled. "And neither will I," he said. "You saved my life."

THE SNOW PALACE

As the sun rose on a new day, Snow Princess Driffa, the Most High and Bountiful, took her Snow Palace back under control. She found her elderly sisters hiding in a cave with the last of the Palace servants – all being driven to distraction by their one remaining sorcerer.

The four sisters now set to work. Soon a well-worn road of compacted snow ran between the Blue Pinnacle and the Palace, on which Driffa's fleet of silver sleighs ran back and forth carrying the exhausted prisoners to sanctuary. Furs were found to keep people warm, beds were made in the guest rooms and fires were laid in the huge brick chimneys that snaked up through the rocks at the back of the Snow Palace. The cooks came out of hiding and got to work.

Leaving Tod and Dan to spend time together, Ferdie, Oskar, Torr and William explored the Snow Palace. They spent hours going from one ice tower to another, travelling the seemingly delicate – but very strong – bridges that joined them. It felt like traversing a huge, sparkling spiderweb, but the spider that had once lurked at the edge was gone.

At the front of the Snow Palace was a wide promenade bounded by ramparts that overlooked the vast SnowPlain hundreds of feet below. It was warmed by braziers of burning logs suspended over fire pits, and people gathered around these, talking contentedly. And when they were warm, they would wander to the ramparts and gaze out at the Plain, watching the progress of the sleighs, the sun glinting off their runners, going steadily back and forth, beginning the long, slow task of setting everything to rights.

It was beside one of the fire pits that the Sarns and the Heaps met Samuel Starr. Samuel had been locked away with many of the other prisoners in one of the Iglopuks, but he already knew every detail of the events in the Orm Chamber. "When I heard the Lady had fled, I knew it was something to do with you, Ferdie Sarn," he said with a broad smile. "I always thought you were more than a match for her."

"It wasn't just me," said Ferdie.

"It was all of them," Rosie Sarn said. "But none of us would be here now, Samuel, if it had not been for your helping them to escape from that terrible ship. We can never thank you enough."

Samuel bowed. "It was my pleasure," he said.

William – dutifully wearing the fur jacket his mother had taken from the Fire Pit – chased off with Torr to explore. "William! Be careful!" Lucy called out anxiously.

"He'll be fine, Lu," Simon said soothingly.

But as Lucy watched her son go running across a slender bridge that climbed precipitously up to the tallest tower, she knew that from now on she would always worry about William. She felt a sudden sympathy for Sarah Heap, with *seven* boys to fret about. Hand in hand, Lucy and Simon wandered along the promenade, Lucy stealing glances up at two small figures cavorting on the bridge. Entranced by the glittering scene, Lucy and Simon stopped to gaze at the the graceful towers of opalescent ice, tall and thin with pointed roofs, each one topped with an elegant blue-and-gold finial. The sun shone down on the frosted snow, for the Enchantment that kept the snow for ever Frozen had not been destroyed here. As Simon looked up, Lucy caught a flash of blue in his right eye.

"Si," she said. "Hold still. You've got something in your eye."

Simon put his hand up to his eye. He had hoped Lucy wouldn't notice – at least not until she stopped being so nervous. "I know I have," he said. "It's lapis. From the palimpsest of the Orm."

"Well, let's get it out, then," Lucy said.

Simon shook his head. "No, Lu. It's part of my eye now. The iris is solid lapis."

The enormity of what Simon had done began to dawn on Lucy. "Can … can you still see through it?"

Simon shook his head. "No. But it was worth it, Lu. Worth it to get our William back. And I've still got one eye left." He grinned and Lucy saw a glint of gold in his lapis-blue eye. It suited him.

"Oh, Si …" she said.

Later that day, wrapped in Driffa's best furs, Tod and Dan too were wandering the vast Snow Palace. Still in a daze from finding her father alive, Tod was revelling in the beauty surrounding them. From that day onward she would always feel a profound happiness in the presence of snow.

They followed strings of sparkling lights strung along the suspended walkways, explored delicate ice turrets suffused with deep blue shadows and took winding stairs of blue down into lapis caves where hot springs bubbled up, filling the air with steam and heat. And as they roamed, Dan told Tod about the day he disappeared.

"It was a perfect fishing day. I was laying crab pots on the far side of the headland where the stream comes out of the Far, when I saw Mitza on the beach. She was waving and – well, you know how clearly sound travels over water – I heard her yelling, 'Dan, Dan, come quick. Alice is hurt!' I set the sails and turned for home but Mitza got even more frantic. 'No!' she screamed. 'She's here. In the Far!'

"I was so worried that I didn't question it. I took *Vega* up on to the beach and Mitza met me. She looked terrified, and that really scared me. I begged her to tell me what had happened but she just grabbed my hand and dragged me into the Far." Dan shook his head. "Suddenly I was surrounded by guards and creatures from a nightmare."

"Garmin," said Tod. "Oh, *Dad*."

"They took me to the Far Fortress and then here. Mitza told me you would be next. It was some old feud she had with Cassi – which she reckoned she'd well and truly won. Tod, I was *so* worried for you. Every day I thought of you being at home with that awful woman and those terrifying creatures coming for you. And there was nothing I could do. *Nothing*." Dan shook his head, and Tod saw tears spring into his eyes.

Tod linked her arm through Dan's and together they walked in silence for a while, simply happy to be together again. After some time Tod said, "Dad … when you dived in, did you know you had gills?"

Dan shook his head. "No. But as leader of the Circle it was my duty to go first."

Tod nodded. She'd thought as much.

They wandered along to the promenade and joined the watchers gazing out anxiously at the Blue Pinnacle. Overnight it had tilted and now looked very unstable. The words "collapse" and "any minute now" could be heard from the gathered crowd.

Far below, a handsome silver-and-blue sleigh pulled by four white horses was setting off. In it rode the ExtraOrdinary Wizard, the Deputy Castle Alchemist, the ex-ExtraOrdinary Wizard and the Snow Princess.

As Dan looked out across the SnowPlain, he felt nervous – and it wasn't about the Blue Pinnacle. There was something he had to ask Tod. "Alice," he said rather formally. "So. Would you like to come home?"

Tod didn't know how to answer.

Dan did not press her. He stood quietly beside his daughter, who he thought had changed so much in the past two long months. Apart from growing at least two inches taller, she had become self-assured and so very much reminded him of her mother. He had noticed also the change in her eyes – a Magykal green was beginning to break through. Dan watched Tod's gaze follow the sleigh and he thought sadly that he knew the answer she would give him.

Five Magyk

Under a clear blue sky, with a bright sun blazing down, four figures — one in white, one in purple, one in black and one shimmering in a cloak of many colours — stood beside the dangerously tilting Blue Pinnacle. They stared down into the pit before them, and far below they saw the empty Orm Tube drained of water, which had poured out through the cracked base where Simon had forced his way through the rock. And although they could not see it, at the very bottom of the Orm Tube was an empty, egg-shaped hollow, where for many thousands of years, the Egg of the Orm had lain.

"It's a disgrace," said Marcia. "To plunder a **Magykal** creature's birthplace in this way." She shook her head. "It makes me ashamed to call myself a Wizard."

Princess Driffa stared down, shaking her head sadly. "This place has nothing. No future. Just a collapsing Pinnacle and a dead Orm, cracked and broken."

"Not necessarily," Septimus said.

The Princess looked at Septimus, her blue eyes the colour of the sky above. "How so?" she asked.

"Because we will restore the earth and the lapis below. We will remake the Chamber of the Orm. We will set the Blue Pinnacle straight once more and renew its **Enchantment**."

Driffa looked at Septimus in disbelief. "No one is that powerful," she said.

"No *one*," agreed Septimus. "But there are four of us here. Each one of us has a different kind of Magyk. But I believe we will need five to make this kind of Magyk. Do you agree, Marcia?"

Marcia did not answer straight away. Five Magyk was an Ancient Art and was highly suitable for anything to do with the earth. It was a little bit Darke, a little bit Witchy, but Marcia was rapidly getting over her objections to both. It seemed that nothing was as clear-cut as she had once believed. She smiled at Septimus. "You're the ExtraOrdinary Wizard," she said. "And I agree with you. *Whatever* you say."

Septimus looked startled.

But old habits die hard and Marcia could not resist adding a little advice. "Of course, ideally the fifth will be a novice. Talented but untainted. First Magyk is powerful Magyk."

They both looked back to the glittering towers of the Snow Palace. Marcia smiled. "I'll go and fetch her, shall I?"

Septimus, Simon and Driffa watched Marcia take the sleigh back, showing the skill that she had learned as a girl of seven, when she would drive her itinerant Magykal father across the Enchanted Plains at breakneck speed. Simon shielded his eyes against the glare. The shard of lapis felt sharp and hot in the sun. But he thought nothing of it. His son was safe and he was needed for his own, personal Magyk. Nothing could be better.

From the promenade, through a pair of eyeglasses, Dan watched his daughter make her first Magyk. He saw her, barefoot on the

363

bare earth, being part of a spectacularly powerful **Five-Star Enchantment**, and he felt immensely proud. And when Tod returned, buzzing with the excitement of being part of such potent **Magyk**, Dan saw her eyes had turned a brilliant green and he knew that Cassi TodHunter Draa had been granted her dying wish. Alice TodHunter Moon was becoming part of the world of **Magyk**.

HOME

But for all her **Magyk**, Tod was still a PathFinder. A few days later when everyone was rested, Driffa escorted Tod, Dan and the PathFinders down through the **Re-Enchanted** walkways. With them came a new villager: Samuel Starr had decided to return to the home of his forebears.

Silently, they followed Driffa along the Sacred Ice Walk, filing down the steps into the beautiful blue Chamber of the Orm. The **Re-Enchanted** chamber possessed a delightful echo. The PathFinders' murmurs of amazement travelled around its smooth lapis walls, until the air was filled with a happy hum. **Five Magyk** had restored all to as it had been.

Except for the Orm Tube, which lay empty and dark.

"Castle **Magyk** will return the Egg of the Orm to us," Driffa said with a smile, thinking of a moonlight promise that the Castle's ExtraOrdinary Wizard had made.

Beneath the two golden eyes of the palimpsest of the Great Orm, Tod waited for the villagers to join her. She lifted the **PathFinder** from its lapis box and slipped the hollow lapis dome over its onyx sphere, then she took her pet rock from her pocket and touched the top of the **PathFinder** to its nose – at least, Tod hoped it was its nose. The arrow swung around and pointed to Way IX, which Tod knew would be the first of many.

A few Grula-Grulas were hanging around – just as they had always done before the Garmin polluted the Ways. The colour of their fur varied from dull brown through to brilliant red, but all possessed tiny, shining pink eyes. A glittering of pink pin-points watched the villagers join hands and followed the long line as Tod led them into the silver-and-lapis arch of the Way. The pink eyes exchanged approving glances. It was good to see the Ancient Ways being used once more.

When the last of the PathFinders had gone, an orange Grula-Grula performed an elaborate farewell bow to his companions and disappeared into Way VI. He had decided to return to the Castle. He thought he might pay another visit to a shop that sold cloaks, of which he had strangely fond memories.

Tod and the PathFinders travelled through five Hubs before they stepped into the Hub of the Far Fortress. Rosie Sarn recognised it immediately. She grabbed hold of Torr, Ferdie and Oskar – she was not letting go of them in such a terrible place. But the Far Fortress was deserted. The Lady and Aunt Mitza were gone and all that was left of the Garmin were dried-up white skeletons – Oraton-Marr's Enchantment had deserted them, too.

Oskar led the PathFinders home through the Far. When Marni Sarn saw them emerge from the trees she thought she was dreaming, but Jerra knew better. He ran to meet them, laughing. "I knew it!" he said. "I *knew* you'd be back." And he picked Torr up and swung him around and around until they both fell to the ground, laughing.

★   ★   ★

Later that night, beneath the Bell, the PathFinders met to talk about rebuilding their village. But before the meeting, Dan had something to say to Oskar and Ferdie. "You know our Path-Finder secret now," he said, "but I am asking you not to tell the little ones. It is too dangerous for them to know. Does Torr understand what happened?"

"No," said Ferdie. "Torr thinks it was all **Magyk**."

"In a way he is right," Dan said. "Things we don't under-stand *are* **Magyk**."

"Anyway," said Oskar, "Ferdie and I are going to forget all about the secret. We want to hear it properly from you next summer in the Circle."

"And so you will," Dan said with a broad smile.

"Will ... will Tod be there too?" asked Oskar.

Dan's smile faded. "I don't know," he said. "You will have to ask her."

But no one did ask Tod, in case she said she wouldn't be.

Over the long, warm autumn, the PathFinders built their homes anew and Tod and Dan cleared their house of wreckage and the smell of fear. At the night of the equinox the village met beneath the Bell to hear the story of what became known as the Great Escape. And Tod realised with a thrill that the name Alice TodHunter Moon would be spoken of for generations to come.

The PathFinders began to reclaim the Far. A wide track was made to the Far Fortress and the villagers knocked down the cells that had held them and their ancestors prisoner. Tod, Ferdie and Oskar made many visits to the Castle, taking the shortcut through Way VII. Ferdie and Oskar spent good times with Lucy, Simon and William, and Tod got to know Dandra

Draa and the Wizard Tower until it felt almost like home, just as her mother had hoped it would.

As autumn turned to winter, the final PathFinder house was rebuilt and Tod knew at last what she wanted to do. One day, Tod brought two invitations to the village – one for the Sarn family and one for Dan. They read:

The Wizard Tower

On MidWinter Feast Day
The ExtraOrdinary Wizard, Septimus Heap,
Invites You to the Apprentice Supper
In Honour of His Apprentice,
Alice TodHunter Moon.

Dan put the invitation in pride of place on the shelf above the fire. He turned to Tod with tears in his eyes. "Your mother would have been so proud," he said.

It was after the Apprentice Supper, when Tod, Ferdie and Oskar were on Snake Slipway looking out over the frozen Moat, that Tod said, "We mustn't let it happen again. Not to our village. Not here. Not *anywhere*."

Oskar and Ferdie knew exactly what Tod meant. "But it might," Ferdie said. "That sorcerer has the Egg now."

"I know," Tod said. "Which is why we are going to get it back."

"But how?" Ferdie and Oskar said together.

Tod gazed up at the moon, imagining that somewhere in the world the moon might be looking down on the Egg of the

Orm right then. "I don't know," she said. "We'll do it somehow. And whatever we do, we'll do it together. Us three."

Oskar grinned. "Tribe of Three," he said, holding up the first three fingers on his right hand. "PathFinder sign."

Tod and Ferdie did the same. "Tribe of Three."

"Cool," said Oskar, who had already picked up Castle slang.

Tod was right about the moon. That moment, in a distant land, it was shining down on an ancient frozen quay – deserted apart from a figure carrying a large, egg-shaped, blue silk sack. As the snow swirled, the figure watched a beautiful ship with *Tristan* emblazoned on its prow sail towards him. Far above him hovered a green dragon, watching him as it had done for many long weeks. Oraton-Marr looked up. "Go *away*, will you!" he screamed. *"Get lost!"*

But just as the dragon had taken no notice of a young Queen shouting at him, he took no notice of a **Darke** old sorcerer, either. The dragon had an Orm Egg to look out for. Orms were family. And family was what mattered, whether you were a dragon, an Orm or just a funny little human being.

Septimus Heap,
Wizard Apprentice.
Magyk is his destiny

Enjoy all of his
amazing adventures . . .

Angie Sage is the bestselling author of the delightfully witty *Araminta Spook* series and the masterful *Septimus Heap* books. She lives in a fifteenth-century house in Somerset and has two grown-up daughters.

LOOK OUT FOR THE NEXT
TODHUNTER MOON
ADVENTURE

OUT IN OCTOBER 2015